EDWARD ADRIFT

PRAISE FOR CRAIG LANCASTER

FOR *EDWARD ADRIFT*

"Craig Lancaster is a perfect novelist. Not only do his characters and stories seep into your heart with incredible longevity, but he manages to get them there in an unfussy, pure manner. He's that skilled of a writer. It's hard to know who I adore more: Lancaster's character Edward Stanton or Lancaster himself for creating him. It's rare that I get so attached and invested in a fictional person, but I find that I think about Edward quite often. It brings me indescribable happiness to be able to return to Edward in *Edward Adrift*, with his endearing eccentricities and his capacity to teach us all more than expected. He's a reminder that we might miss out on spectacular people should we fail to look past societal expectations of what friends should and shouldn't be. I wouldn't miss Edward for the world."

—Jessica Park, author of *Flat-Out Love*

FOR *600 HOURS OF EDWARD* (2012)

"A nearly perfect combination of traditional literary elements, mixing crowd-pleasing sappiness with indie-friendly subversion. A masterful blend of character and action."

—Chicago Center for Literature and Photography

"This is a wonderful book."

—*Montana Quarterly*

FOR *QUANTUM PHYSICS AND THE ART OF DEPARTURE* (2011)

"The success of any short-story collection hinges on the author's ability to create characters that immediately connect with readers. Lancaster excels on this point, ironically so because the inability to connect is his underlying theme."

—*Booklist*

"Have you ever felt in your pocket and found a twenty you didn't know you had? How 'bout a hundred-dollar bill, or a Montecristo cigar or a 24-karat diamond? That's what reading *Quantum Physics and the Art of Departure* is like—close and discovered treasures."

—Craig Johnson, author of *The Cold Dish* and *Hell is Empty*

FOR *THE SUMMER SON* (2011)

"A classic western tale of rough lives and gruff, dangerous men, of innocence betrayed and long, stumbling journeys to love."

—*Booklist*

"Lancaster has crafted a novel that offers readers the most valuable gift any work of fiction can offer: an authentic emotional experience."

—Jonathan Evison, author of *The Revised Fundamentals of Caregiving* and *West of Here*

EDWARD ADRIFT

CRAIG LANCASTER

The characters and events portrayed in this book are fictitious. Any similarity to real persons, living or dead, is coincidental and not intended by the author.

Text copyright © 2013 Craig Lancaster

Published by Amazon Publishing

PO Box 400818
Las Vegas, NV 89140

ISBN-13: 9781611099058
ISBN-10: 1611099056
Library of Congress Control Number: 2012918990

This one's for those who love Edward and wanted to
see more of him. As it turns out, I did, too. And,
as always, for Angie and Zula and Bodie, the
best home team there could ever be.

WEDNESDAY, DECEMBER 7, 2011

I look at my watch at 3:37 p.m., or actually 3:37 and sixteen seconds—I have the kind of watch with an LED digital display for precision—and stop in the kitchen. I have another fifty-four seconds and could easily make it to the couch, but I stand still and watch the seconds tick off. The six morphs (I love the word "morphs") into a seven and then an eight and then a nine and then the one becomes a two and the nine becomes a zero, and I keep watching. Finally, at 3:38 and ten seconds, I draw in my breath and hold it. Time keeps going, and I exhale. I look down again and notice that I am standing on top of dried marinara sauce that sloshed out of the saucepan yesterday. And just like yesterday, I don't have the energy to clean it up, even though it bothers me.

At 3:38 p.m. and ten seconds, twenty-one days ago, on Wednesday, November 16, 2011, Mr. Withers fired me from my newspaper job at the *Billings Herald-Gleaner*. I know it happened at that time because as Mr. Withers said, "I hate like hell to have to tell you this, Edward," I looked directly at my Timex watch on my left wrist, where I always keep it. Its display read 3:38:10, and I made a mental note to write it down as soon as possible, which I did exactly fifty-six minutes and fourteen seconds later, as I sat in my car. A phrase like "I hate like hell to have to tell you this" is a precursor to bad news, and I think the fact that I recognized this is what caused me to look at my watch. I was right about the news. Mr. Withers finished by saying, "But we're going to have to let you go." He said a lot of other things, too, but none of them are as important. I couldn't listen very closely, because I needed to concentrate on remembering the time. The time is now logged, but that's purely academic. I don't think I'll ever forget it, although I hesitate to say that definitively. I can think whatever I want. It doesn't mean things will happen that way. It's easier to stick to incontrovertible (I love the word "incontrovertible") facts.

Needing fifty-six minutes and fourteen seconds to get to the car can be attributed to the fact that getting fired is no simple thing. In the movies and on TV, getting fired never seems complicated. Some boss, generally played by someone like Ed Asner, comes out of an office and says, "You're fired," and the fired person leaves. But Mr. Withers doesn't look like or sound like Ed Asner, and he made me sign a lot of papers—things like the extension of my health care benefits through something called COBRA and the receipt of my final paycheck, which included the hours I had worked in that pay period and what Mr. Withers called "a severance," which was two weeks' pay, or eighty hours at $15 an hour, minus taxes. The severance check came to $951.01. When I asked Mr. Withers why I was being fired, he said that I wasn't being fired per se (I love the Latin phrase "per se," which means "in itself") but rather that it was what the company liked to call "an involuntary separation." He said that often happens when a company needs to cut its costs. Labor, which is to say people, is the biggest cost any company has. Mr. Withers said it was an unfortunate reality of business that people sometimes have to endure involuntary separations.

"So, Edward, don't think of it as a firing," he told me as he shook my hand, after he took my key and my parking pass. "You didn't do anything wrong. If we could keep you on board, we would. It really is an involuntary separation."

I think Mr. Withers wanted to believe what he said, or maybe he wanted me to believe that he believed it. I don't know. I veer into dangerous territory when I try to make sense of subtext, which is a word that means "an underlying, unspoken meaning." I would rather people just come out and say what they mean, in words that cannot be mistaken, but I haven't met many people who are willing to do that. I will tell you this, though—another word I love is the word "euphemism," which is basically a nice way of saying something bad. The incontrovertible fact is that "involuntary separation" sounds a lot like a euphemism to me.

— • —

Getting fired, or involuntarily separated, from the *Billings Herald-Gleaner* has made it a real shitburger of a year. Scott Shamwell, one of the pressmen at the *Herald-Gleaner*, taught me the word "shitburger." Scott Shamwell was always coming up with odd and interesting word combinations, and most of them were profane, which delighted me. One time, the printing press had a web break—that's when the big roll of paper snaps when the press is running, meaning they have to shut everything down and rethread the paper—and Scott Shamwell called the press a "miserable bag of fuck." I still laugh about that one, because the press is almost entirely steel. There's not a bag anywhere on it that I've ever seen, and now that I don't work at the newspaper anymore, I'll probably never see the press again. I don't know. Again, it's hard to be definitive about something like that. If I ever get a chance to see the press again, I'll take one last look and see if there's a bag somewhere. I don't think there is.

— • —

One of the things I learned from Dr. Buckley before she retired—and that is another thing that makes this a shitburger year—is that when times are difficult, I need to work hard at finding stability and things that bring me pleasure. Dr. Buckley, who helped me deal with my Asperger's syndrome, is a very logical woman, and in the eleven years, two months, and ten days that I worked with her, I came to learn that I should act on her suggestions. On that note, I guess I should focus on the brighter news that I continue to maintain my daily logs of the high and low temperatures and precipitation readings for Billings, Montana, where I live. I started keeping these logs on January 1, 2001, when it occurred to me that Billings, in addition to having wildly variable weather, has poor excuses for weathermen. Their forecasts are notoriously off base, so I've come to distrust what they say. I prefer facts. Every morning, my copy of the *Billings Herald-Gleaner* provides me with the facts about the previous day's weather. I then write it down, and my data is complete.

For example, yesterday, December 6, 2011, the 340th day of the year, saw a high temperature of 34 and a low temperature of 16 in Billings. There was no precipitation, meaning we held steady at 19.34 inches for the year. It's been a bad year for precipitation in Montana, and a lot of places have had floods, although not Billings. Scott Shamwell lives in Roundup, which is 49.82 miles north of Billings, and his town flooded badly. He said one time that he was going to start driving "a cocksucking rowboat" to work, but I don't think he ever did. I wasn't there every day that he was, as our schedules didn't fully align, so while it's conceivable that he could have driven a cocksucking rowboat to work, I have to believe that he or someone else would have told me about it. Belief can be dangerous, of course. I prefer facts. We did have an oil spill in the Yellowstone River, which mucked things up, and last year a tornado blew down our sports stadium, so it's not like Billings is getting off light as far as catastrophes go. I guess everybody is having trouble these days.

Anyway, tracking the weather data is how I maintain stability, as Dr. Buckley suggested. She also suggested that I find something that gives me pleasure. That has been more difficult, especially since I was involuntarily separated from the *Billings Herald-Gleaner*. I should just try harder, I guess. But how?

THURSDAY, DECEMBER 8, 2011

From the logbook of Edward Stanton:
   Time I woke up today: 8:23 a.m. The 17th time in 342 days I've awoken at that time.
   High temperature for Wednesday, December 7, 2011, Day 341: 37
   Low temperature for Wednesday, December 7, 2011: 22
   Precipitation for Wednesday, December 7, 2011: 0 inches
   Precipitation for 2011: 19.34 inches

This year just keeps getting worse.

Harry Morgan died yesterday. I read about it in the *Billings Herald-Gleaner.*

It was a small story, on the bottom of page A3. I could quibble with certain things about that story. For one thing, it's too short. Harry Morgan lived to be ninety-six years old, and he worked steadily in Hollywood from 1942 to 1999. It's impossible to give a full accounting of that in a seven-inch-long article. I could also make a credible case that Harry Morgan's obituary should have gone on the front page of the newspaper, but I will concede that this falls into the area of news judgment, and reasonable people and newspaper editors can disagree on that. The one unassailable (I love the word "unassailable") point I would like to make is that the newspaper editor made a huge error by running a picture of Harry Morgan dressed up as Colonel Sherman Potter from *M*A*S*H*. That was a nice role for him, don't get me wrong, but it's clearly secondary to Harry Morgan's role as Officer Bill Gannon on the ninety-eight color episodes of *Dragnet*.

Let's examine the facts of this situation:

Fact No. 1: On *M*A*S*H*, Harry Morgan's character was a replacement after McLean Stevenson's Lieutenant Colonel Henry Blake was killed off at the end of the third season. If Colonel Potter was such a great role, why did it come second? (That's a rhetorical question—I love the word "rhetorical.")

Fact No. 2: Before Harry Morgan ever played Colonel Potter, he appeared on *M*A*S*H* as a character named Major General Bartford Hamilton Steele. Observant viewers, like me, have a hard time reconciling that. Both characters are clearly played by the same man. Did the producers of *M*A*S*H* think we wouldn't notice? (That, too, is a rhetorical question.)

Fact No. 3: At best, Colonel Potter was the number three character on *M*A*S*H*. Officer Bill Gannon was a clear number two on *Dragnet*, and he was much funnier than Sergeant Joe Friday, so that made him memorable.

The facts are on my side. The *Billings Herald-Gleaner* blew this one.

I used to watch *Dragnet* on videocassette, one episode each night at 10:00 p.m. sharp (and then, after I started at the *Billings Herald-Gleaner*, at 12:30 a.m., because I worked nights). I'd start with the first episode and end with the ninety-eighth, and then begin again. That came to an end on April 19, 2009, when the first of my seven *Dragnet* tapes was severed in the guts of my VCR during the eleventh episode of the series, called "The Shooting." Sergeant Joe Friday and Officer Bill Gannon were just about to put the pinch on two hoods who gunned down a fellow police-man when my TV screen went snowy and the VCR started mak-ing an awful noise, and that was the end of the tape. My friend Donna Middleton (now Donna Hays), before she moved away, showed me that I could still watch the episodes on the computer, but I tried and it wasn't the same. I threw out my *Dragnet* tapes, even the good ones.

— • —

I've been dreading today since November 15, the day I made an appointment to go see Dr. Rex Helton, my primary care physician at the St. Vincent Healthcare clinic on Broadwater Avenue. When I had my physical a year earlier, on November 15, 2010, Dr. Rex Helton told me that I needed to lose some weight and that my glucose levels were beginning to alarm him. He told me that I should get more exercise and eat better. The spaghetti that I eat nine times a week had to be reduced, he said. He also said that a quart of ice cream a week was not good for me and that I should try some sugar-free gelatin or some fruit.

For a while I did well at heeding Dr. Rex Helton's advice. I bought a scale and weighed myself daily—which made for an exciting new entry in my logbook—and took walks and tried to eat more lean meat and vegetables without going so far outside my comfort zone that I became "a granola-eating fucknut," as Scott Shamwell called me one day when he saw me with a salad at work. By February 1 of this year, I had dropped my weight from 283.8 pounds to 266.3. But February 1 is also the day that Dr. Buckley told me she would be retiring, and (while I hate to admit this, I have to acknowledge that it's true) I didn't do a very good job with my new routine after that. I haven't stepped on the scale since March 8, and I would be afraid to do so now. There are three quarts of ice cream in my freezer right now. The numbers can't be good. That's informed conjecture, which I'll concede isn't as good as a fact.

— • —

I leave my house on Clark Avenue promptly at 11:15 a.m. for my 11:45 appointment with Dr. Helton. Broadwater Avenue is the next big thoroughfare to the south of my house, which is nice because it means I can get to the clinic by making nothing but right turns in my car. Right turns, statistically, are less risky than left turns, so whenever possible, I plot a course that includes them. I don't want you to think I'm a freak or something, though. I do make left turns; they're unavoidable sometimes. But I prefer right turns.

As I turn right on Broadwater, the R.E.M. song "Losing My Religion" comes on the radio, and I'm reminded anew of the shit-burger year. R.E.M. is my favorite band—or, I should say, they were. They are no longer together. On September 21, R.E.M. said it was disbanding. I couldn't believe it. I still can't, but yet, if I turn on my computer and do a web-engine search for R.E.M., this will be confirmed: the band is no more. I don't understand it. Earlier in the year, they released a new album, and it was one of my favorites. Michael Stipe, the lead singer, said something about knowing when it's time to leave the party, which is a euphemism. I can't begrudge Michael Stipe doing what he wants to do, but I wish I had some way to convince him to keep the party going.

At the clinic, I simply tell the receptionist my name and sign off on my list of medications. The only medication I take is eighty milligrams of fluoxetine daily. Dr. Buckley gave me that medicine twelve years ago, as part of my treatment for Asperger's syndrome and its associated obsessive-compulsive tendencies, which were ruining everything. I'm forty-two years old, and taking fluoxetine is now just part of my life, like breathing or recording the daily temperature readings.

Once I've cleared the paperwork, I set about my usual business. I go from table to table and arrange the magazines by title and edition number. I have to do this every time I am here. The other patients do not take good care with such things, and while that is frustrating, I've learned that there is no way to stop it. I do what I can to offset the damage they're causing.

Here's something that bothers me about seeing Dr. Rex Helton: My appointment time says 11:45, but experience tells me that it could be 11:48 or 11:55 or even 12:01 before my name is called. That never happened at Dr. Buckley's office. With her, I had a 10:00 a.m. appointment every single Tuesday, and she never failed to have me in her office by that time. I can only conclude that the Broadwater clinic isn't as interested in precision as she was.

Here's another thing that bothers me about seeing Dr. Rex Helton: When the nurse finally calls my name, at 11:47 a.m., and after I'm weighed (290.2 pounds—holy shit!) and my blood pressure is taken (138 systolic, 92 diastolic—holy shit!), I'm placed alone in a room at 11:51 a.m. and told that Dr. Helton will see me shortly. (I don't like a word like "shortly." It's imprecise and owes too much to individual interpretation. Dr. Rex Helton's "shortly" and my "shortly" could be two completely different things.)

When Dr. Rex Helton finally comes in—at 12:02 p.m.—he says "Hello, Edward," and then he gets right to it. Directness is the only thing I appreciate about Dr. Rex Helton.

"I'll be blunt. It's not good," he says. "It's not good at all. It's not just the weight, which you know is going in the wrong direction.

We've seen the results of the fasting plasma glucose test you took a couple of days ago, and you've tipped into type two diabetes."

"What was the reading?" I ask.

"Well, your six-month average is two hundred and twelve. It's far outside normal."

Holy shit!

Dr. Rex Helton goes on. "I'm also worried about your blood pressure. We need to get aggressive with this. You have to eat better, you have to exercise, and you're going to have to go on medication."

"How much medication?"

"Fifteen milligrams of lisinopril for the hypertension. Forty milligrams of furosemide, a diuretic to leach some of the water out of your body. Thirty milligrams of actos, which will help increase your sensitivity to insulin. A thousand milligrams twice a day of metformin, which should help control the glucose in your blood. And, finally, a daily potassium chloride tablet to help with your kidney function. That furosemide is going to put a lot of stress on them, so we don't want problems there."

"You mean, I'm going to be peeing a lot?"

"Yep."

"Holy shit!"

I can't believe I actually said this out loud, in front of Dr. Rex Helton.

"Edward, I know it sounds like a lot. It is a lot. But we have to get out in front of this thing. Lose the weight. Control your diet. You don't have to take this stuff forever. I've seen people come off it. But you have to do the work. Is there any reason you can't?"

I could make a lot of excuses about all of the things that have happened to me this year, but I don't.

"No, Dr. Rex Helton. There's no reason I can't. What should I weigh?"

Dr. Rex Helton doesn't know this, but it's better for me when I have tangible goals.

"Less than you do now, OK? It's not just about weight. It's the whole picture. You're tall"—in fact, I am 6 feet 3 $\frac{5}{16}$ inches tall—"but you're still overweight. Lose some of the weight, adjust the diet, and we'll see improvement."

"But how much?" Dr. Rex Helton is not answering my question.

"Let's say you should weigh two hundred pounds."

Holy shit! I do the math in my head. I need to lose 31 percent of my weight. More than that, really. I don't have time to calculate the fractions of a pound before Dr. Rex Helton is talking again.

"Now," he says, "here's what I want you to do. Get a notebook and keep track of how much you exercise. Thirty minutes a day, Edward. It can be as simple as a brisk walk. As for meals, imagine a plate divided into thirds. I want two-thirds of that to be vegetables—salad, carrots, green beans, peas, whatever you like. The other third can be lean meat. You can have pasta, but it needs to be an occasional thing, not the everyday meal it's been. Those days are over. And look into sugar-free options for dessert. There are a ton of them. You need to be serious about this. Do you hear me?"

I smile. Dr. Rex Helton smiles back at me. I hear him. I'm getting new entries in my daily logbook. I wouldn't go so far as to say that type 2 diabetes has been a good development, but I've found a silver lining, at least.

— • —

When I go home, I don't follow my earlier route in reverse. That would transform all of my right turns into left turns. Instead, I get into my candy-apple-red Cadillac DTS, which used to belong to my father, and turn right onto Broadwater, right on Twenty-Fourth

Street West, right on Grand Avenue, and right into the parking lot of the Albertsons on Grand Avenue and Thirteenth Street West.

Dr. Helton has called my new prescriptions in to the pharmacy, and sure enough, when I tell the pharmacist (her name tag says LUELLA, which I think is a pretty name) who I am, she has them ready to go. I pay the $122.57 with my credit card.

From the Albertsons parking lot, I am again a right-turning kind of guy. Right on Grand Avenue, right on Fifth Street West, and right on Clark Avenue, and then a right turn into my driveway.

I'm pretty smart sometimes.

— • —

In my absence, the mailman has come. I used to obsess about the time of the mail's arrival, because it bothered me that there could be such wide variances given that the mailman walks the same route every day. It didn't make sense to me. But Dr. Buckley worked hard with me to help me figure out the difference between things that matter and things that don't. She helped me to see that as long as I receive the mail each day, it doesn't matter what time it arrives. Dr. Buckley is a very logical woman. Besides that, I have been reading a lot in the *Billings Herald-Gleaner* about the financial trouble the United States Postal Service is in—how delivery might be curtailed on certain days and how letters may take longer to go from one place to another. While I don't like conjecture, it's easy for me to imagine that the postal employees are under a lot of stress, and I don't think it would be fair for me to add to it by obsessing about delivery times.

I have only two pieces of mail. I can tell from the script handwriting on the envelope of one that it is from my mother, who is spending the fall and winter months in North Richland Hills,

Texas, a suburb of Fort Worth, where she is from. She and her sister, Corinne, spend about half the year together in Texas now that their husbands are dead, and they do all sorts of things, like traveling and going to concerts and shows and spending time with some of their childhood friends, many of whom have also lost their husbands. All this death makes me wonder sometimes if marriage kills men. I asked my mother one time if she would think about getting married again now that my father is gone, and she wrinkled her nose and said, "Why would I want a smelly man around my house?" I didn't have an answer for that, and she didn't insist on one.

The other piece of mail is from Jay L. Lamb, my lawyer. I don't feel so hot in my stomach when I see that envelope.

I open the envelope from my mother and remove the contents as I step through the doorway into my living room.

Dear Edward,

Here is your ticket to fly to Texas for Christmas. You'll be leaving at 6 a.m. on December 20th, which I know is early, and you'll be going back on December 27th. All of the information is on the ticket that I've enclosed. Did you know it cost an extra $25 for a printed paper ticket? That's highway robbery, or skyway robbery. Be sure to take your credit card and your driver's license when you get on the plane. They'll charge you for your bag, and you'll have to prove who you are.

I can't wait to see you, son. We will have a real good time. Did you know the Cowboys are playing on Christmas Eve? Guess what? You're going!

Merry (early) Christmas!
Love,
Mom

My mother asked me two questions, both of them rhetorical. That means she doesn't really want answers, but I feel compelled to offer them. First, I didn't know that about paper tickets, and I agree with my mother. Second, of course I know the Cowboys play on Christmas Eve. They will be playing the Philadelphia Eagles, whom I hate. Not hate as in I wish them ill health. I just don't like them. The Dallas Cowboys, on the other hand, are my favorite football team, and I have wanted to see them in their new stadium since it opened for the start of the 2009 season. That was a good year for the Cowboys. They finished 11–5 and won the NFC East division, although they lost 34–3 to the Minnesota Vikings in the second round of the playoffs. In any case, it was way better than the next season, when they went 6–10 and didn't even make the playoffs. Right now, in 2011, they are 7–5, but I'm not feeling too good about them. Still, I can't help but root for the Cowboys, because I always have and because my father did. I do understand, however, that not everyone likes the Dallas Cowboys. Scott Shamwell hates the Dallas Cowboys. He calls them "America's Douche-Canoes." I don't like it when he says that, but I have to remember that Scott Shamwell is a Minnesota Vikings fan and has never seen his team win a Super Bowl. The Cowboys, on the other hand, have won five. I will just be thankful for my team's good fortune.

Feeling happy about my Christmas trip and seeing the Dallas Cowboys, I open the letter from Jay L. Lamb and prepare to feel worse. I will concede that this preemptive (I love the word "preemptive") feeling of dread is an effect of years past, when Jay L. Lamb, under my father's direction, would write me letters telling me what to do and threatening to cut me off from my father's support if I did not follow his directions.

Since my father died and my mother yelled at Jay L. Lamb and instructed him never to speak to me without her permission, I have not had any trouble from him. Feeling dread at his letters is what Dr. Buckley would call a "conditioned response," and those are hard to break, like habits. I'm trying. I will try harder.

> *Edward:*
>
> *As I relayed to your mother and she asked me to relay to you, I have found private health coverage for you now that you are no longer employed by the Herald-Gleaner. I will direct the human resources department at the newspaper to suspend your participation in the COBRA program. Though this new insurance will be more expensive than your employer-provided plan, it is in any case less costly than COBRA. I will be in touch soon with plan details and your insurance card. Please let me know if anything has changed on the medical front.*
>
> *Also, some additional good news—the strategic steps we took to position your money in late 2008 have paid off handsomely. We have recovered the recessionary losses and then some, and your holdings as of this writing total $6,123,817. It's safe to say that you need not work another day in your life.*
>
> *With all the best regards,*
> *Jay L. Lamb*

Jay L. Lamb has a talent for saying something that is innocuous (I love the word "innocuous") and offensive at the same time. I appreciate his getting me new insurance and taking care of my money, and I will endeavor to tell him so. As for his comment about my not needing to work, it just goes to show that while Jay L. Lamb may be my lawyer, he doesn't know me. My father made that money in the oil business and in investments after he retired and became a politician. Jay L. Lamb thinks my money is what keeps me alive. He's a fool. But I won't tell him that.

I go into the room adjacent to my bedroom, where my computer desk sits, and I compose a letter to Jay L. Lamb. I'd like to get this in the mail as soon as possible so all the necessary details of my new health coverage can be put in place.

Jay L. Lamb:

Thank you for your note of the 7th. I am writing to you to fulfill your request about details on the medical front. Today, I saw Dr. Rex Helton at the St. Vincent Healthcare Broadwater clinic, and he has informed me that I have type 2 diabetes. I have gone to Albertsons and picked up the medications that Dr. Rex Helton recommends as a deterrent for this new condition, and I am sure Dr. Rex Helton can provide any details you need beyond this letter.

Thank you for attending to this and for the update about my money.

Regards,
Edward Stanton

As long as I'm writing letters, I might as well compose one to Mr. Withers at the *Billings Herald-Gleaner*. I have spent three weeks and a day thinking about the circumstances of how I was fired (or involuntarily separated), and I have built a substantive case for being rehired as soon as possible.

Mr. Withers:

As you may recall, you had to involuntarily separate me from the Billings Herald-Gleaner on November 16th. At our last meeting, which you euphemistically called an exit interview, you suggested that this was a result of "business challenges" and not a commentary on the quality of my work.

While I am not privy to the newspaper's business challenges, I think that once you reconsider things, you will see that I should continue to be employed as the night-shift maintenance expert.

I have included here a short list of the things that need to be done at the Herald-Gleaner. All of these things would have been done by me had I remained an employee:

- *The steps on the south side of the building need to be squared off with a liquid concrete bonding agent. As it is, these steps are a safety hazard.*
- *The landing on the north entrance needs to be retiled.*
- *Given the unseasonably warm December we have been enjoying, there is time to prune the trees on all sides of the building.*
- *Again, given the unseasonable warmth, the parking lot lines can be repainted.*

As I wrote earlier, this is just a sampling of the chores left undone by my involuntary separation. By the time I finish these items, there will no doubt be many more things for me to do. I'm sure I don't have to tell you that maintenance at so large a plant is an ongoing concern. I stand ready to assume my previous position and assist you with these tasks.

I look forward to hearing from you.

Regards,
Edward Stanton

I am proud of this letter. I fill out the envelopes for Jay L. Lamb and Mr. Withers, seal the letters inside them, affix a stamp upon each, and clip them to the mailbox so they go out first thing tomorrow.

For the first time in three weeks and a day, I feel content. I like it. I feel so content, in fact, that I will lie down for a nap after I take my medicine. It's not even 3:00 p.m.

— • —

When I wake up with a start at 10:48 p.m., four unrelated thoughts are in my head.

The first is that I have to pee really badly. I run into the bathroom, which fortunately is adjacent to my bedroom, and I just manage to get my pants down before the pee comes. It's like my tallywhacker (I love the word "tallywhacker") is a miniature fire hose, the way the pee shoots out of me. It is a clear, strong stream, and just when I think I'm about to be done, more comes out. I don't think I've ever peed this much, although I must concede that it has never occurred to me to measure my pee output on a consistent basis. While the idea has some appeal—I love keeping data on things—I quickly recognize this as one of the compulsions that Dr. Buckley always told me I had to work hard to control.

In any case, I can now see that Dr. Helton was right: my new medicine will make me pee a lot. Not enough to lose 31.08 percent of my body weight, but a lot. (I just made a joke. I'm pretty funny sometimes.)

My second thought concerns the new TV show I'm trying to get into. When I call it a new show, I mean it's new to me. It's actually an old show called *Adam-12*, and it was produced by Jack Webb, the star of *Dragnet*, so it ought to be good. My mother gave me the DVDs for the first season of the show back in February, after I got the news about Dr. Buckley's retirement. My mother thought it might cheer me up, but it didn't. I just put the box on a shelf in my den. It wasn't until Mr. Withers fired me twenty-two days ago that I started watching *Adam-12*, since I had nothing else to do. While I can definitely see some similarities to *Dragnet*, in that it's about Los Angeles cops, I'm a little frustrated by the show. That's what I'm thinking about now. Take as an example the episode I was supposed to watch tonight, if I hadn't fallen asleep. It's the twenty-second episode, and it's called "Log 152: A Dead Cop Can't Help Anyone." It comes immediately after "Log 102: We Can't Just Walk Away From It," and immediately before "Log 12: He Was Trying to Kill Me." I'm sure you can see what my trouble is. The stupid logs don't go in order. I guess the characters, Officer Pete Malloy (played by Martin Milner) and Officer Jim Reed (played by Kent McCord), are all right, although they're no Sergeant Joe Friday and Officer Bill Gannon. But this show leaves a lot to be desired in terms of consistency.

My third thought, however, is the reason that I'm getting up and putting on my clothes. If I wait for Mr. Withers to answer my letter and rehire me at the *Billings Herald-Gleaner*, precious time that could be spent on shoring up the property will be wasted. Furthermore, the unseasonably warm weather we have been enjoying could turn quickly—I have years' worth of data that show this tendency conclusively—and preclude my accomplishing some of the tasks I outlined for Mr. Withers. It's already been a very cold day. More bad weather could be on the way.

As I am fully awake and dressed, there is no reason I cannot start on these chores now. I will be happy to do them without recompense (I love the word "recompense").

In the basement, I pull together the things I will need for this task: safety goggles, a chisel, a sledgehammer, a whisk broom, a hammer, a stiff paintbrush, boards to build forms, nails, and a plastic drop cloth (and it occurs to me now that "drop cloth" is a silly term for something made of plastic—it's not cloth at all). It takes me three trips, but I manage to hustle all of that upstairs, out the back door, and into the trunk of my Cadillac. In the garage, I get a garden hose, a wheelbarrow (which I strap to the roof of the car), a shovel, a bag of ready-mix concrete (I am glad I always keep one on hand), and the bonding agent.

I count everything off one more time, just to make sure I have it, and then I remember: It's nighttime. I'll need light, too. I run inside and grab one. And that's when I'm reminded of my fourth thought. I'm terribly hungry, not having eaten all day. I grab a package of cheese-and-peanut-butter crackers out of the pantry as I pass back through the kitchen. These are not on my new diet. I hope Dr. Rex Helton doesn't find out.

— • —

It is 11:38 p.m. and, after brushing away the accumulating snow—a potential trouble spot on this job—I have begun hammering together the wooden forms for the concrete steps when Elliott Overbay, the fat man who runs the copy desk at the *Herald-Gleaner*, comes outside.

"What are you doing?" he asks me. He must be stupid.

"I'm repairing these steps. You need to move. You're standing in my light."

"Why?"

He's really stupid.

"As you can see, they're crumbling. You could see that if you ever looked, Elliott Overbay."

"I mean, why are you doing it now? Are you supposed to be here?"

I decide to answer him with a rhetorical question.

"Why not?"

"What does that mean?"

"What do you think it means?"

Elliott Overbay is really stupid, and as much as I am enjoying this, it is interfering with my work.

"You need to go away now," I say. "I'm busy."

Elliott Overbay shakes his head and walks away. I really don't like him. I never worked directly with him, but every time I was in the newsroom at night, he was really loud and obnoxious about all the grammatical mistakes he was fixing. I'm glad to see him leave.

— • —

At 11:46, I hear the door open and I look up. Now it's Scott Shamwell walking toward me. I wonder what he's doing out here. At

11:46, he should be hard at work on the press, getting it ready for the local run of newspapers.

"Edward, what the fucking fuck, man?"

"What?"

"I heard they shitcanned you. What are you doing here?"

"Fixing these steps."

"It's snowing."

"They're still damaged."

"You can't be here, bro."

"Why not?"

"Because you don't work here anymore, man."

"That will change."

Scott Shamwell arches an eyebrow, and just for a moment he looks like John Belushi in the excellent movie *Animal House*, which always makes me laugh.

"How do you figure?" he asks.

"I wrote to Mr. Withers and asked for my job back."

"What did he say?"

"I haven't sent the letter yet."

Scott Shamwell comes closer, until he's less than a foot away from me. His eyes look sad. He reaches out a big freckly arm and sets his hand on my shoulder.

"Ed, buddy, I really hope that works. But unless you get the job back, you can't be here, man."

I drop a board.

"Why?"

"It's just not the way things are done. If you got hurt—"

"I'm not going to get hurt," I say.

"I'm just saying, if you do, it will be a bad scene, man. You wouldn't want that, would you?"

"I guess not," I say.

"All right, man. Let me help you put this stuff back in the car."

We gather up my things and dump them in the trunk. Scott tells me to leave the wheelbarrow, that he'll bring it by my house in a few hours with his truck so it doesn't scratch the roof of my Cadillac.

I'm about to leave when Scott Shamwell, who has on a short-sleeve pressman's shirt and is holding himself in the cold, whistles and motions for me to roll down the window. I hit the button, and the glass recedes into the door.

"Eddie, call me after Christmas, and we'll go out and do some radical shit."

"OK," I tell him.

He turns and goes back into the building at a jog. I head for home, with a right turn on North Twenty-Seventh, a right on Third Avenue, a right on Division, and lefts on Lewis and Fifth Street West before another right onto Clark Avenue, which leads me home. I don't even care about the left turns. I'm that disappointed.

I leave the tools in the car and trudge into the house. I don't feel very good. I don't know what to do with my time. If my life right now were an *Adam-12* episode, it would be called "Log 152: An Involuntarily Separated Employee Can't Help Anyone."

FRIDAY, DECEMBER 9, 2011

From the logbook of Edward Stanton:
  *Time I woke up today: I'm not sure what to put. After the deba-
cle (I love the word "debacle," although I hate actual debacles) at the
Herald-Gleaner, I didn't fall asleep again until after 1:00 a.m., and
I woke up to pee at 2:14, 3:31, 4:16, and 5:27. I finally woke up for
good at 10:22, when the phone rang.*
  High temperature for Thursday, December 8, 2011, Day 342: 26
  Low temperature for Thursday, December 8, 2011: 13
  Precipitation for Thursday, December 8, 2011: 0.06 inches
  Precipitation for 2011: 19.40 inches

At first, the ringing phone folds itself into the haze of my
dream, a sandy vision in my head that slips away from me the
moment I realize that I am awake.

I push myself off the bed and run to the extension in the
kitchen wearing my underwear and just one sock, on my left foot.

"Hello?"

"Edward, thank God."

A funny thing happens when I hear the voice of Donna
Middleton (now Donna Hays, since she got married), my best
friend. It's as if my brain fast-forwards through the time that I've

known her. I remember when she moved across the street from me: September 12, 2008. I remember when I met her for the first time: October 15, 2008. I remember that she didn't like me, and because of that, I didn't like her very much, either. But that didn't last. She and her son, Kyle, became my very good friends. We had good times together. I even built Kyle a super-awesome three-wheeler called the Blue Blaster. And then Donna met Victor Hays and married him, and he became my friend, too, but later he took them away from here.

"Donna, why are you calling me?"

I realize immediately that I have said the wrong thing. The phone call surprised me.

"Please forgive me, Donna," I say. "I had a bad night."

Her words come at me fast.

"Edward, I promise you, I'm going to double back and ask you about your bad night, because I'm really sorry to hear about that. But can I tell you something first?"

"Yes."

"It's about Kyle." Her voice is urgent.

"Kyle?"

Any vestiges (I love the word "vestiges") of sleep clear my head immediately. My heart beats faster, and I wish at once that I were six hundred miles away in Boise right now with Donna and Kyle and not here in my stupid kitchen in stupid Billings.

"He's been expelled. It happened just this morning. Holy crap, Edward, I was on my way to the grocery store, and I got a call from his principal, and he says Kyle can't come back to school the rest of the semester at least. My kid! My beautiful, smart kid. I...I just...how do you even..."

There are a million—not literally a million, but a lot of—things I want to ask Donna, including whether her grocery store has self-checkout stands, but instead I say, "Slow down." In my head, I hear Dr. Buckley's voice and the things she said to me many times. *Slow down. Take it in small pieces. Tell me what happened. Tell me what's wrong.* My memory of Dr. Buckley whispers the words in my ear, and I say them out loud on the telephone.

"Tell me what happened."

"Edward, it's all so incredible, I just don't even know how to begin. I mean, you know it hasn't been an easy transition for Kyle here."

"I know."

"He had a lot of friends there, and seventh grade is a really tough time to change schools, because all of these other kids, they've been together for years, and Kyle's had to figure out how to find a place with them. It's been hard. His grades have been slipping all year, and at first, you know, we figured maybe it's just the adjustment and a different set of teachers here. We were confident he'd catch up, but he hasn't. If anything, it's gotten worse."

"OK."

I rub my bare right foot on the kitchen floor, and it feels something hard and raised against the linoleum. I look down and see the marinara stain. I resolve to scrub it up today. I've waited long enough.

Donna keeps going. "On his last report card, he had a D in algebra. A *D*! Math is his favorite subject. His marks for conduct were bad, too, and we knew then that we were up against something big, because he's never had that kind of trouble."

"OK, but how did he get expelled?"

I rub my foot against the stain again.

"I'm getting to that. I just wanted you to, you know, have some background. He got expelled because…God, I can barely say it." Donna's voice goes into a low whisper. "Edward, he called his English teacher a cunt."

I giggle.

"Edward!"

I giggle again.

"I'm going to hang up."

"No, don't. I'm sorry."

I hold the phone away from my face and cough real loud to clear my throat.

"I'm sorry."

"I want to know where he could have heard such a word," she says.

I have no idea. Scott Shamwell is the only person I know who uses the word "cunt" without any shame, but he gets away with it only because there are no women on the press crew. Anyway, I don't think he's met Kyle.

"He probably picked it up from another boy," I say, trying to be helpful.

Donna starts crying. "I don't know what to do. I asked Kyle what in the world has happened with him, and he said he hates living here, he wants to be back in our house across the street from you, that you're the only friend he has."

I silently thrill at this, although I immediately wonder if I should let Donna know that. Donna and Kyle and Victor left here in June, and I miss them.

"What did you say?" I ask.

"I didn't say anything. I sent him to his room so I didn't kill him. Not kill him, kill him. You know I'd never do that. I need to talk to Victor, but he's out of the office this morning and he's not picking up his cell. I know Kyle misses you. We all do. But I can't see that just giving him whatever he says he wants is going to fix what's wrong here. You know?"

"Yes."

The crying has stopped. "Would you have room for him? If we were to let him come see you, I mean?" she asks.

"Yes. Of course."

She sniffles. "OK. Let me talk to Victor. We'll figure out what to do from here."

"Good."

Again, I slide my foot along the soiled linoleum.

"Edward," she says, "why did you have a bad night?"

"Um…"

"I feel really bad that this has been all about our problems. What's going on there?"

I press at the edge of the sauce stain with my toenail, trying to lift it. It's no use.

"Donna, I'm going to have to call you back. OK?"

"What—"

I hang up.

— • —

The spilled, hardened marinara comes up without any problem once I apply a rag soaked in hot water and some scrubbing to it. It then occurs to me that this will leave me with one spot on my kitchen floor that's cleaner than the rest, which is, of course, unacceptable. I go back to my bedroom, pull my grubby clothes from the bottom drawer of my bureau, slip into them, and then I return to the kitchen and fill the mop bucket with warm water and floor cleaner.

It's when I'm sweeping up, clearing the floor for washing, that I'm thinking of 8:17 a.m. on Saturday, June 4, as I stood in the driveway of Donna's house, across the street from mine, and I waved good-bye to her and Victor and Kyle. They moved to Boise because Victor's job with the railroad got transferred there.

I can't say I was surprised. I mean, I can actually say the words "I was surprised"—that's easy—but I wouldn't believe them if I did. Victor was talking about the possibility all the way back in October 2010. It was October 31, which I remember because we were handing out Halloween candy to the neighborhood kids when he said something about it to Donna and she nodded. I badly wanted to ask why he would even consider moving to Boise, Idaho, and leaving this great neighborhood, but I didn't say anything. I just wished hard that it wouldn't happen, and you can see what wishing leads to—nothing good. By March, all that remained was for Kyle to finish up school here so they could pack and move.

I've noted before that it's silly to think that time actually speeds up. It doesn't. It's just an illusion. But it sure seems to move quickly when something you don't want to happen is imminent (I love the word "imminent"). June came so fast, figuratively speaking. My three best friends—my only three friends, really—left town, and I've been sad ever since. I talk to them on the phone, but it's not the same. I don't like talking on the telephone. I also exchange e-mail with Donna and Kyle, but that's not the same, either. Donna is the best friend I've ever had. She really knows how to call me on my bullshit without being a beeyotch (a word I learned from Kyle, and one I still don't quite understand). Seeing her words on my computer screen is better than nothing, I'll concede, but I would prefer that I could see her in person every day, like I used to. I liked how her hair would get lighter in the summertime and the freckles on her nose would look more pronounced, even though all of that was just a trick of the light. I liked how she walked really fast and stiff when she was angry. I liked how she could make me smile by smiling at me, when everybody else who smiles at me just makes me nervous.

As for Kyle, I met him on October 15, 2008, and so I've known him for 1,148 days of the 4,684 days he's been alive. (That means Kyle was born on February 9, 1999, making him twelve years, nine months, and twenty-nine days old.) I've known Kyle for more than 24 percent of his life. That means I'm invested, and that's why it hurts that I don't see him every day. He's been gone from here for 187 days, and that's 187 days of getting smarter, growing taller, and becoming closer to a man. I used to measure Kyle's height once a month along the side of my little garage, because I could plainly see that he was growing fast, but what my eyeballs told me was no match for solid data. The data is still there on the garage, written in blue ballpoint pen for anyone who wants to see it, but the last measurement happened on June 1 of this year. Between March 1, 2009, when we took the first measurement, and June 1, 2011, when we took the last, Kyle went from 4 feet 10 ⅜ inches tall to 5 feet 6 ⁷⁄₁₆ inches tall—taller than his mom. It's a shame I can't tell you how tall he is now. I'll never paint that garage again, so I at least have the measurements we took to remember that he was here.

I've tried to blame Victor for my friends being gone, because if Donna hadn't met Victor, she wouldn't have married him and there would have been no railroad job in Boise to take them away from here. The problem with blaming Victor is that it forces me to assume that nothing else would have changed, and I'm not comfortable assuming anything. That Dr. Buckley retired and I lost my job go to show that a lot has changed, not just the presence of Victor and his job in Boise. I prefer facts, and while it is a fact that Victor's job led my friends away from me, it's also a fact that Donna and Kyle love him and want to be with him and are happy they found him, and I think that should be given at least as much consideration as anything else. And even though I'm unhappy that my friends are gone, I like Victor too much to blame him. Donna and I were already good friends when he came along, and he tried hard to be my friend, too, which isn't always easy. He even asked me to serve as a witness when he married Donna at the courthouse, which was nice of him to do.

All this thinking about my friends moving away inspires another thought. If Donna and Victor are willing to send Kyle here for a few days, I'll have time to spend with him before I have to fly to Texas. We can watch football games, go for walks, build things in my basement workroom. I will ask him about his troubles at school. I will tell him about the shitburger year I've been having. We'll go outside and get a new measurement of his height on the garage, something that we badly need. It could be a good thing for both of us, and I remember that Dr. Buckley once said that "mutually agreeable" outcomes are the best kind. She's a very logical woman.

I mop the floor, and I'm happy about this idea I have. When I'm done, I'll call Donna back and tell her what I'm thinking, and then I'll hope that she and Victor are amenable (I love the word "amenable") to this course of action.

Happily, I dip the mop, like I'm Fred Astaire and it's Ginger Rogers.

I'm pretty funny sometimes.

— • —

I've finished in the kitchen, taken the wheelbarrow back into the garage (Scott Shamwell left it outside, just like he said he would), had a shower, put on my good clothes, and had my breakfast of oatmeal—along with my fluoxetine and new diabetes drugs—when the phone rings.

"Hello?"

A voice I know instantly comes back at me.

"Edward, it's Nathan Withers."

This is incredible. The mailman hasn't even picked up my letter and already it's gotten results.

"Hello."

I hear him clearing his throat.

"Edward, my boy, I've always shot straight with you, haven't I?"

I've never seen Mr. Withers use a gun, but I recognize this idiom.

"Yes."

"I intend to keep doing so," he says. "I heard you were here last night, trying to fix those steps on the south side of the building."

"Yes."

"You can't do that. I don't want to hear about you being here again. Am I clear?"

I want to cry. "Yes."

"Now, listen," he says, more softly than when he told me never to visit the *Herald-Gleaner* again. "I know it's hard. My boy, I would have never let you go if I'd had any other choice. Now, I'm not supposed to tell you that, but again, I'm shooting straight with you. Working here is something you're going to have to let go. It's hard, and you did good work, and you don't deserve what happened to you. Have you ever heard the phrase 'deserve's got nothin' to do with it'?"

"Yes. Clint Eastwood said that in *Unforgiven*."

"That's right. You're a talented man and a good worker, and somebody will appreciate that and give you a job, if you want one. But it won't be here. If you need a recommendation, I will write you one. If you want to have lunch sometime, I'll buy it. But you're not getting your job back. Do you hear me?"

"Yes."

"OK. Edward, have a good Christmas. Life is so much more than where you work. Find something you want to do, something that belongs to you and nobody can take away, and do that happily for the rest of your life. I know you can."

"I will try."

"That's good. Take care."

Mr. Withers hangs up.

I want to go back to bed.

Unfortunately, I have to pee first.

— • —

It's 1:57 p.m. when I wake up for good. I woke up thirty-three minutes earlier and an hour and twelve minutes earlier to pee. While I have no statistical data to back this up, I can say with near-certainty that I've never peed this much in my life.

The reason I woke up for good is an idea. It's one of the best ideas I've ever had. Again, tracking my number of ideas and their respective qualities is not something I ordinarily do, so I'm making this statement not based on empirical fact but on gut feeling. I don't imagine that I'll ever completely warm up to gut feelings, given their intrinsic (I love the word "intrinsic") lack of reliability, but in recent years I've learned to accept that I have them.

Now that Mr. Withers has stated without equivocation (I love the word "equivocation") that I will not be going back to work at the *Billings Herald-Gleaner*, I am not bound to be in this house or in Billings. Furthermore, as my lawyer, Jay L. Lamb, has made clear, I'm fucking loaded. I have never really thought of it that way, but I remember that was Scott Shamwell's reaction when I told him how much money my father left me when he died. "Bro," he said, "you're fucking loaded. Why are you working here?" He meant it as a rhetorical question, but in time, Mr. Withers answered it for him by involuntarily separating me.

But back to my current situation. The world is my oyster, as the saying goes, and a stupid saying it is. Kyle doesn't need to come here. I will go to him. I am not due anywhere for eleven days, when I'm scheduled to fly to Texas to see my mother. I have plenty of time.

I head for the phone, detouring to the bathroom first.

— • —

This is going to be so great.

Donna said she and Victor would love to host me in Boise, that they have a finished basement like mine and a good bed down there. She even puts Kyle on the phone, and although he sounds glum when he says "Hi, Edward," I am sure that our being together again will improve his mood. It's hard to be sure about something like that, but again, I have a good feeling.

I tell Donna that because we have been enjoying unseasonably mild weather, I would just as soon drive my Cadillac DTS to Idaho. It has been a long time since I got out and saw the western part of Montana, and by a long time I mean that I haven't seen it since June 15 to 23, 1986, when I was seventeen years old and I rode along with my mother and father on a family vacation to Seattle and back.

Donna tells me to be very careful and that before I leave, I should go to the cell phone store at Rimrock Mall and get myself a cellular telephone so I have a way of getting help should I run into trouble. She's a very logical woman.

When I think about going to Rimrock Mall, I feel a little queasy in my stomach. I don't really like it there, with all the people. Also, there's just no way to get there without taking left turns. I know. I've tried.

I'm also thinking about all the other things I have to do to get ready. I have to pack. I have to plot out a route, including gas stops and food. I have to get the oil changed in my Cadillac DTS. And I have to call Dr. Bryan Thomsen and tell him that I will not be at our 10:00 a.m. appointment Tuesday.

This will be weird. I've seen Dr. Buckley or Dr. Bryan Thomsen every Tuesday of every week of every month of every year since June 11, 2002, when Dr. Buckley moved my appointment from its regular 10:00 a.m. to 11:00 a.m. and it was nearly a disaster. She never made that mistake again, and from then on, my appointments were at 10:00 a.m. No matter what else has been unreliable in my life, my Tuesday counseling session has held steady. Now I'm going to miss one by choice. That's difficult for me to believe.

On the other hand, I'm troubled by the fact that Dr. Bryan Thomsen, whom I've been seeing now that Dr. Buckley has retired, has missed the 10:00 a.m. mark seven times in our thirty-two one-on-one meetings. I've held my tongue because I haven't wanted to wreck things with him, but if his sloppiness continues, it will have to be addressed. By skipping an appointment, I will avoid that potentially uncomfortable conversation for now.

"Are you sure about this, Edward?"

This is something I do not like about Dr. Bryan Thomsen. What kind of question is that? Of course I'm sure. That's why I called him and told him he wouldn't be seeing me Tuesday.

It's not like Dr. Buckley never questioned me about my choices. Believe me, she did. But her questions would always have a degree of specificity (I love the word "specificity") that Dr. Bryan Thomsen's lack. She would say something like, "Have you thought about 'blank,'" with the blank being some consequence of my decision that I would have to account for before committing myself to a course of action. But Dr. Bryan Thomsen just asks me a lame question with no specificity whatsoever.

"I'm sure. I'm driving to Boise, Idaho."

"When will you be back?"

"Before December twentieth, because I have to go Texas."

"Will you promise to schedule an appointment as soon as you can after you get back? I don't want to lose momentum on the good work we've been doing."

"I promise."

"Do you have my numbers? If you need to call me from the road, you can."

"I have your numbers."

"OK, Edward. I'll talk to you when you get back."

"OK."

I hang up, and as I do, I realize something: December 20 is a Tuesday. Even if I weren't going to Boise, my streak of every-Tuesday counseling sessions would have ended this month. How did I not notice that before?

It seems like everything I can rely on is slipping away from me.

— • —

If not for the fact that I have to do it, I would not choose to be at Rimrock Mall today.

First, the parking lot is so full that I have to park way in the back, almost to Twenty-Fourth Street West, the busiest street on

the west end of town. Here's how bad it was: I had to make six
left turns in the parking lot as I drove up and down the lanes
before I finally found a spot for my Cadillac DTS. Those were six
highly dangerous traffic maneuvers. I should feel fortunate that I
emerged from them without crashing, but it's hard to feel fortunate when my heart is pounding.

It's also hard to feel fortunate when I have to pee and the
entrance to the store is so far away.

I make my way through the parking lot at a light jog—fast
enough to get me into the mall before I wet my pants, but slow
enough that the agitation does not aggravate my impulse to pee.
This is a difficult balance to strike.

— • —

When I emerge from the men's room—stopping in the food court
to pull up my zipper—I see what I am up against. This mall is
teeming (I love the word "teeming") with people, and though
looks can be deceiving, I must say that not many of them look
merry and bright. I'm intimidated.

I stick close to the wall as I walk toward the center of the
mall to ensure that I touch as few people as possible. When I was
here a few years ago, some woman plowed directly into me with
her giant Orange Julius, and that is a scene I wish to avoid today.
When I reach the intersection of all the mall paths, I stop and jam
my back against the wall as I look for the cell phone kiosk. At last
I see it. It's manned by a pretty young woman wearing a Santa
hat. She looks friendly. Maybe this won't be so bad after all. Both
of those things—the woman's apparent friendliness, the notion
that this won't be bad—are conjecture, and conjecture is not good
enough. I need facts, and there is only one way to get them.

The woman in the Santa hat sees me coming.

"Happy holidays, sir," she says. "How can I help you?"

"I need a cellular telephone for my trip to Idaho."

She gestures at the array of phones adorning the kiosk.

"Well, we can certainly help with that. Did you have a particular model in mind? We have Blackberries, iPhones, Androids…"

"Just a phone that calls other phones."

She smiles.

"You're funny, sir. Let's look at this Droid Razr. It's has one gig of LP DDR2 RAM, a four-point-three-inch display, it runs on the 4G LTE network—"

"Does it call people?"

"Yes, of course it does. It also has some bitchin' apps."

"What?"

Her face flushes.

"I'm sorry. I shouldn't have said 'bitchin' "

She flummoxes me.

"I don't care," I say. "If it's bitchin', you should be honest about that."

"Oh, good. What kind of data plan do you need?"

"What's a data plan?"

"You know, web browsing and stuff."

"I have cable Internet at home."

"Right, but for your phone, I mean."

"This phone has that?"

"Of course. And it has a camera so you can send pictures to people, and text-messaging capability."

"Text messaging?"

"Absolutely!"

"Is there any other kind?" I ask.

"Any other kind of what?"

"Messaging."

"Not on this phone."

"OK. I like to send messages."

"OK, so you'll want to go unlimited with that."

"Yes, I don't want to be limited."

"You know what?" she says. "The Razr is good. But I think I have the right phone for you, sir. You want the best."

"Yes."

She brings out what she calls the Apple iPhone. It has everything I would ever want to do, she says. I can talk on it, I can use it to surf the Internet, I can send and receive messages, I can listen to music, I can take pictures. She says it's the best phone there is.

She also tells me that it's $399 and that the full data plan—"You'll want that," she says—will run me about $150 a month. Both of those numbers seem steep to me, but I remember that (a) I'm fucking loaded and (b) I wouldn't want to disappoint this woman who keeps telling me how smart I am for zeroing in on the iPhone.

I give her my credit card.

— • —

It's 11:23 p.m. I have spent the past six hours and thirty-four minutes playing with my bitchin' iPhone, minus the time it took for eight pee breaks.

It is the greatest thing I have ever owned. That might be hyperbole, but I don't care.

I will be able to get rid of my television set.

I will be able to get rid of my VCR, which I don't use anymore anyway, now that my *Dragnet* tapes are gone.

I will be able to get rid of my DVD player.

I can watch Dallas Cowboys games anywhere.

I barely need my computer anymore.

I have every song R.E.M. has ever released saved to my phone.

I just plotted out the entire trip to Boise, including gas stops, food, and lodging in Butte the first night, then I sent the files to my printer from my "cloud" so I have backup paper copies, which is just smart planning.

I love my "cloud."

I don't think my bitchin' iPhone is enough to countermand (I love the word "countermand") my declaration that 2011 has been a shitburger of a year, but maybe it can make 2012 the best year ever.

I leave tomorrow.

FROM BILLINGS TO BOISE: A TWO-DAY
ITINERARY BY EDWARD STANTON

Dates of travel: December 9–10, 2011.

Beginning address: 639 Clark Avenue, Billings, Montana.

Ending address: 1313 N. 25 Street, Boise, Idaho.

Beginning odometer reading: 27,156.8 miles.

Anticipated ending odometer reading: 27,848.3 miles (this accounts for the 686.5 miles from here to Donna and Victor's house, plus gives me 5 extra miles for getting off the highway for food and gas. I wish there were some way to be precise about this, but there isn't).

Anticipated gas mileage: 22.7 miles per gallon on the highway, based on current figures.

Size of gas tank: 18 gallons.

Number of fill-ups needed to complete trip: Two. In Butte on Day 2, and later that day in American Falls, Idaho.

Anticipated amount/cost of fill-up in Butte: 9.925 gallons at $3.23/gallon, for $32.06. Gas prices are highly volatile, however, and this estimate is based on online reports of the average cost of gas in Butte, Montana, today. I have no way of knowing what the prices will be the day after tomorrow.

Anticipated amount/cost of fill-up in American Falls: 12.078 gallons at $3.18/gallon, for $38.41. See my note above about the volatility of gas prices.

Anticipated amount of remaining gas upon arrival at Donna and Victor's house: 8.666 gallons, or enough for 156.9 miles of city driving at 18.1 miles per gallon. That's way more than I should need, I would think. The facts will reveal themselves in due time.

Planned accommodations in Butte: I have reservations at the Best Western Plus Butte Plaza Inn on Harrison Avenue. It has a four-and-a-half-star rating on the basis of five reviews on Google. Pros: Easy access from the interstate, a Perkins restaurant adjoining (I love the word "adjoining"). Con: $110 a night. But fuck it. I'm loaded.

Snacks procured: Dr. Rex Helton would no doubt prefer that I eat carrots and celery, but I cannot do that. Aside from the fact that I don't like celery, there is the issue of freshness to be considered. I am driving 691.5 miles. Therefore, I have unsalted sunflower seeds and a case of bottled water.

Music: Everything R.E.M. has ever released, piped in through my bitchin' iPhone.

Other details: A few things I need to keep in mind:

1. *Remember the medicine and take it every day.*
2. *Remember to take a walk every day and to keep a log for Dr. Rex Helton. I haven't started this yet, and I need to.*
3. *Keep the car at 65 miles per hour at all times on the interstate. Others may drive faster. At 65, I will get excellent fuel efficiency at a legal speed, thus better ensuring that my fuel usage estimates have a high degree of accuracy.*

4. *Be on the lookout for interesting things on the drive. Stop and take pictures with the bitchin' iPhone camera. Enjoy the trip.*
5. *Be safe.*
6. *Stop making this list.*
7. *OK, stop now.*
8. *Now.*
9. *Shit.*
10. *I can't end on 9, so I will end here.*
11. *Thank goodness.*
12. *Shit!*
13. *I*
14. *Guess*
15. *I'll*
16. *End*
17. *It*
18. *At*
19. *Number*
20. *20.*

SATURDAY, DECEMBER 10, 2011

From the logbook of Edward Stanton:
   Time I woke up today: 6:17 a.m. The first time all year I've been awake at this time.
   High temperature for Friday, December 9, 2011, Day 343: 33
   Low temperature for Friday, December 9, 2011: 21
   Precipitation for Friday, December 9, 2011: 0.00 inches
   Precipitation for 2011: 19.40 inches
   Addendum: I will be on the road for a few days, so I will have to rely on out-of-town newspapers for the official Billings weather data. That should not be a problem, although I am worried about whether those newspapers use the same source of information that the Billings Herald-Gleaner does. I will have to accept their numbers, I guess, and reconcile them against the Herald-Gleaner when I get home. It's not an ideal situation.

Because I wish to travel light, I am not carrying my full accompaniment of weather data notations, so I say this in the admittedly sketchy vein of personal recollection: this is the prettiest December I've ever seen. I notice this in particular at 8:03 a.m., twelve minutes after I departed, as I'm merging onto Interstate 90 westbound, staring at a clear sky and the Crazy Mountains in the distance.

I've eaten my oatmeal and consumed my fluoxetine, lisino-pril, potassium chloride, metformin, actos, and furosemide. I've packed a large duffel bag with all the clothes I will need for at least a week. Donna and I did not agree on a date when I would return home. It's unlike me to be so informal about things, and yet somehow, today, that does not bother me. Which bothers me.

I set the Cadillac DTS on cruise control at exactly 65 miles per hour, and I take a swig of water from the bottle in the cup holder beside me. I've always heard singers pay tribute to the open road—it seems that you cannot be a singer for long with-out singing about being on the road, as if that's required by the international singers' union or something—and for the first time, I think I understand what they mean. I'm not sure why I waited until I was forty-two years old to do this.

Michael Stipe, incidentally, is not singing about the open road. He's singing about a crush with eyeliner through my bitchin' iPhone, which is plugged into my Cadillac's speakers. Michael Stipe is pretty inscrutable (I love the word "inscrutable") some-times.

— • —

Thirteen-point-seven miles into my trip, Michael Stipe is sing-ing about how everybody hurts—a song that has resonance with me—when I realize that I hurt, or at least my tallywhacker does.

I have to pee really bad.

Luckily, I am close to the exit for Laurel, the town directly west of Billings, when the urge to urinate strikes. I pull off the interstate and into the parking lot of a gas station, and I hustle inside, holding my tallywhacker through my pants as I look for the men's room.

As I'm standing there, draining my ever-filling bladder, I think of a word I like: "retromingent." This means "to pee backward." I am not retromingent; I pee forward. Cows are retromingent, though. I find this curious.

In the gas station's store, I buy a pack of sugar-free gum. I don't like gum very much, but I don't think it's right to use the store's facilities without contributing to its economic well-being. This seems like the right choice.

Soon I'm back on the interstate and headed west again. Michael Stipe is singing about his harborcoat. I have to say, putting my extensive collection of R.E.M. music on shuffle was a smart move by me. While I know that each song will be R.E.M., I have no idea which exact song is coming up until the first notes are struck. I am enjoying this spontaneity.

And yet this enjoyment is balanced by a sadness I haven't been able to shake since September 21, when R.E.M. announced that they were disbanding. I still wish I knew why Michael Stipe and the rest of R.E.M. had to leave me.

— • —

I want to talk about why I'm going only 223 miles on the first day of my trip. Certainly, driving the entire 686.5 miles from my house to Donna and Victor's would not be impossible to achieve in a single day. If my father were still alive and making this trip with me, I have little doubt that he would say something like, "Teddy, buckle up. We're going the whole route." I don't like to be called Teddy; my name is Edward. But if it meant that I could see my father again and hear his voice, I would be willing to endure it.

The reason I am going only 223 miles today is it's hard for me to concentrate on a singular task like driving for much longer than that. This is one of the byproducts of my condition, Asperger's syndrome with a strong streak of obsessive-compulsive disorder. My mind wanders, and that can become a dangerous situation when one is driving a car, especially alone without anyone to talk to. I'm going to try to drive the remaining 463.5 miles tomorrow. If I make plenty of stops to allow my brain some rest time, I should be able to do that, and once I am at Donna and Victor's, I will be able to get as much rest as I need to recover from the arduousness (I love the word "arduousness") of the trip. If I cannot go 463.5 miles tomorrow, I am prepared to spend a second night in a motel. My condition sometimes allows me to do some dumb things, but failing to make contingency plans for a trip like this is not one of them. I have already scouted out the lodging options between Butte, Montana, and Boise, Idaho. I am developmentally disabled. I'm not stupid.

— • —

It's 140.7 miles from my driveway to Bozeman, Montana, and it took me two hours and thirty-two minutes to cover that distance. That segment of my trip took longer than I anticipated because I had to stop to pee twice.

The first time was just outside Columbus, Montana, at mile marker 418. The rest area sits atop a high hill that overlooks the Yellowstone River valley. After taking care of my business, which is a euphemism, I walked along the sidewalk and took in the view. On an unseasonably warm December day like this one, with the sky clear and no haze, it was as if I could see forever, which is of course an optical illusion.

As much as I was tempted to sit down in the grass and look at the scenery for a while, I pushed on. I had many miles to go, and

I would not want to disappoint Donna, Victor, and Kyle by being later than necessary.

Thirty-eight miles on, near the small town of Greycliff, I stopped again. This peeing business is getting a bit ridiculous, although I suspect that I make it worse by drinking so much water. By the time I got to Greycliff, I was on my second bottle, and I hadn't yet covered a hundred miles. As unlikely as it seems, I may have to invest in a second case of water.

It's also possible that I did not maintain a constant 65 miles per hour on the interstate. In Livingston, for instance, 27 miles from Bozeman, the Cadillac DTS was blown aggressively by the wind. And as I came through the mountain pass into Bozeman, I deviated between going faster than 65 miles per hour down hills and slower than 65 on tight turns. The mountain pass between Livingston and Bozeman is a good representation of why I am taking this trip in small chunks. It stresses me out to drive through mountain passes.

Now I am in Bozeman, at a coffee shop on Main Street because I am hungry. I left the house at 7:51 a.m. having eaten only oatmeal and three handfuls of sunflower seeds (which I have now abandoned because they're messy and I do not like messes), and it's now 10:23 and I am a bit lightheaded. That's not good.

I order a sugar-free chai tea which I'm eager to try, never having heard of such a thing, and a granola bar that the nice lady at the counter said would be OK for me to have in my condition.

"I'm diabetic, you know," I tell her.

"Well, I didn't know that, but we can work out something just fine," she says.

I appreciated that, both for her willingness to work around my dietary needs and for her pointing out that she had no way of knowing about my condition. It was silly for me to have suggested she did.

I'm on my second gulp of the chai tea, which is really good and comes in a tall, thin glass that I find visually appealing, when a young man with close-cropped blond hair comes up to me and says, "Oh, you're a bright boy, aren't you?"

I look around. I haven't heard anyone say "bright boy" since I saw the 1946 movie *The Killers*, in which William Conrad says it several times in the opening scene.

"Me?" I ask.

He points at my sweatshirt. I look down. It reads: University of Montana, 2001 National Champions.

"Yeah, you," he says.

"Well, I am pretty smart sometimes," I say.

He pokes me in the chest with his finger, and it hurts.

"It's not smart to wear a Griz shirt in Bozeman."

I look past the young man to the counter, but the woman who gave me the tea and the granola bar doesn't seem to notice. He and I are alone in the back of the coffee shop.

"I don't care about the University of Montana Grizzlies," I say. "I'm a Texas Christian University fan."

This makes him angrier.

"So you're just fucking with people then?"

"No."

"It seems like you are."

"Conjecture can be a risky thing," I say. "It seems that you're assuming the reason for my wearing this sweatshirt, and as it turns out, you're incorrect."

My father received it from a friend of his, a University of Montana supporter, and I got it from my mother when she was sorting out my father's clothes to give away after he died. I wore it today because I was thinking of him.

"You're a real smart-ass, aren't you?"

"No, just smart."

What happens next is so abrupt I have no way to prepare for it. The angry young man hits me square in the nose with his fist. Intense pain spreads across my face, and my eyes begin to water. I almost fall off the chair I'm sitting on, but I catch the edge of the table with my left hand and hold myself up. I taste something tinny in my mouth, and I touch my nose. It's bleeding.

"Fuck you," the young man says, and he turns and heads for the door.

The woman who was working the counter runs past him the other way to check on me.

"Are you OK?" she asks.

"I'm bleeding."

I want to cry, and I probably could because my eyes are watering, but I don't want to do that in front of this woman.

"Let me grab something," she says.

She runs back to the counter and runs a washcloth under the hot water. She then brings it to me.

"Tilt your head back," she says.

I do as she tells me. She gently passes the washcloth over my nose, which still hurts. When she lifts it, I can see that it's inundated (I love the word "inundated") with blood.

"I'll be right back," she says.

As she leaves me again, I call out, "Who was that? Why did he hit me?" The first question is real; the second one is rhetorical. There is no good reason for hitting someone square in the face like that.

"I don't know," she shouts to me across the room. She holds up a hand to a couple waiting at the counter, to tell them she'll be back in a moment.

"Here," she says, handing the clean washcloth to me. "Keep your head back and hold this on your nose."

"I didn't do anything to him," I say.

I've begun to cry. I can't help it.

"I know you didn't. Do you want me to call the cops?"

I don't like the police. I'm not going to get into it with her, but the truth is, the cops were called on me a few times before my condition was brought under control with Dr. Buckley's help, and it's a conditioned response that I just don't like to see them.

"No," I tell her.

"Are you going to be all right?"

"I don't know."

"OK. Listen, I have to see what these folks want. Let me know if you need anything."

"OK."

After she leaves, I stand up, holding the washcloth on my face, and I make my way to the far back of the coffee shop, where the restroom is. I don't have to pee.

The single bulb in the restroom casts a dim light. I push my face forward until it's about an inch from the mirror, and I examine the damage. My nose is inflamed, and I see swelling around the bridge of it. Flecks of dried blood line the edges of my nostrils.

I touch the swollen parts of my face, and pain shoots to the spots where my fingers have been. I will have to be very careful until things have had a chance to heal.

All things considered, though, it seems that the damage is minimal, except to my feelings. All I wanted was a snack and a few minutes to relax, and I got a punch in the face.

I didn't deserve that. It was wrong of that young man to punch me like that.

But then I remember that deserve's got nothin' to do with it.

— • —

It is 83.15 miles from Bozeman to Harrison Drive in Butte, where my hotel room is waiting for me. The route covers some of the wondrous country Montana is known for—river valleys, mountain ranges (I particularly enjoy the Tobacco Root Mountains, which have a great name), and the sky that is so impressive that the state has been given a special name: Big Sky Country. I take all of this in, but aside from a pee break at the Town Pump in Whitehall, I do not stop. I do not take photos with my bitchin' iPhone. Periodically, I look at my face in the rearview mirror, and I see that the swollen areas around my nose have not receded much and, in fact, have begun to turn a violent shade of purple. This sucks elephant balls. It's ruining my trip.

Finally, at 12:37 p.m., I pull into the parking lot of the Best Western Plus Butte Plaza Inn. I retrieve my duffel bag from the trunk and trudge inside to check in.

"Whoa, buddy, what happened to your face?" the desk clerk says.

"I got punched."

"By who?"

"By whom, you mean."

"Yeah."

"Somebody who didn't like my sweatshirt."

He peers over the top of his glasses at my chest.

"Huh. Good team."

"Are they?"

"You don't know?"

"I don't care."

He shakes his head.

"Well, they are."

I start to say something but abandon it. His attention is on his computer screen, and he doesn't seem interested in talking to me anymore, which is fine. I sigh, and he frowns. Finally, he hands me my keycard. I take it and walk away.

"We have a continental breakfast starting at six in the morning," he calls after me.

— • —

After a shower, I lie across the motel room bed in my robe and close my eyes. I keep thinking about the young man who punched me, and I keep wishing I could see Dr. Buckley again, because this is something she and I would have talked about extensively. My trust in her was complete, and that's something I don't enjoy with Dr. Bryan Thomsen—which, I suppose, is why I don't call him and tell him what happened.

I think back to Tuesday, February 1, the day when Dr. Buckley told me that she would be retiring at the end of April. She said that her husband had already retired from his job as a cardiovascular surgeon at Billings Clinic, which I didn't realize because, first, Dr. Buckley and I talk mostly about me and not her and, second, my family gets its medical attention at St. Vincent Healthcare. My father was on the board of directors there and was loyal to it. He died there three years, one month, and ten days ago. I haven't thought about it before, but I hope wherever he is—if he is anywhere at all other than the Terrace Garden Cemetery—he's happy that he died at St. Vincent Healthcare instead of Billings Clinic. I think that would have mattered to him.

Dr. Buckley said she and her husband wanted to do some traveling before "we're too old to get around anymore," and I told her that was silly, that she looked young and vibrant and ambulatory (I love the word "ambulatory"). She said, "You're sweet, Edward," but I wasn't trying to be. She really does look good, or at least she did on Tuesday, April 26, which was the last time I saw her. It would be conjecture to say what she looks like now. In any case, I have no way of knowing whether her husband is healthy, as I have never met him. Maybe he's about to die. Maybe Dr. Buckley's haste is warranted.

Before Dr. Buckley and I parted ways, we had five joint sessions with Dr. Bryan Thomsen. Dr. Buckley said this would allow me and Dr. Bryan Thomsen to "ease into" a patient-doctor relationship. She said that she was sure we would "hit it off" and that Dr. Bryan Thomsen, being more my age, might even relate to me in a way that she could not. I had my doubts about this, because I never saw any evidence that the age gap between me and Dr. Buckley was an impediment (I love the word "impediment"), but I told her that I would try.

I've been right so far in my suspicions about Dr. Bryan Thomsen. He's been a poor substitute for Dr. Buckley. Most of the time, that doesn't bother me, but it sure does right now.

— • —

Unable to sleep because I keep touching the part of my face that hurts, I decide to watch *Adam-12* on my phone. I am so far behind. I have not been good about watching this show daily like I used to do with *Dragnet*. But I'm trying to hang in there. Dr. Buckley and I worked diligently to break my destructive compulsions while properly channeling those that brought balance to my life, like the daily complaint letter I used to write. But in this shitburger of a year, it seems that many of my routines have been shattered.

I hope that reestablishing a balance with my show watching will help settle me down. Hope, of course, is fleeting and unpredictable. I'd rather have facts.

I'm watching the twenty-second episode of the first season, called "Log 152: A Dead Cop Can't Help Anybody." I should have watched it two days ago, but I fell asleep, and then the excitement of planning my trip overtook me.

It has taken me a while to figure out things about *Adam-12*, and while I still think it is vastly inferior to *Dragnet*, I'm starting to warm up to it. Neither Officer Pete Malloy nor Officer Jim Reed is as wise and logical as Sergeant Joe Friday, but between the two of them, they make almost the perfect cop. Malloy is older and more crotchety (I love the word "crotchety"), while Reed is a young hotshot. Their respective attributes—wisdom and reserve, youth and strength—serve them well as they tackle crime in the streets of Los Angeles.

I think I will keep going with this series.

— • —

After eating a grilled chicken dinner at Perkins, I take a walk around the immediate area. It's a nondescript place close to the interstate. Tomorrow morning, in fact, I'll have to go west for 6.6 miles farther on Interstate 90 to get to Interstate 15 South, which will carry me into Idaho.

The sky has gone dark. While the weather is variable, the time of sunset is not. We have not yet reached the winter solstice, when the stretches of daylight will begin growing longer. The sun was down before 5:00 p.m. I pull my coat up to cover my ears. It's quite cold here—much colder than it is back home in Billings.

I'm adrift. That's the feeling I've had since setting out today—and, really, for much of this shitburger of a year—and I've finally found the word to describe that feeling. My home is 223 miles behind me, and my destination is still 463.5 miles away. I don't feel comfortable here, my feelings are still badly hurt over getting punched, and I'm nervous about seeing Donna and Victor and Kyle again. That seems strange to me. If you'd asked me on any of the 189 days since they moved whether I'd like to see them, I would have jumped up excitedly and said, "Yes, please, that would be very nice."

Now I'm about twenty-four hours away, and I feel scared.

That flummoxes me. It's hard to know how much of that feeling is because I'll be seeing my friends again and how much is because of everything else. I don't like not knowing things.

TECHNICALLY SUNDAY,
DECEMBER 11, 2011

I wake up at 2:37 a.m., and I'm discombobulated (I love the word "discombobulated") and short of breath. As my eyes adjust to the absence of light, I stop fighting for air, and my heart rate slows. I remember now where I am.

I had a weird dream.

In it my father was alive. I frequently have dreams in which my father is alive and with me. Usually, he is showing me how to do something or telling me something he thinks I ought to know. I never dreamed about my father while he was alive. At least, I don't remember doing so. I've dreamt about him often in the three years, one month, and eleven days since he died. It's odd, but it's also comforting, so I do not complain.

This dream was strange in that what happened in it also happened in real life, many years ago. I was with my father in a bar in a little town called Cheyenne Wells, Colorado. I was nine years old. I remember that because the Dallas Cowboys had beaten the Denver Broncos in Super Bowl XII earlier that year. A few months later, after school was finished, my mother let me go with my father to Cheyenne Wells, where he was going to oversee some work on the oil pumps that the company he worked for owned there. That's how we ended up at the bar.

We were sitting on stools. My father was on my left, engaged in an earnest bullshit session with the bartender, and on my right was this old man with long, white whiskers. He had his hands clenched together, and he kept bringing them to his face and peering into them with one eye.

This sparked my curiosity.

"What do you have in there?" I asked him.

"It's a mouse. Would you like to see it?"

I didn't believe him. A mouse could not fit into the small space between his clenched hands. Even if it could, it would probably try to bite the man. I thought he was playing games with me.

"No, I don't want to see your mouse."

I don't remember everything—I can't even guess when the last time was that I thought about this—but I do know this went on for some time, with the old man looking into his hands and inviting me to take a look. I declined every time.

At some point, I got up to go to the bathroom and pee— because I was a young boy with a small bladder, not because I was medicated like I am now. When I emerged from the bathroom, the old man was waiting for me, and he grabbed me by the wrist and tried to hurt me.

I screamed for my father, and he got there in what seemed like a millisecond, although I know that's impossible. He grabbed the old man's hand and my wrist and yanked them apart, and then he threw an elbow into the old man's chest, knocking him to the floor.

"Get the hell out of here," my father said, and the old man did.

After the old man scrambled away, my father turned to me. He looked concerned. "Teddy, are you all right?"

I nodded. I couldn't say anything.

My father held out his hand.

"Come on, Son."

He led me back to the bar and told the bartender to set me up with a fresh root beer.

— • —

I have to be honest about my father. He was an inscrutable man sometimes. We got along great when I was a young boy, but in later years, especially when I was a teenager and even older, we fought a lot. There were times when he was cruel to me, like when he directed Jay L. Lamb to write me nasty letters upbraiding (I love the word "upbraiding") me for what he perceived to be my failures.

When he died, which was quite sudden and unexpected, we had not resolved many of our disagreements, and that left me regretful.

Dr. Buckley said that as I adjusted to my father's death, the good memories would replace the bad and perhaps I could have a relationship with him in death that I could not manage while he was alive. This has been true for the most part, but not entirely. The truth is, I alternate between happy memories, ones where it almost seems as if he's by my side, and regretful ones, where we're still fighting and still finding it impossible to understand each other. The one constant, regardless of memory, is that I wish he were here for real. As I lie on my back in bed, staring into the dark, the blanket pulled up around me, I think that I have never wanted him here more than I do right now.

If my father had been with me yesterday, he would have protected me from the intemperate young man in Bozeman. If he were here right now, he might be able to tell me why I am suddenly so scared of figuring out how my life is supposed to go. I don't know anymore. I used to have a job and friends whom I saw every day, or nearly so. I used to have routines and things I could rely on. I don't have many of those things anymore. I don't know how to replace what I've lost. I don't know if it's even possible.

I would want to tell my father this, but I also would want him to know that I am hanging in there. My father admired people who hung in there. Troy Aikman was his favorite football player ever because he seemed to be fearless, even when other teams were hurting him bad. I am not fearless. I cannot even pretend to be. But I am hanging in there. I'm trying to make sense of things. I think that's why I'm on this trip. Yes, Kyle is in trouble, and I want to help him if I can. Yes, I want to see Donna and Victor again. But maybe I want something for me, too, such as not feeling so adrift. That seems selfish, but I think it's OK. I think my father would think it's OK, too.

I'm glad I could think about this, even if it did interrupt my sleep.

OFFICIALLY SUNDAY, DECEMBER 11, 2011

From the logbook of Edward Stanton:
Time I woke up today: 2:37 a.m. to deal with the dream about
my father. 7:38 a.m. for good. The 208th time all year I've been
awake at this time.

High temperature for Saturday, December 10, 2011, Day 344:
43 (according to the Butte newspaper)
Low temperature for Saturday, December 10, 2011: 27
Precipitation for Saturday, December 10, 2011: 0.00 inches
Precipitation for 2011: 19.40 inches
New entries:
Exercise for Saturday, December 10, 2011: 47-minute brisk
walk after dinner.
Miles driven Saturday, December 10, 2011: 223.4
Addendum: While I had a bowl of oatmeal this morning at the
complimentary continental breakfast—where I consumed all of my
medicine—I thought a lot about the dream I had early this morn-
ing and my fear about where my life is headed. There is nothing I
can do to magically make the fear go away. There is no such thing
as magic. Maybe the fear means something. Maybe it is guiding

me toward something. This is all more touchy-feely than I prefer to be, but perhaps I will stress out about it less if I believe I'm headed toward something new and important. I have nothing against belief, although I will concede that it is not nearly as good as fact.

I've also thought a lot about being punched by the intemperate young man in Bozeman. I'm going to try not to stress out about that, either.

I have a long purplish-blue streak that runs vertically along the right side of my nose, and the fleshy area under my right eye is turning black. What a whipdick that intemperate young man is.

— • —

Before I leave, I do something smart—I wait for an hour after I've taken my medicine before loading up the car and leaving Butte. In that time, I pee twice, which should mitigate (I love the word "mitigate") my having to pee while in transit. I still manage to gas up and be on the road by 10:02 a.m. My fill-up requires 10.023 gallons of unleaded gasoline at $3.1499 a gallon, for a total of $31.57. By my figures, I got 22.3 miles per gallon yesterday. My projections were way off, and that disappoints me. There is just no way to fully anticipate your costs when you're at the mercy of oil companies.

It's a cold, clear morning. The external thermostat on my Cadillac DTS, which displays on the control panel inside, says it's twelve degrees outside. The external thermostat on this car is not as reliable as the official temperature-gauging machinery used by the National Weather Service, but it is sufficient for my driving needs.

— • —

As I pass a weigh station, where the transportation department checks the paperwork and cargo size of large trucks and other commercial vehicles, I remember sometimes being with my father when he would take long drives like the one I am on. He hated weigh stations. His hostility didn't come from direct personal experience. Only once did I ever see my father driving a large truck, and that was in November 1974, when he bought an International Paystar 500 in Denver and drove it to Midland, Texas, so it could be outfitted with a drilling rig. My mother sent me along with him on that trip. I was five years old. Their marriage was in trouble, although I didn't know that at the time. I don't recall that we had any difficulty with weigh stations on that trip. I'd remember it if it had happened.

Anyway, my father hated weigh stations. Every time we would pass one, he would say something like "money-grubbing assholes" or "two-bit quasi-cops." I asked him one time why he hated weigh stations so much, and he said the people in them liked to give a hard time to the drilling crews he supervised. He told me about this one time when a driller named Jim Quillen got stopped at a weigh station near Grand Junction, Colorado. The weigh station personnel came out and checked the paperwork on his big drilling rig and a smaller truck with a water tank on the back. They climbed onto the cab of the drilling rig, measured the overhang on the mast, and told Jim Quillen that it went too far over the snout of the truck.

"Quillen was a hothead, but he was smart, too," my father said. "He knew that if he kicked up a fight, they'd just shut him down permanent. So you know what he did, Teddy?"

I did not know what he did, and I told my father so.

"He brought that water truck around front of the rig and backed it right up till they were almost touching. Then he lashed the trucks together, and he hauled out of there. No more over-hang. Quillen said that when they went by the shack, those guys' mouths were open to the floor. Serves 'em right, the fuckers."

My father told me this story and he laughed so hard that his face turned red. I could tell that it was one of his favorite stories. It was a pretty good story, I guess. I don't rate these things, but it's not the best story I've ever heard. All the same, I'm thankful that he told it to me, so I could remember it now and think of him.

— • —

The route I'm traveling, Interstate 15 South into Idaho, takes me through some beautiful country, and twice I pull off to take a picture along the Beaverhead-Deerlodge National Forest. I've never been much of a picture taker. I tend to remember so many things that I don't need the pictures to remind me, but I must concede that I've been glad to have all the pictures of Donna and Kyle and Victor that have been taken and given to me in the past few years. When I'm feeling especially lonely, I bring them out and remember the good times when they were taken. These pictures from this trip, which I'm taking with my bitchin' iPhone and sending to my "cloud," might serve a similar purpose for me sometime. Part of me wishes I could leave the interstate and do some exploring. Virginia City, which was the territorial capital of Montana, is not too far away. Neither is Bannack, which was the territorial capital before Virginia City. I learned about these places in my Montana history class in the eighth grade at Will James Middle School, and I would like to see them someday, but I have hundreds of miles to go and can't deviate (I love the word "deviate") that far.

My predeparture peeing program seems to have paid dividends. Before I cross over into Idaho, I stop only once to drain my main vein and make my bladder gladder, and that's in Dillon, 66.1 miles into my trip. I drive into the parking lot of an Exxon station and half-jog inside. I've planned well. Unlike yesterday, I don't feel as though I'm about to burst, and so I'm able to get to the bathroom without drawing attention to myself by holding my tallywhacker. Two minutes and seven seconds later, after I've washed my hands thoroughly, I pay the store cashier for a pack of sugar-free gum and I'm headed back to the car.

At 11:28 a.m., I am on the interstate and headed for Idaho.

This is a good day already.

— • —

I'm 24.7 miles beyond Dillon when my bitchin' iPhone makes a noise at me.

I pick it up, and this message is on the screen: *Whats up. LOL.* That doesn't make sense.

With one hand on the wheel, and glancing repeatedly between my phone and the road, I type back: *Who is this?*

I put my right hand back on the steering wheel and try to keep my eyes focused on the road, but curiosity is stronger than my desire to drive in the recommended safe manner. I keep moving my eyes so I can see the phone's screen.

Finally, another message comes through: *The cops. LOL. Turn around and go home. LOL.*

I'm really flummoxed now. Again, I split my attention and spell out a reply: *How did you get this number? And what's so funny?*

I'm not stupid; I know that LOL means "laughing out loud." I also know what ROFLMAO means, and I have figured out most of the things that are known as emoticons. I do not like them.

Internet culture is destroying the way we communicate with each other.

I look down again at my phone, waiting for a response. When I look up, I've drifted too far to the right, and I have to pull hard on the steering wheel to keep the Cadillac DTS from leaving the road. That was a close one. My heart pounds.

In comes the next message: *I know everything. LOL.*

As I reach down to respond yet again, blue lights fill my rear-view mirror. A Montana Highway Patrol car is pulling me over.

Well, slap my ass and call me Sally. That's just a saying, by the way. Scott Shamwell used to say that sometimes. I don't want my ass slapped, and I prefer to be called by my own name, which is Edward.

I pull over and wait for the officer.

— • —

After the patrolman gives me a $250 ticket for reckless driving—and scolds me for texting while driving, saying that I'm lucky I didn't kill myself or somebody else or worse, which seems silly to me because what could be worse than killing or being killed?—I remain in my turned-off car on the side of the interstate.

Who is this, really? I type. *Don't lie.*

A few moments pass. *Kyle. LOL.*

You just cost me $250 and got me in big trouble with the Montana Highway Patrol.

LOLOLOLOLOLOLOLOLOLOLOLOLOLOLOLOLOLO-LOLOLOLOLOLOLOLOLOLOLOLOLOLOLOLOLOLO-LOLOLOLOLOLOLOLOLOLOLOL!

— • —

The taunting messages from Kyle keep coming. He tells me to be a "gangsta" and not pay my ticket. He tells me that the Dallas Cowboys suck and that the Denver Broncos and Tim Tebow rule. He tells me that he's going to whip my butt on all his Wii games, which is probably true; I never was very good at Wii. He tells me that his parents are stupid and that his school is full of "douches."

I watch the messages as they continue to come through as I drive, which I'm probably not supposed to do, but I can't help it. I'll be stopping to eat in American Falls, which is 170.6 miles away, and I can answer his many text messages when I get there. In the meantime, I will monitor them.

At 12:37, however, I receive a message that causes me to turn off the bitchin' iPhone.

Dont be all stupid when your here.

I blink twice when I see it. The words sting me. Kyle, as much as anybody, should know that I'm not stupid. I explained my condition to him soon after I met him, and I know Donna has told him about it, and still he saw fit to message my bitchin' iPhone and call me stupid. I'm not stupid at all. I'm very smart. I know a lot of things, and I know how to do a lot of things. The world sometimes doesn't make sense to me. Other people regularly flummox me. I'm bad with crowds, and I don't know what to do when people are emotional, but none of that means I'm stupid. The irony is now I'm the emotional one. Kyle's message makes me want to stop this car and beat on it with a hammer.

Also, Kyle has some nerve calling me stupid when he doesn't know the difference between "your" and "you're."

I try to imagine what Dr. Buckley would tell me to do, which is a poor substitute for actually hearing from her. For one thing, it forces me to use conjecture, and I've been clear all along that conjecture can be a dangerous thing. I guess I have no alternative now.

I suppose Dr. Buckley would say that Kyle is a boy, and boys can be cruel. She might also say that his ugliness toward me is just a misplaced manifestation (I love the word "manifestation") of his frustration with himself. Dr. Buckley often said that when we say nasty things about other people, we're really criticizing something in them that we don't like in ourselves. I'm not sure I ever fully understood what she meant by that, but taking that and applying it to Kyle somehow makes it easier to process. I know Kyle is having a tough time in his new town and at his new school. Maybe people are calling *him* stupid. Maybe he's putting that on me so it's not on him any longer. That's a lot of maybes, which makes me uncomfortable.

Finally, I remember Dr. Buckley once telling me that the children who would make fun of me when I was young were, in many cases, simply dealing with differences the way children often do. Children are perceptive about differences, and they sometimes fall victim to a sort of mob mentality where a lack of conformity is identified and punished. It saddens me to think that this might now describe Kyle, because up until this point, he and I have never let our differences—like our age—keep us from being good friends. When he and Donna and Victor left Billings 190 days ago, he hugged me in their old driveway, and I hugged him back, which is hard for me. Now he's speaking (writing) to me this way. What if we can't be friends anymore? I don't think that's something I want to contemplate.

I resolve to leave the bitchin' iPhone off until I arrive at Donna and Victor's. I won't get to take pictures of Idaho, and if I'm late in arriving, I won't get to follow the Dallas Cowboys' game tonight against the New York Giants, but I also don't want to be confused by Kyle any more than I already am.

— • —

After dinner at the Pizza Hut in American Falls, I settle back into the seat of my Cadillac DTS and turn on my bitchin' iPhone. I can't help it.

A voice mail is waiting for me.

"Hi, Edward, it's Donna. I got hold of Kyle's phone and saw the crap he's been sending you. I am so, so sorry about the ticket. We'll pay for that. And you can bet you won't be getting any more messages. This young man seems intent on digging himself a bigger hole than the one he's already in. Gosh, we're really so excited to see you, if you can stand to come still. See you in a few hours. Call if you're going to be delayed. Bye now."

Hearing Donna's voice makes me feel funny, but not ha-ha funny and not bad funny, either. It's like a warmth inside my body, something similar to the way I would feel when I was a little boy and I was sick and my mother would stroke my forehead and tell me stories about bunnies who live in the clouds, which is of course impossible. It's something I haven't felt at all since Donna has been gone. She is my best friend. Kyle was also my best friend, and I'm hopeful that he can be again, but right now Kyle and I are in difficult circumstances. Kyle seems to be in difficult circumstances with a lot of people.

That Donna would offer to pay my traffic ticket just shows what kind of person she is. That's silly, though. I would never let them do it. I know Donna and Victor are financially comfortable, but $250 is a lot of money, and it's not like they did anything wrong. If anybody should pay the ticket, it's Kyle; he's the one who caused it. But Kyle is just a boy, and he probably doesn't have $250.

I'll pay the ticket. Regardless of what Kyle did, it's my responsibility. And fuck it, I'm loaded.

— • —

A half-hour's drive down the road, after the sun has dipped below the horizon, I see the headlights coming at me from the eastbound lanes as long streaks of light. I've already stopped once to pee, which I should have done back at Pizza Hut. I'm close now, less than three hours away if my calculations are correct, and they usually are. (I'm not including gas in that statement, as those calculations continue to flummox me. In American Falls, I needed 13.013 gallons of gas to fill up, at $3.0699 per gallon. That came to $39.95, which sounds like a television commercial price. From Butte to American Falls, I traveled 278.3 miles, which means I got 21.4 miles per gallon.)

Despite my relative freshness, I do not like driving in the darkness, and I especially do not like it on a road that I haven't been on before. At home, in Billings, I know the roads just fine, and I even know most of the right-turn-only routes through town. Here, on the interstate, at least I have the knowledge that I will be heading in a consistent direction: west. What I don't know are things like where the rises are, if any patches of the interstate are in disrepair, or whether lanes will be closed due to construction. I will find these things out as I go, in the darkness. And that's why I'm ill at ease.

I remember that one time my father had a bad wreck in the darkness. He and my mother had been in Sheridan, Wyoming, visiting some friends, and my father hit a deer on Interstate 90 as they were coming back that night. It was a bad wreck. The car—a Cadillac, naturally—wouldn't drive anymore, and a tow truck had to come and get it and bring my father and mother the eighty-something miles back to Billings (I do wish I knew the exact distance, but I never did find out). The insurance company said the car was totaled, and it gave my father the money to buy a whole new Cadillac, which he of course did. My father wouldn't drive any other kind of car. He used to call the Cadillac the greatest negotiating tool in the world. He would say, "When they see you coming in a Cadillac, they know two things: first, that you know quality, and second, that you don't need their deal. You know why? Because you're driving a goddamned Cadillac, that's why."

I also remember that my mother was very angry with my father about that crash. Every time the subject would come up, her face would twist and she would say, "Ted, you should have never been driving." I'm not sure what she meant when she said that. My mother never drove, not when my father was around.

I will be seeing my mother in nine days. It will be the first time since August 28, which makes it 105 days since I've seen her. She spends only part of the year in Billings, and it seems like her stays have been getting shorter. Last year she went to Texas in September and she came back to Montana in April. The year before, she came back in March.

It's been a long time since I talked to my mother about my father. Lately, I have been thinking about him more than ever, and that surprises me, because I've had a lot of time—three years, one month, and eleven days—to get used to the fact that he's gone. I wonder if she thinks about him, too. I wonder if she misses him, like I do.

I will have to ask her, I guess.

— • —

It's 7:53 when I see the lights of Boise, and Michael Stipe is singing about bang and blame, and I have this rush of happiness inside me that feels like a Coke bubbling over into my cranial cavity. I try to concentrate, though, because I know I'll need to stay alert. It's four right turns—and, unfortunately, two left turns—to get to

Donna and Victor's street, but finally, the Cadillac's tires are on the pavement of North Twenty-Fifth Street. I drive along slowly, because it won't be far now and because I cannot see the house numbers in the dark, and I've only seen pictures of their place. Michael Stipe is telling somebody not to go back to Rockville.

The house is not hard to find. Victor's red Dodge pickup truck is parked in the driveway.

I pull along the curb and park.

When I pull myself out of the seat of the Cadillac, a dull ache is in my legs and my shoulders. I stretch.

I close the door to the car and head for the trunk to retrieve my things.

And then I hear her voice. "Edward!"

I pivot back toward the house, and Donna is bouncing toward me—she is literally bouncing; this is not hyperbole. She is running and leaping and calling my name, and behind her is Victor with a big smile, and he's extending a hand for me to shake.

I walk toward them and Donna hugs me around the neck. Victor shakes my right hand and slaps me on the back friendly-style with his left hand.

They are happy to see me.

I am glad to be here.

In the doorway, under the light, Kyle stands.

He's gotten so big.

TECHNICALLY MONDAY, DECEMBER 12, 2011

It's 12:09 a.m. and I haven't been able to keep my eyes closed for more than seven minutes and twenty-seven seconds since I came down to the basement at 10:04.

I don't know what to do.

Victor and Donna were great. They understand me completely and work hard to be good friends to me. After we finished greeting each other on the street, they helped me bring my things in. Once we were inside and in better light, they saw my bruised nose and they were very concerned when I told them what had happened in Bozeman.

Kyle, for the first time, said something.

"He hit you?"

"Yes."

"Why?"

"I don't know. He doesn't like the University of Montana, I guess."

"Did you hit him back?"

"No."

"Why?"

"It didn't occur to me."

"You should have."

"He was gone by the time I was exactly sure what had happened."

Donna and Victor told me to sit down on the couch in the front of the TV. The Cowboys were playing the New York Giants, and the second half was just under way. They knew I'd need to see the rest of the game, and even though what I probably should have done is focus on visiting with them, they made allowances for me. That's what good friends do for each other.

"It's a tight one so far," Victor told me.

He said Tony Romo had played great in the first half, with two touchdown passes, and the Cowboys led 17–15.

Donna asked Kyle to come over and sit with me and watch the game. He was standing against the far wall and hadn't said anything after all the questions about my being punched.

"I hate the stupid Cowboys," he said.

I worked hard at not responding to that. Kyle and I have been over this subject before, and while I understand and appreciate that he is a Denver Broncos fan, he has never been willing to appreciate that I am a Dallas Cowboys fan. I have been ascribing (I love the word "ascribing") that to his youth, which often comes with bullheadedness. But he's getting older—he's now 191 days older than he was when I last saw him in Billings—and still he persists. It's getting to be a pain.

Donna was calmer than I would have been, so I'm glad she's the one who spoke first. "But you like Edward, so maybe you ought to focus on that."

Kyle didn't say anything to that, but he did walk over and sit on the far edge of the couch, away from me. He still had a twisted look on his face, the kind of face that my grandpa Sid used to call "puckered up like a chicken's asshole."

I waited for a commercial break to talk to him.

"How tall are you now?" I asked.

"I don't know."

"You were five feet six and seven-sixteenths inches tall on June first. You look a lot taller than that now."

"Duh."

"Can we measure you?"

"No."

"Why not?"

"Because that's weird, you douche."

"Hey!" Victor said.

Donna, clearly mad, came over from the recliner she was sitting in and put her face directly in front of her son's.

"You know I hate that word. I won't have it here, or anywhere else. You apologize to him right now."

Kyle didn't even look at me. "Sorry."

The game was back on now, so I left him alone. After stopping the Giants on their first second-half possession, the Cowboys were trying to get moving, but Tony Romo got sacked.

"Come on, Romo," I said.

I have said this many times since Tony Romo became the Cowboys' quarterback—far too many to count, and I'm glad I don't keep track of such things.

"Suck," Kyle said.

"Huh?"

"They suck."

"They're still ahead, Kyle."

"You suck."

Donna was on her feet. "That's it. You're done, kid. You can't be with civilized people, you'll be alone."

She grabbed Kyle by the arm, lifted him to his feet, and led him out of the living room. Kyle swung his left arm violently and dislodged her hand. That's when Victor left his chair and stepped toward Kyle, who seemed to shrink physically, although that's not technically possible. But he definitely knew that he was in trouble and that he didn't want to tangle with his stepfather.

"Bed," Victor said. "Now."

Kyle didn't protest further. He left the room, with Donna trailing him.

Victor sat back down and faced me.

"He doesn't mean it, Edward. He's angry. Confused. There's a sourness in him that we just have to ride out."

"Why?"

"I don't know. Hormones, maybe. It hasn't been an easy transition for him, being here. He doesn't know these kids very well. Junior high is a pretty tough time under the best circumstances, as I recall."

I nodded. All of school was tough for me—not necessarily the subjects, although some of them were. I didn't have friends, and that's hard for a kid. That's hard for anybody, as I've learned since all my friends left Billings. I've been so frustrated with Kyle today, and now, remembering what things were like for me thirty years ago, when I was his age, I feel like I understand him. I wouldn't want him to live through the kinds of things I experienced.

"He's so big," I said.

Victor laughed. "Tell me about it. Four inches, at least, since the end of the summer. He wears a size ten shoe. We've had to buy new clothes twice."

"What should I do?" I asked.

Victor's face went from laughter to solemnity (I love the word "solemnity") in a single moment.

"To start with, keep being his friend. He needs one. We'll see how it goes."

That's what I'm contemplating here in the darkness. Being Kyle's friend.

The fact of the matter is that Kyle was my first good friend. Donna and I are close now, and I can feel myself becoming better friends with Victor. But Donna and I didn't start out that way. I didn't like Donna when I first met her, and I don't think she liked me very much, either. Kyle, though, made things fun the first time I met him, on October 15, 2008, when he helped me paint my garage.

Maybe that's what is missing from Kyle—fun. He looks miserable, and he surely is making his parents miserable. He's making me miserable, too. As Dr. Buckley would say, that's an awful lot of power we have given one boy over all of us.

In fairness to Kyle, he's not the only reason I'm in a bad mood. The Dallas Cowboys really messed up tonight. They led by twelve points, 34–22, with five minutes and forty-one seconds left in the game, and they still managed to lose. Eli Manning passed for one touchdown, and Brandon Jacobs ran for one, and with a two-point conversion, the Giants won 37–34. The Dallas Cowboys blow a lot of big leads. In this case, it wasn't Tony Romo's fault—he threw for four touchdowns. A lot of times, though, it is Tony Romo's fault.

I shake my head and remember that I'm here for Kyle, not for the Dallas Cowboys. I make myself a promise in the dark, but not like the kind in the Pat Benatar song. I promise that I will work hard while I am here to have fun with Kyle, to show him what fun is, to remind him of the good times we used to have together and can have again.

It feels good to have settled on a course of action. It's 12:48 a.m. now. The fun starts in a few hours.

OFFICIALLY MONDAY, DECEMBER 12, 2011

From the logbook of Edward Stanton:

Time I woke up today: 8:33 a.m. (not counting the hours I stayed up past midnight). Fifth time this year I've been awake at this time.

High temperature for Sunday, December 11, 2011, Day 345: 43 (according to the Boise newspaper). Same as the day before.

Low temperature for Sunday, December 11, 2011: 26. Just one degree colder than the day before.

Precipitation for Sunday, December 11, 2011: 0.00 inches

Precipitation for 2011: 19.40 inches

New entries:

Exercise for Sunday, December 11, 2011: None, unfortunately. I drove, I ate, I watched the Dallas Cowboys, I went to bed. I need to rectify this today.

Miles driven Sunday, December 11, 2011: 464.9

Total miles driven: 688.3

Addendum: I'm in Boise now. "Fun" is the key word. Kyle clearly isn't having any, and neither are his parents. Neither am I, if I'm honest about the situation, and I always like to be honest. I *am here now, and I want to make the best of this visit, because soon enough I will be going home and then on to Texas to see my mother, and I do not know when I will see my friends again.*

Fun. It's the most important word there is right now. That seems odd to say. I've never considered whether words ought to be ranked in terms of importance, although I know that etymologists like to track the frequency with which words are used. But frequency and import are not necessarily the same thing. Let's just say that fun is a very important word for Donna, Victor, Kyle, and me right now. There is no need to give it any more gravity than that.

I have a breakfast of oatmeal, which is fast becoming one of my favorite foods now that Dr. Rex Helton has recommended it to me as I battle my type 2 diabetes. Donna sits with me and we talk. I tell her about my diagnosis, and she's greatly interested in that, because she's a nurse and has seen the effects of unchecked diabetes up close.

"Helton is absolutely right, Edward," she says. "This is different than juvenile diabetes. You can beat this thing. You can shed the weight and get your sugars under control, and you can come off this medicine."

"It makes me pee a lot." I pop a hand over my mouth. "I'm sorry. It's impolite to talk about peeing."

I hear Kyle's voice coming up from behind me. "Peeing is cool."

He says it like those cartoon characters on the music television channel, and then he chuckles stupidly like those two guys do.

"OK, wise guy, come have some breakfast," Donna says.

She slides a bowl toward him, and he sits down in the chair to my right. I get a better look at him in the morning light, and he gets a better look at me.

"Looks like your face is healing, dude," he says.

I touch the skin around my nose.

"Really?"

"Yeah. Man, you really got your ass kicked."

Donna snaps, "Don't even start, young man."

He looks up at her, then digs into his breakfast.

"Had you ever been beaten up before?"

"You don't have to answer that if you don't want to, Edward," Donna says.

I put down my spoon. I don't mind answering.

"Beat up? No. I got picked on a lot. There were even boys who might have tried to beat me up, if they thought they could have gotten away with it. But, no, nobody ever did that before. I wasn't ready for it."

"Are you going to learn to fight so it doesn't happen again?"

Kyle's interest in this topic flummoxes me.

"I don't want to fight," I say.

"But what if someone wants to fight you?"

"I'll walk away."

"What if you can't?"

"I can't imagine that circumstance. That doesn't mean it wouldn't happen. I just can't imagine a situation where I wouldn't have a chance to leave and extricate myself from what was happening. 'Extricate' is a good word, by the way. I love it."

"Whatever. Maybe you don't have much of an imagination."

Kyle is a very perceptive young man.

"I don't."

"So maybe it will happen again."

This conversation has become circular, but I am loath (I love the word "loath") to end it because Kyle is actually talking to me. The problem is that I don't know what to say to him that will keep the conversation alive without going over the same things we have already addressed. That will exhaust me and make me cranky.

Donna, however, does know what to say.

"How about we talk about something other than who is going to be beat up by whom and when?"

I love that Donna uses her pronouns properly.

Kyle does not seem interested in another topic. He goes back to eating his cereal, and we sit in silence.

And as we do, I keep thinking back to the question Kyle asked me. What *would* I do if someone wanted to beat me up and I couldn't walk away?

I think about it and think about it. Kyle isn't talking and Donna is reading the newspaper, so I have time to give the question the proper attention. The problem is that I just don't know what I would do. It's too much hypothesis and not enough fact for my brain to process it. I'll just have to hope it never happens.

— • —

Donna tells me that she has cleared her entire day for the three of us to do things together. First, she says, we're going for a nice, long walk so I can get my exercise regimen going. Donna Middleton (I keep forgetting that her new last name is Hays) is a very logical woman.

"I'm not going," Kyle says.

"Oh, yes, you are," Donna says. "Young men who are polite and respectful get to spend time alone if they want, because they've earned that right. Young men who get expelled from school are made to spend endless, agonizing hours with people who love them."

She picks up his bowl and mine and carries them into the kitchen. Once her back is turned, Kyle makes a very rude gesture toward her that is known as flipping someone off. I am horrified, and I guess the look on my face tells Kyle that, so he flips me off, too.

— • —

We go north on Donna's street, North Twenty-Fifth, and pass cross streets with names like Lemp and Heron and Hazel, all of which are interesting names to me. This subdivision doesn't seem like the ones in Billings. In the neighborhood I live in, the street names are on a theme: Lewis, Clark, Custer, Miles. They're names of important people in Montana's history. But here, I don't know. I will concede that I don't know my Boise or Idaho history, but I don't see any order to these names. I don't know what a "lemp" is. A heron is a kind of bird. Hazel is an old woman's name, or a color. Farther up, we cross Bella Street and then Irene Street—those are definitely women's names. Bella is a very popular name right now because of those vampire books and movies. So is Edward, unfortunately. When I worked at the *Billings Herald-Gleaner*, people kept telling me that I was on Team Edward, which I guess has something to do with those movies. I didn't like that.

On the other side of Irene, we turn right and walk down to a pretty park on the corner. Donna has hooked her arm in mine, and we're talking—well, she is, mostly—the whole way and smiling at each other. Kyle hasn't said a word on the whole walk, and most of the way he's been a few feet behind us, his head down.

"Do you like it here?" Donna asks me.

"It's a very nice town. Do you like it?"

She doesn't answer immediately. I look across the street as I wait.

"I miss Billings," she says. "I was there a long time, and I had a lot of friends. But there are possibilities here, and Victor has such a good job. I can see a future."

Kyle, from behind us, says: "Ha."

"You don't see a future?" I ask Kyle.

To be honest, I too am a little flummoxed by what Donna said. I'm not sure I trust the idea of seeing a future. I don't like predictions, and I don't think they are reliable. I prefer facts.

"No, all I see are a couple of douches."

Donna turns around to face her son. She is twitching. I have seen her this angry before, and I remember hoping that I would never see it again. This is what hope gets you.

"Who are you?" she says.

"What do you mean?"

"Not so many days ago, I had a son. He was a good kid. He was sweet and he was kind. But he's not here anymore. Do you know what happened to him?"

"Maybe you left him in Billings, you bitch."

My left arm shoots out, and my hand grabs Kyle by his coat. This surprises me, as I did not ask my left arm and hand to do any such thing.

"Let go of me, you fucking freak."

Donna slaps Kyle across the face. Hard. The sound of her hand against his skin reverberates (I love the word "reverberates") through the cold in this empty park.

Kyle looks at her. He looks shocked, like someone told him something incredible and scary. He looks at me. Donna is twitching beside me. I want to start running and not stop until I am away from here and what just happened.

And then Kyle starts crying. He cries and he cries and Donna stops twitching, and she reaches for her boy, and he tries to shove her off, but she reaches for him again, and he lets her pull him in. He sobs into her shoulder, and Donna is crying, too. There's a very small voice inside of me that says I should hug them, but that impulse does not prevail.

I sit down on a park bench and I watch them.

I wish I weren't here, but I also feel like this is where I am supposed to be.

Those two things, together, make no sense.

How can I help my friend when I am lost, too?

— • —

By Kyle's own action, he is stuck in his bedroom again, the door closed. Donna says she isn't sure if Kyle is locked away from the rest of us, or if we're locked away from him. This is one of the things I like about Donna. She is clearly hurting for her son, and though she can cry and hug him when he needs it, she's also not one to let him slide when he acts inappropriately and calls her a nasty name like "bitch." (I'm setting aside, for a moment, the fact that he called me a freak. That hurt my feelings, but I'm trying to remember that none of these things with Kyle are about me. He will have to do something to repair his relationship with me. That much is clear. But that can wait for another time.)

Donna takes away his Wii and his computer. She tells him that he needs to sit quietly and think about things, and that he can come out when Victor comes home. Together, as a family—and it makes me feel good that Donna includes me in that word, "family"—we will all sit down and talk about Kyle and where we will go from here.

Even though these are awful circumstances, I'm glad to be part of this. I usually don't get to help sort out adult situations with other adults. When I think about it rationally, which is what I always try to do, I can see that this is an understandable response, given some of the things I have struggled with, but being left out of things for my own benefit still frustrates me. What few people outside of my friends and family seem to grasp is that I am not too stupid to understand adult problems. I am not stupid at all. I'm developmentally disabled, and so I process information in ways that often don't make sense to the people they call neurotypical. (I love the word "neurotypical.")

There's something else that people don't realize. Because of my long association with Dr. Buckley, I have come to know something about rage and how to control it, or at least mitigate it. When I began to see Dr. Buckley, I was consumed with rage, although I didn't realize it, and I did not know how to let it go or channel it into something constructive. I had been ordered to stay at least five hundred feet away from Garth Brooks and to not send him any more letters of complaint, even though I still contend that he ruined country music. I had been fired from a job—that time for my conduct and not as an involuntary separation. I had been banned from an Albertsons in Billings—not my favorite one, the one on Grand Avenue and Thirteenth Street West, but the one on Sixth Street West—because I had knocked down an old lady, even though I still contend that was not my fault.

Dr. Buckley helped me overcome all of that. She helped me see that writing my letters of complaint could be a positive action, in that it would allow me to blow off steam in the act of writing. I could then file the letter away without ever sending it. That didn't make a lot of sense at first, but it really does work. These days, I no longer write a daily letter of complaint, although I will write one if someone genuinely wrongs me. In those cases I even send the letter, and I've often seen positive results (in November, for instance, I got ten free pizzas because one that was delivered to my house arrived soggy and I wrote a letter of complaint). When Dr. Buckley and I began working together, I would not have thought it possible that I could write a letter of complaint and not get in trouble for it later.

In addition to all of that, Dr. Buckley taught me coping strategies for rage and frustration. Sometimes I close my eyes and let the flash of anger pass before I take any action. Sometimes I sleep on things and wake up with a new perspective. And sometimes I even get angry and show it, although not very often. The point is that most reasonable actions, even anger, have their place. It's just a matter of learning how to judge the situation and the propriety (I love the word "propriety") of the moment. That, among other things, is what Dr. Buckley has helped me to do. I am not saying I'm perfect at it; no one is perfect. I am saying that I'm better than I was before I started seeing her.

I know this sounds like bragging. I do not wish to do that. I'm simply trying to say that if Kyle needs my help developing any of these coping strategies, I will be happy to provide it. I've had practice.

— • —

Donna and I are having coffee at the kitchen table. She is having coffee, anyway. I am having sugar-free hot chocolate, because I don't like coffee and because Donna didn't have any chai tea, which I do like. Discovering that was the only good thing to come of my misadventure in Bozeman, although I'm not sure that chai tea was worth a punch in the face from the intemperate young man.

Donna has a grave look, which I understand. Today has not been easy, nor has it been fun.

"Edward," she says. "I want to talk to you about something. I want us to talk about it now so when it comes up tonight when Victor's home and we all sit down to chat, you won't be surprised by it."

"OK."

"I think you're going to need to go back home."

I feel an ache in my stomach.

"OK. Why?"

She looks at me, and tears have begun to build up in her eyes. I reach out and catch one on my thumb before it runs down her face. This surprises her. It surprises me, too.

"I hate to say it," she says. "I hate it. But this thing is so much bigger and more awful than I imagined, and I think we're going to need all the time and effort we can muster to save Kyle from whatever's got hold of him."

I agree with what Donna is saying, and I try to communicate this to her by nodding.

She goes on. "You're a part of this family, Edward. I want you to know that. When Kyle came home after being expelled, he said he wanted to go back to Billings and visit you, and, honestly, we considered it. We'd still love to do it. But we can't while he's like this. It wouldn't be fair to you. He's way, way out of control. Do you get what I'm saying?"

I nod again. I get it. It still hurts me in my gut, but I think Donna is only making sense. She is a very logical woman.

"I will do whatever you think helps the most, Donna," I say.

Donna sets her head down. She grinds her forehead into her arms, which are crossed on the table. Her shoulders heave. She is crying again.

I sip my sugar-free hot chocolate and I wait for her to finish.

I'm going home, but there's nothing for me there.

I am adrift. I hate that word.

— • —

I'm leaving the bathroom—this medicine continues to make me pee prodigiously (I love the word "prodigiously")—and passing by the door to Kyle's room. He cracks it open and speaks to me.

"Don't let them make you leave," he says.

I look around, afraid that we'll both be in trouble, but Donna can't hear him. She's in the kitchen cutting vegetables for dinner.

"Kyle, you're not supposed to be out here."

"Screw her."

"*Kyle.*"

"Why are they making you leave?"

If he's managed to eavesdrop enough to know that I will be going home, he should know the answer to his own question. Still, I tell him.

"Because you're being bad and they don't know what to do. I'll get in the way."

For just a moment Kyle looks mad, and I brace myself in anticipation that he will call me another name that hurts my feelings. But he doesn't do that. He's just defiant.

"So what? They're doing it because they want to punish me. And you're going to leave because you want to punish me, too."

"I don't want to punish you."

"Then why are you leaving?"

"Because your mom thinks it would be better if I did."

"She's wrong."

"She's very logical, Kyle."

"You're wrong."

"I don't think so. We'll have to see what the facts bear out."

Donna's voice calls out from the kitchen. "Edward, can you help me with something real quick?"

"Close the door," I tell Kyle.

"Don't let them make you leave."

"Close it!"

Kyle, at last, does as he's told.

I head for the kitchen.

I'm flummoxed, to say the least. No, I guess to say the least would be to say nothing at all—another phrase that doesn't make much sense.

TECHNICALLY TUESDAY, DECEMBER 13, 2011

It's 4:47 a.m.

My father visited my dreams again. This is not an altogether rare occurrence, especially since he's been dead, but my recent dreams about him have deviated from the norm in that they've been set earlier in my life, when I was just a boy. Most of the time, my father appears in my dreams as I knew him around the time he died, and I am generally around the age I was then or am now. I don't like to use phrases such as "most of the time" and "generally," as they provide no precision about the frequency of occurrence, but dreams are hard to enumerate (I love the word "enumerate") and categorize. Science has proved that all mammals dream, and I certainly am a mammal, but just because I have dreams doesn't mean I remember all of them when I am awake. Sometimes I can't remember a single dream. Sometimes I remember only pieces of dreams and it's hard to make sense of them in the conscious world. And sometimes I remember entire dreams with vividness, as if they were a movie or a TV show I watched. When my father appears in a dream, for better or for worse, I remember it in the latter way.

This time we were again in Cheyenne Wells, Colorado, on that long-ago trip, only it was a blend of that time and a time much earlier, one I've only read about in books. My father and I were out in the oil fields, where he oversaw a crew of men who were doing cathodic protection on oil pumps to keep them from corroding. That image is based on something that really happened. While in the field, in my dream, we met up with two men who were traveling in a wagon train, and this is where the dream becomes illogical. They introduced themselves as John Charles Fremont and Charles Preuss, and although this seemed perfectly natural in my dream, as I sit here now, eyes open, I know it is absurd. They were men of the 1840s. Fremont was a man who made important expeditions to the West, seeing many things in this part of the country before any other white man did, and Preuss was his long-suffering cartographer, who hated the very thing he was great at doing.

In my dream, my father told me that Fremont and Preuss were men who had the courage to set out for frontiers that no one had seen before. The actual truth of the matter is that my father never said any such thing. If he knew anything about Fremont or Preuss, I never heard him talk about them. Furthermore, I know for a fact that my knowledge of both men comes from books and television. The question of how my brain came to blend Cheyenne Wells—which is far south of where Fremont and Preuss traveled—with two early-nineteenth-century explorers is likely to remain a mystery. There is just no logical explanation for it, and I am a person who values logic over all else.

So now I lie on my back and try to make sense of something that defies conventional order, and this is perhaps the hardest thing anyone can ask me to do. In the time I've been on this trip, my father has shown up in my dreams twice, both times we have been in Cheyenne Wells, Colorado, and I have been a little boy. I wonder what that means, or if it means anything at all. If I were an oneirologist, which is a person who studies dreams, I might have some basis for understanding this. I am not an oneirologist. And what of Fremont and Preuss? I can't make sense of that, either. I remember watching a program on their expeditions and thinking that Preuss was the kind of person I would like, because he was very particular about things, just like I am. This quality made him a good cartographer but a bad explorer, and the program noted that Preuss never seemed to grasp the import of the things he saw. For example, Preuss once happily wrote in his journal that some of the men in the traveling party had successfully negotiated with the Indians for some salt, which would make their food taste better. The program I saw noted that Preuss said nothing about the fact that they discovered Lake Tahoe around the same time. The narrator seemed to find this humorous, but, to be honest, I saw Preuss's side of it. It's hard to be impressed by big things when the little things are all messed up. He just wanted his salt, just like I want to know why I am adrift and why I'm being shown these things in my dreams.

There is a deductive device called Occam's razor. The way it works is that when someone is trying to sort through multiple possible explanations for something, the hypothesis (I love the word "hypothesis") that makes the fewest assumptions is generally the correct one. In other words, the simplest explanation is the best explanation, until and unless more information emerges that suggests a different reason. I like Occam's razor for a lot of reasons, but the disdain for assumptions is my favorite part of it.

I decide to apply Occam's razor to things. I turn on the bedside light, pull a notebook from my bag, and begin writing.

1. *I came here to help Kyle, but he's beyond my reach.*
2. *I also came here because I was feeling adrift.*
3. *I still feel adrift.*
4. *My father has visited my dreams twice, and both times he has been with me in Cheyenne Wells, Colorado.*
5. *John Charles Fremont and Charles Preuss visited my dreams, and they were explorers who mapped the way for others.*
6. *I need to find my way, and it doesn't seem that anyone can map it for me.*
7. *Though I have to leave Boise, I don't have to go home. I have eight days, including this one, before I leave Billings for Texas.*
8. *I'm going elsewhere. I think I will go to Cheyenne Wells, Colorado. Even if my father's appearance there in my dreams is completely random, I would like to see the town again.*
9. *I'm done with the list now.*
10. *Now.*
11. *Shit.*

I'm determined to stop writing, even though the last thing on my list is a curse word and an odd number. I manage to do it—I'm very proud—but I have to snap the pen in half to keep from writing down the number 12.

I feel better having made a decision about what to do next, but then my mind goes back to Kyle, and I feel bad all over again.

When Victor came home earlier tonight, all four of us sat at the kitchen table and talked. Victor impressed me. He was disappointed that Kyle called his mom a bitch and me a freak, but he did not yell at the boy. Kyle did all the yelling.

"You made me come to this stupid place and this stupid school. I never wanted to leave!"

Victor spoke to his stepson softly. "Kyle, you're not the first kid who's moved. I lived in four different cities when I was a kid."

"That's your problem!"

"No, it's our problem. What are we going to do about it?"

"Like you'd give me a choice anyway."

Donna spoke. "I think we need to talk to someone together, all of us, as a family."

"Him, too?" Kyle pointed at me.

"Edward is going home."

"Why?"

"Because we're going to be busy here, and because he has to go to Texas to see his mom."

"Not for eight days," I said.

"Can he stay until then?" Kyle asked.

"No," his mother said.

"Why not?"

"I just told you. Because we're going to be busy."

"This sucks."

Victor pointed at Kyle with his left index finger. "Young man, I've warned you…"

"Yeah, whatever."

Kyle stood up and shoved his chair hard against the table, and then he ran down the hallway to his room and closed the door.

Victor looked at Donna and then at me. Donna looked at the table. I looked out the sliding glass door to the backyard. The sky was purple and orange, and the leafless trees looked like spindly (I love the word "spindly") black monsters against the sky. I don't think I ever noticed how spooky trees can look. I'm noticing a lot of things I've never noticed before, and I'm finding that I don't like all of the things I see.

It's 5:34 a.m. now. I kick off the covers. I have a new route to plot. Time is wasting.

OFFICIALLY TUESDAY, DECEMBER 13, 2011

From the logbook of Edward Stanton:

Time I woke up today: 4:47 a.m. First instance this year that I've been awake at this time.

High temperature for Monday, December 12, 2011, Day 346: 23 (according to the Boise newspaper). Twenty degrees colder than the high the day before.

Low temperature for Monday, December 12, 2011: 20. Six degrees colder than the low the day before.

Precipitation for Monday, December 12, 2011: a trace amount.

Precipitation for 2011: 19.40 inches

New entries:

Exercise for Monday, December 12, 2011: Donna, Kyle, and I took a walk but came home early after Kyle mouthed off.

Miles driven Monday, December 12, 2011: None.

Total miles driven: 688.3

Addendum: Much earlier than I'd anticipated, I'm leaving Boise and cutting short my visit with Donna, Victor, and Kyle. I wrote yesterday that "fun" was the key word, and I'm sorry to report that we never managed to have any. I'm sad that I will not *get to spend any more time with my friends, but I understand why Donna thinks I should go. As I still have a week before I'm due back in Montana for my flight to Texas, I will be turning south today and heading toward Cheyenne Wells, Colorado, in the southeastern part of the state. Though I do not believe that dreams hold any particular power, I am intrigued that my father has been showing up in mine and that he has been in Cheyenne Wells when he does. On the off chance that I'm wrong about dreams, I figure I better go there. It is 998.9 miles, and I am going to try to make it in two days, which means I'll be driving farther each day than I ever have before. If I manage to do that, I can spend two days in Cheyenne Wells and still be back in Billings with a day to spare.*

I realize I'm doing something unusual for me, in that I'm driving off the course I originally set and I'm doing so on a whim. But I think this venture will be worth it. If I'm correct and dreams hold no answers about why I am so adrift, at least I will have seen some countryside and a town I visited when I was a little boy. If I'm wrong and my dreams have been guiding me toward something, I will have to reconsider my strict adherence to facts and allow for the possibility that unexplained things, like my dreams, can have profound implications.

Whatever the case, I think Dr. Buckley would say that I'm allowing myself to live in the moment, and I think she would find that to be worthwhile. Maybe even Dr. Bryan Thomsen would think so, too. I will find out when he and I speak.

I leave Donna and Victor's house at first light. Victor shakes my hand, and Donna pulls me in for a big hug and a kiss on the cheek, which makes me feel warm inside. That always surprises me, because I usually do not like to be touched. Kyle, she says, is asleep, and she doesn't want to wake him because rest has been hard for him to come by lately. I understand and will talk to him another time, after he has overcome his present difficulty.

"We will do this again, Edward, and we'll get it right," Donna says. "Just give us some time."

"Yes," I say, and I hope a single word communicates to her that I will give her and Victor and Kyle all the time they need. They are my friends, and I love them. I wish I could tell them that right now, but such an overt (I love the word "overt") display of affection is not the way I do things.

— • —

Behind the wheel of my Cadillac DTS, I first look for a gas station so I can begin my long journey with a full tank. It's a clear, cold morning, and flecks of purple—the last bits of the nighttime sky—mingle with the yellow of the sunrise. I'm driving south and east, into the rising sun. Before the day is out, if I can stick to the schedule I've plotted, I will see Idaho and Utah and Wyoming, and I will spend the night in Rock Springs, Wyoming, before heading into Colorado tomorrow. As I stand beside the car, filling it up at a Chevron on West State Street, I think of how the weather has favored me on this trip. No snow is on the ground in Boise, and I have encountered no storms since I left Billings. Given the time of year and the massive shifts in terrain and weather tendencies I'll be encountering over the next couple of days, I do not expect this good fortune to hold out. Still, expectation and supposition are poor stand-ins for facts. I shall see what the weather brings.

I peek through the tinted window into the backseat and see the sleeping bags and blankets I made sure to pack in Billings, along with the water and the sunflower seeds I'm not eating anymore. If I should be stranded by inclement (I love the word "inclement") weather, which has been known to happen this time of year, I will be able to survive with my car as a sort of emergency shelter. I hope this is something I don't have to prove, but hope is powerless against the forces of nature. I prepared for the worst-case scenario. That is all I can do.

After fueling—9.747 gallons at $3.0199 a gallon, for a total of $29.43—I make my way through the early-morning traffic of Boise to the ramp for Interstate 84 eastbound.

Michael Stipe is singing about how he waited for someone to call and he's sorry. I'm sorry, too, about a lot of things. I'm sorry it didn't work out with Donna, Victor, and Kyle. I'm sorry I don't know when I'll see them again. I'm sorry I don't know exactly why I am heading to Cheyenne Wells, Colorado, as such displays of whimsy tend to be in conflict with my desire to rigorously plan everything. Still, I am determined to go there. When I plotted the course early this morning, I noticed that much of my route today and tomorrow will take me along the path John Charles Fremont and Charles Preuss followed when they mapped the Oregon Trail. Alanis Morissette would call that ironic, but it's really only a coincidence. Even so, it's a very interesting one.

At least I think so.

— • —

At the 114.6-mile mark of my trip, as Michael Stipe is singing about being the king of birds and as I near the town of Jerome, Idaho, I hear something shift in the backseat. I know I'm supposed to keep both hands on the steering wheel and my eyes forward at all times, but it's a straight stretch of interstate, so I lean over the seat and try to secure the case of bottled water on the seat so it doesn't tumble to the floorboards.

That's when Kyle throws back the blanket and says, "Good morning, douchebag!"

It's hard for me to describe what happens to me physically, because I do not like to use similes. Still, I will try: It's as if someone sets off a bomb in my chest. The Cadillac veers hard to the left, and I try to pull it back into the right lane. I step on the brake as hard as I can, the car's tires make a screeching noise, and I can smell burning rubber as I get control of the car and pull it over onto the shoulder. Kyle, the whole time, is laughing at me, and I get extremely angry.

"What the fucking fuck, Kyle?"

He's still laughing. "Oh, man, you totally should see your face. That was awesome."

It was not awesome. It was scary and awful. I sit in my seat, my hands still clutching the steering wheel so hard that I can't feel them anymore, and I expel my breath in short bursts as I wait for my heart to stop doing flip-flops in my chest.

Kyle can't stop laughing. Holy shit! How did he get in my car? I am going to have to turn around and go back to Boise. There's no way I can make it to Cheyenne Wells, Colorado, on time now.

— • —

I reach Donna on my bitchin' iPhone and tell her that Kyle is with me. She is incredulous (I love the word "incredulous"), and I hear her walking down the hallway to his room and opening the door to see if he's in there. I'm certain he's not, because he is right here with me. I can imagine the entire scene. Donna twitches when she is angry, and as I hear her saying, "Oh my god, oh my god," I know that she is most assuredly angry at what her son has done.

"I will bring him back now," I tell her.

Kyle, to quote Scott Shamwell, goes "apeshit."

He starts screaming, so loudly and shrilly that I cannot hear Donna anymore, and he begins to plead in run-together words.

"*Pleasedon'tmakemego, pleasedon'tmakemegoback, pleaseplease pleaseplease!*"

Donna hears this, and she asks me to put him on the phone. I hand my bitchin' iPhone to Kyle, and he listens to his mother for a few moments. Tears are running down his cheeks.

At something she says—I cannot hear her end of the conversation—he says, "Please let me stay with Edward for a few days. *Pleasepleasepleasepleaseplease.* I will do anything when I come back, just please let me stay."

Donna says something else, and he hands the phone back to me.

I hold the phone to my ear and say hello.

"Edward, can you just wait there for a few minutes? I need to call Victor and talk to him, and I'll call you right back."

I tell Donna that I will wait. Kyle looks at me with expectation, and I shrug. I don't know what to tell him.

— • —

As we wait for Donna to call back, Kyle tells me how he was able to stow away in my car. It turns out that he's an ingenious (I love the word "ingenious") little shit. When Donna and Victor were in the basement with me, helping me to collect my belongings and bring them upstairs to be placed in the car's trunk, Kyle slipped out his bedroom window, ran around to the front of the house, climbed down onto the Cadillac's floorboards, and covered himself in blankets. When I was at the gas station in Boise and looked in, I thought the blankets appeared to be a little askew (I love the word "askew"), but I also thought maybe that was just because they had shifted in transit. I will have to begin investigating my observations more rigorously. If I'd found Kyle at the Boise gas station, I wouldn't have lost much time at all today.

Kyle tells me that he had a hard time staying quiet for almost two hours, especially when I was singing along with Michael Stipe.

"Your voice sucks, dude," he says.

This hurts my feelings because I did not realize I had an audience and might not have sung at all if I'd known he was listening.

He says he wanted to make sure we were a ways down the road before he revealed himself.

I tell him that it was wrong and mean to reveal himself the way he did and that we're lucky we didn't crash. I want to tell him that I also think he's ingenious, but I suspect that would only encourage more bad behavior, so I remain silent on that point.

Thirteen minutes and seven seconds after Donna and I hung up, the bitchin' iPhone tells me that she's calling, and I answer it.

"Edward, I'm going to tell you the truth. We don't know what to do. We've never seen this kind of behavior out of Kyle, and we're really at a loss here. He says he wants to stay with you for a few days. How do you feel about that?"

I look at Kyle, and he's looking back at me hopefully.

"I don't know," I say.

"That's our answer, too. It seems like to give him what he wants, after he's behaved so badly, is the wrong thing to do. But Victor and I also talked about how maybe he'll talk to you about things he's scared to tell us, and we need that to happen, somehow. Does that make sense?"

It makes sense.

"Yes," I say.

"How long do you plan to be in Colorado?"

I tell Donna that if I get to Cheyenne Wells tomorrow evening, as planned, I'll stay two nights and then head home. I also tell her that I don't have time in my schedule to go back to Boise on the way home to Billings. She says that's OK and that she and Victor will meet me in Wyoming to retrieve Kyle.

"Will you do this, Edward? I know it's a lot to ask. We clearly can't control him, so maybe it's just silly to think that he'll be tamer for you. We're operating on a gut feeling here. He trusts you, or at least he used to. Maybe he'll let you in. It's worth a shot."

I agree. It's worth a shot. I feel happiness and fear. I'm happy that I'm being allowed to help solve an adult problem; it's the kind of thing I'm not often trusted to do. I'm fearful that Kyle will keep being mean to me and will make my trip to Cheyenne Wells, Colorado, frustrating and maybe even dangerous. While I am sympathetic to Kyle's problems, I have my own struggles, and I'm hopeful—despite all the limitations of hope—that I will find some answers. I don't want Kyle to mess that up.

"I will take Kyle with me," I say, and Kyle makes a fist pump.

"Thank you," Donna says. "And, Edward, I want you to know—if he gives you trouble you can't handle, you call us. We will come get him, wherever you are. Impose whatever restrictions on him you feel are necessary. You're in charge of him. Don't let him manipulate you."

I think that's good advice. I also think it's ironic—the real kind of ironic, not the Alanis Morissette kind. Kyle has been manipulating all of us. That has to end. I decide that I'm not driving another mile with him until I've set some rules.

"Reach into the backseat and hand me my notebook," I tell
Kyle, who obliges.

It makes me feel good that he obeys my first order.

— • —

RULES FOR KYLE ON OUR TRIP TO CHEYENNE WELLS, COLORADO

1. *Kyle is not to do anything that compromises my safe operation of the Cadillac DTS. This includes but is not limited to making loud, scary noises; attempting to cause me to look away from the road, intentionally or unintentionally; grabbing the steering wheel or manipulating any of the car's propulsive (I love the word "propulsive") machinery; being in any shape or form a bad kid. "Bad kid" is subject to my definition.*
2. *Kyle cannot call me names.*
3. *Kyle will follow my instructions when I give them. This has to be an absolute rule, because I cannot anticipate every situation that will emerge.*
4. *Kyle must stay with me at all times.*
5. *Kyle cannot curse anymore. Each time he curses, I will write it down and I will show these marks to his parents.*
6. *These are the rules.*
7. *Stop writing.*
8. *Stop.*
9. *Shit.*
10. *OK, that's it.*

I draw a line through numbers six through ten, and
then I hand the notebook to Kyle and tell him to sign it,

acknowledging that he understands the rules and agrees to abide by them.

"What if I don't sign?" he asks.

"I will call your parents right now and they will come get you." He signs the paper.

"And what's this about cussing? You cuss."

He's right. Shit. "I am a grown-up," I say.

"So what? If I can't cuss, you shouldn't be able to cuss, either. How about if you cuss, I get a dollar?"

I consider this. It seems reasonable. I shouldn't curse as much as I do. I take the paper from him and add an asterisked entry:

Each time Edward curses, he owes Kyle one dollar.

"There," I say, showing it to him. "But I'm going to amend the terms to say that if you curse, you have to give up one dollar, if you've accumulated any, and that I will tell your parents."

"That's not fair."

"Yes, it is. You're the one who's in trouble, not me. All you have to do is stay out of trouble and collect the money if I say 'shit' or something."

"You owe me a buck."

"For what?"

"You just said—" Kyle almost says the word but stops. "You just said the s-word."

I pull out my wallet and hand Kyle a dollar bill. "You owe me two dollars," he says.

"How do you figure that?"

"Look at the paper," he says. "I can see where you wrote 'shit.' Writing it is as bad as saying it."

"I'll keep the dollar," I say.

"Why?"

"Because you just said it."

"When?"

"Just now, when you were telling me I'd written it."

"Shit!"

I reach over and pull the first dollar bill out of his hands.

"You did it again," I say.

Kyle's face gets red, and he starts flopping violently in the passenger seat as he screams.

This is going to be an interesting trip.

— • —

We've gone 17.2 miles when Kyle asks if we can listen to something else. Michael Stipe is singing about a parakeet that is colored bitter lime.

"I don't have anything else on the iPhone," I say. It pains me not to call it my "bitchin' iPhone," but I don't want to lose money. "I put all of the R.E.M. I had on it before I left."

"They're boring."

"They're not boring. They're great. They *were* great. They're my favorite group. You would like them."

"You've been telling me that since I was nine years old. I've never liked them."

There's an old saying: You can't account for taste. I don't think this is true. I think if you had the time and access to everyone in the world and could ask them questions about what they like and don't like, you could account for taste. As I think about it now, that sounds like something I would enjoy doing.

"Do you have something else we could put on?" I ask Kyle.

I don't really want to do this, but Kyle is now my guest, and I will have to try to be accommodating to him, within reason. Fortunately for me, Donna has given me the authority to define what reason is.

"My mom has my phone."

I remember now that Donna took it from him.

"Too bad," I say.

"Can we just turn it off for a while?"

This seems like a reasonable request. I unplug the bitchin' iPhone from the auxiliary cable that carries the music into my Cadillac's sound system.

"Thank you," Kyle says.

He's almost being polite—I say "almost" because he's still clearly glum. Still, it is a nice change from him calling me a fucking freak, which I don't say out loud because I want to hold on to my dollars.

We drive on, and I hum the downbeat from the R.E.M. song we just cut off.

Kyle looks at me. "Can we turn you off for a while, too?"

I stop humming. We wouldn't want the politeness to come on too strong, would we?

I just made a sarcastic joke.

I'm pretty funny sometimes.

— • —

Even though it's early, only 10:23 a.m., we take exit 211 and drive the 3.8 miles from the interstate into Burley, Idaho, so we can have lunch. As we cut through the southeast corner of Idaho, we're not going to see many towns until we get into Utah, so it's best that we eat now. Plus, I have to pee.

We find a JB's restaurant that is serving lunch and breakfast, and that works for us because Kyle says he wants pancakes. As we wait for our food, he asks if he can use my bitchin' iPhone to download some different music.

"It will cost some money, but not very much," he says.

"How much?"

"Twenty or thirty dollars."

I think it's funny—not ha-ha funny, but interesting funny—that Kyle considers this "not very much" money. When I worked at the *Billings Herald-Gleaner*, before I was involuntarily separated, I made $15 an hour. It would have taken me two hours of patching concrete or repairing the press or snowblowing the parking lot to earn what he proposes to spend while we're sitting in a restaurant booth in Burley, Idaho, waiting for pancakes. (I decided to have breakfast, too. I like pancakes, even though they're not on my approved diabetic diet.)

"Go ahead," I say. "I'm fucking loaded."

Kyle doesn't even have to tell me. I take out my wallet and push a dollar bill across the table to him. A stern-faced lady at the table to our left looks at me and shakes her head.

"He earned it," I tell her.

"As long as you have the wallet out," Kyle says, "you better hand over two more dollars."

"Why?"

"You remember when I jumped out of the blankets in the backseat?"

This is a silly question. It happened just a little more than an hour ago. Of course I remember it.

"Yes, I remember."

"Do you remember what you said?"

"Not really."

"You said—" Kyle stops short. "I almost messed up. You said, 'What the *f*-ing *f*, Kyle?' That's two *f*-bombs and two dollars for me."

The woman at the next table is looking over here again.

"I'm not paying," I say.

"Why not?"

"Our agreement was not in force when I said those things, and there is no codicil in our contract that allows you to collect on things said before you signed the agreement. Also, 'codicil' is a really good word. It means 'supplement.' "

"You still shouldn't have said it."

"That may be true, although I would argue that it was a natural response to your scaring me. In any event, it's still not covered by our agreement."

"That's not fair."

"It's completely fair. Do you think I should be able to mark down nasty things you said to me and your mother yesterday? Or what you said to your teacher last week?"

"No."

"What's the difference?"

Kyle is stumped. Kyle is also unhappy.

"This is a big *f*-ing load of *s*," he says. The woman at the next table looks horrified.

"You shouldn't use stand-ins for cursing," I tell him. "It's not much different than actually saying the real words."

He digs into his pancakes, which have just arrived.

"Yeah? Well, there's no cod-i-something in our agreement that covers stand-in words. So shove it up your *a*-word."

The woman at the next table picks up her plate and moves to a table at the far end of the row. I don't blame her. Kyle used to be a nice boy, but he's gotten sour somehow, as Victor told me that first night. If I weren't responsible for him, I'd probably move to another table, too.

— • —

As I'm paying for our meal, I ask Kyle what kind of songs he downloaded on my bitchin' iPhone, although I'm careful not to actually say "bitchin' " so I can remain fucking loaded.

"Country songs, mostly," he says.

I stick out my tongue, which I'll concede isn't mature. I will have to be careful about such things, since the question of Kyle's maturity is now such a hot topic.

"What's wrong?" he asks.

"I like rock 'n' roll better."

"Well, too bad."

"I'll make you a deal," I say. "We'll listen to three of your songs, then three of mine, then three of yours, and so on."

"We just listened to maybe ten of your songs before we got here, so I think we should get to listen to ten of mine before we start going back and forth."

"That's not the deal I'm offering you. It's three of yours, then three of mine, as soon as we leave. That way, I can minimize my exposure to bad music."

I'm thinking now about when my OCD was out of control and I got in a lot of trouble for writing Garth Brooks forty-nine letters complaining to him that he had ruined country music. The "Garth Brooks incident," as my father always called it, is what led to my being kicked out of my parents' house and being put under the care of Dr. Buckley starting in 2000. As it turned out, this was a good thing, as I wouldn't have met Donna and Kyle if I hadn't been forced to move, and I wouldn't have gotten better as quickly as I did with Dr. Buckley. That doesn't erase the fact that Garth Brooks ruined country music, the detritus (I love the word "detritus") of which I will now be subjected to, but it's hard to hold a grudge.

"It's not bad music," Kyle says. "It's so awesome. Like, I got 'Honky Tonk Badonkadonk' by Trace Adkins."

I reach over and flick a piece of pancake off Kyle's shirt.

"What's a badonkadonk?"

Kyle giggles. "It's a girl's butt."

"They write songs about girls' butts? It sounds stupid."

"Dude," he says, "it's an awesome song. It's the country song answer to 'Baby Got Back.' "

"The Sir Mix-A-Lot song?" I am impressed that Kyle knows a song from 1992, and I cannot lie.

"Yes."

"You weren't even born when that came out."

"It's one of my mom's favorites."

I don't know where to begin unraveling this young man. Kyle is in the clutches of terrible music, and it sounds like his mother is helping to drive him there. I will have to hit him with strong doses of R.E.M. and hope they have some kind of cleansing effect. I wish now that I had added some Matthew Sweet—my other favorite musical artist—to my collection. If Kyle is in thrall (I love the word "thrall") to silly words like "badonkadonk," there may be no rescuing him with just R.E.M. Michael Stipe, Mike Mills, Peter Buck, and Bill Berry are good, but as far as I know they are not miracle workers. Miracles are hard to quantify, anyway. I prefer facts.

— • —

At 7:07 p.m., I'm in my sweatpants and a T-shirt, lounging on one bed in our room at the Holiday Inn in Rock Springs. Kyle is on the other bed, watching something on MTV that is called *Jersey Shore*.

This show flummoxes me.

Kyle tries to explain how it works, that these eight young people—he calls the guys "guidos," which I guess would make the women "guidesses"—share a house and try to get along with one another, but I watch the show with him and I don't see much getting along. I see people talking on phones, or yelling at each other, or getting drunk and having sex. In other words, this is quality programming.

I just made another sarcastic joke. I am pretty funny sometimes.

Kyle says one of the guys, someone known as "The Situation," is his favorite.

"And that one there," he says, pointing to a very short woman with very tall hair, "that's Snooki."

"What's a 'Snooki'?" I ask.

"It's not her real name," he says. "That's just what they call her."

I watch her as she walks up to the "The Situation" and starts yelling at him.

"Look at the badonkadonk on her," I say.

Kyle giggles.

I was going to propose that we watch the next episode of *Adam-12* on my bitchin' iPhone, but Kyle is having so much fun watching *Jersey Shore* that I skip it. I'm woefully (I love the word "woefully") behind on establishing any sort of pattern with *Adam-12*, and this both surprises me and disappoints me.

I'm surprised because I'm starting to like the show, even if it's not nearly as good as *Dragnet*, and so it stands to reason that I would be eager to view more episodes and become even more acquainted with Officers Pete Malloy and Jim Reed. It disappoints me because a rigorous schedule of show-watching used to be essential to how I went through the day. When I met Kyle and Donna, for example, I was on a strict regimen of watching *Dragnet* every night at 10:00. I couldn't even contemplate skipping it.

But then work and friends—things I had been without—came into my life, and when my *Dragnet* tape broke, I stopped watching.

Now, however, I am adrift. My job is gone. My friends live somewhere else. My mother is in another state most of the year. My father is dead. It seems to me that a little rigor in my schedule would do me some good, and yet I cannot seem to muster the energy to impose that on myself.

There's something else, too. I feel a sense of longing, only I cannot identify what it is I'm longing for, and that is worrisome for someone who values precision the way I do. I am not good at thinking in abstract ways, but I will try to describe this. When I had my job, my best friends across the street, and my house on Clark Avenue, Billings, Montana, was where I wanted to be. It was familiar and it was mine. Now, I am in a hotel room in Rock Springs, Wyoming, a place I have never been before, and, because Kyle is here with me, I do not want this moment to end.

— • —

I am scanning through the songs loaded on my bitchin' iPhone, and I say to Kyle, "How many songs did you purchase?"

"I don't know. Thirty or so."

This is not close to being the correct answer.

"Kyle, you purchased one hundred and ninety-three songs."

"I did?"

"Yes, you did. And at a dollar and twenty-nine cents per song, that comes to two hundred forty-eight dollars and ninety-seven cents."

"It does?"

"Yes, it does. I think you know that."

"I do?"

I look over at Kyle, and he is trying hard to keep from grinning, but I see him. I think that I should feel entitled to scold him for spending $218.97 more than his upper estimate of what his songs would cost, but I don't want to scold him. I want to grin, too. This is a conundrum (I love the word "conundrum") for me, because it seems to me that part of the problem we've been having with Kyle is that we let him get away with such things. And yet, I think that if I scold him over what he has done, he will become angry and make things difficult for me on this trip.

I quickly devise a plan to deal with this.

"How much money did you get from me today because I cursed?" I ask him.

"Three dollars."

That's right. There was the buck in Burley, Idaho, when I said "fuck," and then I had to give him another when I said that the Great Salt Lake looked "pretty fucking awesome," and finally, I gave him a dollar when I referred to my "bitchin' iPhone" at dinner. I have to be more careful.

"OK," I say. "I figure you owe me two hundred and eighteen—"

"What? That's not fair. I don't—"

"Just hold on. I'm not going to make you pay it back in actual dollars. But you have to pay it back in deeds."

"What do you mean, deeds?"

"Every time you take a walk with me, I'll credit ten dollars to your account. You refused to walk tonight, and that wasn't nice, because I had to stay here with you instead of getting the exercise I need to beat my diabetes."

"OK."

"Every time you call your mother and tell her you love her, I'll credit ten dollars to your account."

"This will be easy."

"It might be. But listen—every time you call me a name I'll charge ten dollars to your account. Every time you're rude to someone, like you were with that woman at Wingers when you said, 'You need to fill my drink more often,' I'll charge ten dollars to your account. If you curse, I'll add ten dollars to your account."

Now Kyle looks less sanguine (I love the word "sanguine").

"OK," he says.

"Now," I say, "show me those three dollars."

Kyle digs in his pocket and pulls out three crumpled bills.

"Let me hold them."

He hands them between the beds to me.

"I'll keep these," I say. "Now you owe me just two hundred and fifteen."

He sits upright. "No!"

"Yes."

"That was a dirty trick, douche."

I grab my notebook off the end table and make a notation. "Make that two hundred and twenty-five."

Kyle flops onto his back, covers his head with a pillow, and lets out a muffled scream.

— • —

He doesn't talk to me the rest of the night. He watches his shows, and when I try to talk to him, he pretends not to hear me. I do not like the silent treatment. My father used to do this to me, especially after I became a teenager and he and I did not get along very well. I don't think it is mature. However, it would be a stretch to say Kyle is being rude about it. He is just sending me a very clear, silent message. I wish now that I had put a codicil in our agreement that would reward him for being sociable.

At 10:00 p.m., I tell him that it's lights-out, that we have another long day of driving ahead of us. He doesn't answer me, but he does turn down his bed and climb in. I shut off the light.

I lie on my back and stare into the darkness. Tomorrow, we will drive 517 miles to Cheyenne Wells, Colorado, a route that will take us most of the way across Wyoming, down into Colorado near Denver, and then, finally, on smaller roads into southeastern Colorado and to our destination.

I close my eyes and my brain provides a picture of how I remember Cheyenne Wells from 1978, the last time I was there. Not much comes to mind—grain elevators, a railway line, and a big, wide-open sky that always seemed to hold huge clouds. Southeastern Colorado, in my recollection, has a lot in common with the eastern part of Montana, where I am from. Neither place has the big mountains that outsiders seem to associate with the states they're in. It occurs to me that it has been so long since I saw Cheyenne Wells, this will be like visiting it for the first time. Even as detail-oriented as I am, I know that memories are imprecise renderings of places and times. I am eager to see it again and to reconcile what I see with what I remember. I hope sleep comes soon. Strangely, I hope my father visits my dreams again. I realize that I find comfort in that.

"Edward?"

Kyle's voice is soft. I'm surprised to hear it.

"Yes?"

"Can I tell you something?"

"Yes."

I hear rustling in the bed next to mine as he shifts his weight under the covers.

"I just want to say thanks for letting me come with you."

"You're welcome."

I listen as he flops over in bed, and soon I can hear that he's asleep.

Maybe Kyle is still a sweet young man. I hope so. He's sending conflicting signals—that much is certain. If he were on *Jersey Shore*, they would probably call him "The Enigma." (I love the word "enigma.")

WEDNESDAY, DECEMBER 14, 2011

From the logbook of Edward Stanton:

Time I woke up today: 7:38 a.m. A very familiar time for me. The 209th time this year I've been awake at this time.

High temperature for Tuesday, December 13, 2011, Day 347: 32 (according to the Rock Springs newspaper). Nine degrees warmer than the high the day before.

Low temperature for Tuesday, December 13, 2011: 20. Same as the low the day before.

Precipitation for Tuesday, December 13, 2011: a trace amount.

Precipitation for 2011: 19.40 inches

New entries:

Exercise for Tuesday, December 13, 2011: Kyle refused to walk with me, so I didn't do it. I've decided that we will walk at lunch, even if it costs us time on our 517-mile trip to Cheyenne Wells.

Miles driven Tuesday, December 13, 2011: 490.8

Total miles driven: 1,203.8

Gas usage Tuesday, December 13, 2011: Filled up in Boise: 9.747 gallons at $3.0199 per gallon, for a total of $29.43. Filled up in Brigham City, Utah: 13.209 gallons at $3.2399, for a total of $42.80. I am giving up on trying to project my gas usage and costs; the variables in price and consumption are too great. I will, of *course, continue to write down the actual amounts as I accumulate them.*

What Kyle owes me for the music he purchased: $215. He called his mother this morning and told her he loves her, and I credited $10 to his account. After he handed the phone back to me, Donna said, "What did you do to him?" She meant that I had done well, I think. That made me feel good.

Addendum: I am excited today. It will take many hours, but I will see Cheyenne Wells, Colorado, and that makes me happy. However, my happiness is kept in check by my reminding myself that it's highly unlikely that I will arrive in Cheyenne Wells and the townspeople will congregate (I love the word "congregate") around me and say, "Edward, we are so glad you came. We've been waiting for you." Life doesn't work that way. Yes, my father has been showing up in Cheyenne Wells in my dreams—although he did not last night, as far as I remember—and, yes, I have begun to wonder whether that means he wants me to find something there, but I have to remind myself that I am someone who trusts facts above all, and this idea that my father is guiding me toward something is not a fact. It is a fantasy. I have to remember that so I am not disappointed.

I am glad Kyle is with me on this trip. I wasn't sure I would be, but aside from a couple of small problems, it's been good to be with him. I hope that continues.

After I stop the car for the second time on the 107-mile stretch between Rock Springs and Rawlins, Wyoming, so I can pee, Kyle asks me this question:

"Why do you pee so much?"

I think it is reasonable for him to ask, given the frequency of my urination. So I tell him. "I take drugs that cause me to pee. It's so my body doesn't retain water. It's part of my treatment for my type two diabetes."

"That's weird."

"It's called a diuretic."

"How many times do you pee a day?"

This is an astounding question, and I instantly feel foolish for not having an answer. I really should be tracking this on my data sheets.

"A lot," I say. "In the first four hours after I take my pill, it's especially frequent. Also—I hope this doesn't gross you out—but it's much more pee than it has ever been before. I can't prove this empirically, because I never bothered to measure my pee before I started taking this pill. That would have been gross. But I can tell."

It now seems to me that we've gone about as far as we can with this subject, but Kyle keeps going.

"I bet I can pee more than you," he says.

I laugh. This is ha-ha funny. "No, you can't."

"Wanna bet?"

"Kyle," I say, "you're being silly. I'm older than you, I'm bigger than you, and I'm sure I have a bigger bladder than you do. There is just no way you can pee more than I can, unless you have a bad medical condition, in which case we should get you to a doctor."

"If I pee more than you, will you erase what I owe you?"

This question flummoxes me. On one hand, I don't want Kyle erasing his debt by any means other than being nice to his mother and being sociable with me. On the other hand, this idea that he could pee more than I can is anatomically laughable. I counter with my own question. "This is purely hypothetical, because there is no way you can pee more than I can, but if you do, will you still call your mother and still take walks with me?"

"I guess."

"I want a yes, or it is no deal."

"Yes, OK, I will."

I take my right hand off the steering wheel and offer it across the seat to Kyle, who shakes it.

We're strange.

— • —

Kyle and I agree that we will store our pee in empty water bottles for comparison's sake, and he drinks the contents of two to make room. He wants to drink three bottles of water, but I tell him that he can't because I don't want him to get water poisoning, and he laughs at me as if I'm making something up.

"Water isn't poison."

"Well, no, it isn't technically," I say. "But if you drink too much water, it can kill you."

"No, it can't."

"Yes, Kyle, it can."

I wish he wouldn't do this to me. I don't make things up; it's against my nature as a fact-loving person. I proceed to tell him about a story I read in the *Billings Herald-Gleaner*, long before I worked there. It seems that a radio station in Sacramento, California, held a contest called "Hold Your Wee for a Wii," in which it challenged a woman to drink as much water as she could to win a video game console. She didn't win the game. She died.

"You're lucky," I tell Kyle. "You got your Wii from Santa Claus." I don't like telling Kyle a piece of fiction like this, but I also don't think it's my place to tell him the truth about Santa Claus if he doesn't already know it. That's up to Donna and Victor.

He already knows it.

"Yeah, right," he says. "Santa Claus is my grandpa. You're stupid if you believe in Santa Claus."

"Now you did it," I say. "You are back up to owing me two twenty-five."

"Wait a minute!"

"You called me stupid."

"No, I said you're stupid *if* you believe in Santa Claus. Do you believe in Santa Claus?"

"No."

"Then you're not stupid."

I don't say anything for a few seconds. I don't like being outsmarted.

"You owe me two fifteen," I say.

Kyle slaps the leather seat happily.

We're driving past Rawlins on the interstate now, and I do something I'm not supposed to do and look away from the road and at Kyle, just for a second.

"What?" he says.

"When did you find out that Santa Claus isn't real?"

"Two years ago. I found where Mom hid all the presents."

"Did you tell her?"

"No."

"Why not?"

"I don't know. She likes Christmas and stuff. Anyway, I think she knows that I know."

"How?"

"She's not making a big deal out of it this year."

"Do you know what you're getting?"

He laughs, only it's not a ha-ha-funny laugh. "Probably nothing, the way things are going."

"They'll get you something."

"I guess."

"Do you know what I want for Christmas, Kyle?"

"No."

I feel my cheeks getting hot, which is strange. And then I realize that I'm embarrassed to say what I've been thinking. But I do it anyway.

"This trip with you."

He doesn't say anything. I make sure my eyes stay fixated on the road. I'm afraid that I've embarrassed him or made him uncomfortable, so I don't want to make it worse by looking at him.

"Edward?"

"Yes?"

"When did you find out about Santa Claus?"

I'm glad he asked me this question. I remember it exactly. It was December 24, 1975. I was six years old. I tell him this, and then I tell him why.

"I remember Christmases by the best gift I got each year. For example, in 1975, I got a five-speed bicycle, and the year before, I got a G.I. Joe, and the year after I got Connect Four. So that's how I remember what year it was. But the way I figured out there was no Santa Claus was I heard my father say 'cocksucker' late that night while he was trying to put my five-speed bicycle together in the living room after I had been sent to bed. I don't think Santa Claus would say a word like 'cocksucker,' and even if he would, he wouldn't sound like my father."

Kyle laughs and laughs at this story, and I laugh, too, because it is funny. As I think about it now, I realize that my father and Scott Shamwell, the pressman at the *Billings Herald-Gleaner*, are a lot alike in that both like to curse in loud and creative ways. Maybe that's why I like Scott Shamwell so much—because he reminds me of my father in the best ways and doesn't remind me of him at all in any of the bad ways. It's a good theory. Theories are fine, but I prefer facts. The facts are that I like Scott Shamwell and I miss my father.

Kyle taps me on the shoulder, and I look over at him.

"That's two more bucks to my account," he says.

"Why?"

"You just said—" Again he stops himself. He's better at this than I am. "You said c-sucker twice."

Well, shitballs, I think (but don't say). I guess we're down to $213.

— • —

We're at mile marker 228 near Sinclair, Wyoming, when we have our first chance to go head-to-head on peeing.

"Edward, you better pull over," Kyle says. "I have to go."

Once we're parked he gets out of the Cadillac and runs to the bathroom, empty bottle in hand. I'm following with my own bottle but not running, because that only aggravates my urge to go.

I'm at a urinal, trying to aim my tallywhacker at the small opening of the bottle and having a difficult time of it.

"Dammit," I say as I splash a little urine on my hands.

"That's another dollar!" Kyle yells from the adjacent stall.

"Yeah, yeah," I say. "Two hundred twelve."

Finally I get everything coordinated, and my bladder empties into the bottle, the stream of urine making a drumming sound against the plastic. A fat man on my left, who's wearing a mesh baseball cap, looks at me, and I look back at him. He frowns.

"It's a contest," I say.

He shakes off his tallywhacker, zips up, and leaves without saying anything—or, more importantly, without washing his hands. That's gross.

— • —

Back at the car, I hold the bottles up for comparison. I have to give Kyle credit. The boy can pee prodigiously (I love the word "prodigiously").

"OK," I say. "You beat me on that one. To be fair, though, you just had a lot of water, and I've been peeing a lot all day. Let's see if you're still beating me at the end of the day."

"No way," he says. "That's it, it's over. I don't owe you a dime. We didn't say anything about doing this more than once."

Kyle is probably correct in his contention. Our agreement on the peeing contest was reached informally, and I never bothered to write down an extended deal. Still, I want to keep going. I don't want him to beat me.

"Are you afraid you can't keep peeing better than I can?" I ask.

"I'm not afraid of anything."

"You sound afraid," I say. "You sound like a chicken." I set the bottles down on the leather seat and put my thumbs in my armpits and flap my elbows. "Bock-bock-be-gock!"

"You're being immature," he says.

"Come on, chicken." I flap my elbows some more, and finally Kyle laughs.

"OK, dude, you're going down," he says.

We high-five, and I feel as happy as I have in a long time. It's as if the Kyle I remember from Billings, the one who was nowhere to be seen in Boise, is back with me. I hope he washed his hands.

— • —

It is 2:47 p.m. when we park at a McDonald's off the interstate in Denver. I implore (I love the word "implore") Kyle to pick a different place, but he's insistent that he wants McDonald's, and I am reluctant to do anything that stops our good momentum.

The shopping center holding the McDonald's has many stores and good pathways for walking, and I tell Kyle that after we eat, we need to walk. He doesn't appear keen on this, until I remind him that his debt will be down to $202 if he walks with me.

At the restaurant, Kyle orders a Big Mac, large fries, and a large Coke. I order a grilled chicken sandwich, no fries, and an unsweetened iced tea. It's not an ideal diabetic meal, but it's better than what Kyle has.

I'm the first to notice that six men in this restaurant are wearing Denver Broncos jerseys with Tim Tebow's name on the back. I'm usually the first to notice such things. I point it out to Kyle.

"That's because Tim Tebow's the best," he says.

This is so far beyond absurd that I cannot believe it.

"He's the best what?"

"He's the best quarterback in the NFL."

"Kyle," I say, "that is a laughable contention. I know you are a Denver Broncos fan, but you're being ridiculous."

"Who's better?"

I laugh a ha-ha laugh. I even snort a little bit, which is strange. "Aaron Rodgers is better. Tom Brady is better. Drew Brees is better. Ben Roethlisberger is better. Tony Romo is better. Lots of other guys, too. I can prove this statistically."

"Tony Romo! That's a laugh!"

"He is, Kyle." It's a strange feeling. I know that I'm being defensive because Tony Romo is the Dallas Cowboys' quarterback, and the Dallas Cowboys are my favorite team. But I am also correct about this. Also, my voice is getting loud.

"Tony Romo is a punk," Kyle says.

"He's better than Tim Tebow." I'm being really loud now, and people are starting to look at us. Three of the men wearing Tim Tebow jerseys begin walking toward our table. I ignore their approach and keep arguing with Kyle. "Do you know what Tony Romo's completion percentage is? It's sixty-six-point-three percent. Do you know what Tim Tebow's is? It's forty-six-point-five percent."

One of the jersey-wearing men, a guy who looks to be in his mid-twenties and is so large that he probably shouldn't be eating at McDonald's, says, "Tim Tebow wins. A lot more than Tony Romo does."

"OK," I say, "but you have to acknowledge the fact that one player can't do everything. Tim Tebow has a better defense than Tony Romo does. That makes a difference."

"All I know," says another man with a Tebow jersey, "is that the Broncos were one-and-four before Tebow started playing. They're seven-and-one since he got in there."

Kyle looks at me with a big smirk on his face. "Yeah!" he says.

"I'm not talking about wins and losses," I say. My eyes are moving back and forth between the two men who have rudely injected themselves into my discussion with Kyle. "The debate is quarterback ability. Tony Romo is better than Tim Tebow."

Everybody around us groans, and now the third man wearing a Tim Tebow jersey jumps in. "What's the point of being a quarterback other than to win?"

"I'm just—" I say, but I'm cut off, because now the second one is back at it.

"You've got big balls, bad-mouthing Tim Tebow in Denver, dude."

A chorus of "Yeah" goes up in McDonald's. Kyle is sitting there with a shit-eating grin on his face. I'm not even sure where that saying comes from. Why would anybody grin after eating shit?

I try to talk, but everybody in the restaurant boos me, and a couple of people—including Kyle—throw french fries at me.

This sucks.

— • —

On our seventh lap around the big shopping center parking lot, Kyle, who is walking a couple of steps behind me, says, "Will you buy me a Tim Tebow jersey?"

I stop, turn, and stare at him. I am incredulous.

"You must be kidding. After what happened in there? You have big balls." I didn't like the men in the Tim Tebow jerseys, but I like this saying that one of them introduced me to.

"You owe me a buck," Kyle says.

"'Balls' isn't a curse word."

"So I can say 'balls' as much as I like?"

Kyle has me cornered. I don't think I should lose a dollar on a word like "balls." On the other hand, I don't think Donna will be pleased with me if I send her son home and he's saying "balls" all the time. I think she will be especially angry if she finds out that I gave him permission to say it.

"OK," I say. "Your debt is now down to two hundred and one."

"What about the Tim Tebow jersey?"

He has incredibly big balls.

"No."

"If I'm good the rest of the trip?"

"Maybe."

"If I call my mom twice a day?"

He has relentlessly big balls.

"Yes."

— • —

Back in the Cadillac DTS, we take a big loop around Denver, out past the new airport, to Interstate 40 East. For part of the trip, Kyle chats happily on my bitchin' iPhone with his mother, and as he hangs up, he tells her that he will call again when we reach Cheyenne Wells. After the phone is back in my hands, he reminds me that he's part of the way to a Tim Tebow jersey. This annoys me.

Near the small town of Deer Trail, 119 miles from our destination, Kyle tells me to pull off at a rest stop so he can pee. It's good timing—I have to pee, too, and we're now able to renew our contest.

We're alone in the restroom, which is a nice development, as I'm feeling a little silly about this even as I'm powerless to stop it. This is one of the struggles of my condition, particularly the obsessive-compulsive part of it. I wonder what Dr. Buckley would say if I told her that a twelve-year-old boy and I were comparing our levels of urination. It's difficult for me to even imagine telling her such a thing, although I surely would if she were still my therapist, because I told Dr. Buckley everything. I have not reached that level of trust with Dr. Bryan Thomsen. I suspect that Dr. Buckley would say this is the sort of compulsion I should work harder at controlling.

Having learned how to pee into the bottle at our previous stop, I fill mine with no trouble. From the stall next to me, where Kyle is, I hear a gurgling sound.

"What's that?" I ask.

"Nothing."

I walk around to the front of the stall and peek through the opening between the door and the wall. I can't believe what I see.

Kyle is kneeling at the commode, and he has pushed the bottle into the toilet water to fill it up. This is cheating. This is also really, really gross.

"Kyle!"

He jumps and drops the bottle into the toilet.

"Shit!" he yells, and I make a mental note to add $10 to his debt.

"I can't believe this," I say. "You're cheating. Did you cheat at the last rest stop, too?"

He leaves the bottle in the toilet water and slams through the stall door, almost hitting me in the face as it swings open.

"Shut up, Edward."

"That's another ten dollars for being rude. With that and the s-word you just said, you're at two hundred twenty-one."

Kyle's hands are balled up into fists. "Do you think I care? I'm never paying you, so you can just forget it. You can forget your stupid game, too."

"It's your stupid game, Kyle. You're the one who wanted to do it, and that's what I'm going to tell your mom when I tell her that you've been cheating."

"'That's what I'm going to tell your mom,'" Kyle mocks me in a sing-song voice. "You're not going to tell her about this, you big tattletale. Don't be stupid. How do you think that's gonna look? 'Hey, Donna, Kyle and I were peeing into bottles.' You're an idiot."

Kyle has really hurt my feelings now. I'm not an idiot. I'm developmentally disabled, not stupid. He's right that I probably shouldn't say anything about this to Donna. I suspect that her reaction would be similar to Dr. Buckley's, if not worse, and while I do not like to trust supposition, I'm not willing to seek out the facts on this matter.

Kyle is already out the door of the restroom. I follow him, tossing my bottle of urine into the trash as I go. I call for him, but he doesn't look back. He just flips me the bird, which is a euphemism for holding up one's middle finger. He's at $231 now.

I jog to try to catch up to him. The whole thing flummoxes me. We were doing so well, and now we're not. Kyle is sitting in the passenger seat of the Cadillac DTS, and his face is pressed against the window, as if I'm holding him prisoner.

I climb into the driver's seat and start the car. Kyle doesn't face me and doesn't acknowledge me.

Darkness is coming. We have two hours to go on our drive. Michael Stipe is singing about going all the way to Reno. I look to the west, where Reno is. That's where John Charles Fremont and Charles Preuss went, or close enough. Charles Preuss didn't like it out there. I don't like it out here. I wonder why I came, but I can't stop now.

I put the car into drive and head back to the interstate.

I feel alone. I used to like that. It's the worst feeling ever now.

TECHNICALLY THURSDAY, DECEMBER 15, 2011

I'm glad we're here for only two nights. This bed is too hard. I cannot blame that for why I am awake at 4:21 a.m., however. My father visited me in my dream again, and now I am flummoxed, because we were not in Cheyenne Wells, Colorado, although I am physically in Cheyenne Wells right at this moment. We were in our old house in Billings, the one I lived in with my parents before I was kicked out after the "Garth Brooks incident."

It's hard to remember now that I'm in the conscious world rather than the dream world, but I think I was the same age as in the Cheyenne Wells dreams. I'm going to assume that I was, although assumptions are dangerous things. That, at least, would make the dreams track.

In the dream, I'm nine years old and my father and I are in the front yard, and he is chasing me. I run and laugh and try to elude my father, until finally his big hand clutches the back of my shirt and pulls me in. He wraps me in a bear hug and we tumble to the ground, and I am not scared. I am laughing and having fun, and my father rolls me onto my back and lies gently across my chest, binding up my legs with his right arm so I cannot move.

"One…two…three," he says, and then he gets to his feet and makes noises like a crowd is cheering for him and says, "And the new champion, Ted 'The Bear' Stanton!" He holds his arms aloft and dances back and forth on his toes like Muhammad Ali and makes more cheering noises.

That's when I get up and I run at him, full force. He says "Oof" as I hit him, and he tumbles to the ground in an exaggerated fall. I lie down across him, the same way he did to me, and I try to bind up his legs, but he's too big for me. He thrashes and he could surely throw me off, but he doesn't. I count off "One… two…three," and I jump up with my arms in the air.

The last I remember of the dream is my father picking me up, even though I was a big nine-year-old, and carrying me around the yard. "The champ," he says. "Meet the champ, Teddy Stanton!" I cup my hands and hold up my arms for an adoring, imaginary crowd.

And now, here in Cheyenne Wells, I'm lying in a bed that isn't mine and I can feel tears on my cheeks. I sniffle, and then I hold my breath, until I hear Kyle snoring in the bed next to mine. I wipe my cheeks and try not to cry anymore, but it's no use. I'm not in control of this, and that is a helpless feeling.

I don't know what it all means. I cannot even remember if what I saw in the dream happened in my real life. I don't think it did. I'd like to think I would remember a great day like that. I do know that my father found it much easier to be my friend when I was nine years old than he did later, when I wasn't so young anymore and as he grew more exasperated (I love the word "exasperated") with my condition. While he was still alive, I would often wish that we could go back to those younger days, and I certainly do now that he's gone, but it's impossible to do that unless you're in the dream world. We didn't get a chance to work it out when he was alive, and ever since he died three years, one month, and fifteen days ago, I've been trying to work it out with my memories. It would be nice to think that his appearances in my dream are an effort on his part to work it out with me, but that requires way too much wishful thinking for my fact-loving brain to handle.

And yet, if I allow myself that wishful thinking, I wonder now whether my father has been guiding me not to a place but to a conclusion. I will try to explain this. Kyle was nine years old when I met him. I'm nine years old in the dreams about my father I've been having. When Kyle was nine years old, relating to him was easy for me. He was a friendly young man who made having fun seem easy, who wanted to be my friend when I didn't really have any friends. When I was nine years old, my father found relating to me to be easy. I didn't challenge him the way I did in later years, as I began to learn things and feel things that put me at odds with him (and, it's important to note, as my condition deteriorated before I got the help I needed).

Maybe the memories of my father are telling me this: I won't have the same relationship with Kyle that I once had. He's growing up, he's struggling in his own way as he does, and it's unfair for me to expect him to be the kid I once knew. Maybe I have to accept that this is who he is now and be friends with him on those terms—or, if neither of us can handle it, not be friends anymore.

That's a lot of maybes, which means my information is not at all precise. A lack of precision bothers me. Having only theories bothers me. Not knowing where to look for answers bothers me, too.

I will close my eyes now. I will try to get some rest. Tomorrow, I will start fresh where Kyle is concerned (and I will hope he finally talks to me again, as he didn't from Deer Trail to here). He owes me no money. He can call his mother or not call his mother.

He can walk with me or not walk with me. The choices are his. I cannot make him do anything.

I hope we can find our way back to being friends. I will even try to believe in him. Hope and belief have flaws, because you can attach all of your aspirations to them only to find out later that you were wrong.

I prefer facts. Right now, facts are hard to come by.

OFFICIALLY THURSDAY,
DECEMBER 15, 2011

From the logbook of Edward Stanton:
Time I woke up today: 4:21 a.m. and then again at 10:36 a.m., a time I hadn't awoken a single time this year. After putting on a T-shirt and some sweatpants, I went to the lobby for the continental breakfast, but the woman who owns this motel said, "Sorry, breakfast's over. You have to wake up earlier. You can get something at the Kwik Korner if you want." Well, crud. (I'm trying not to curse so much.)

High temperature for Wednesday, December 14, 2011, Day 348: 42 in Billings (according to the Denver newspaper, which I find crumpled in the motel lobby). Ten degrees warmer than the high the day before.

Low temperature for Wednesday, December 14, 2011: 20. Same as the low the two previous days.

Precipitation for Wednesday, December 14, 2011: 0.01 inches

Precipitation for 2011: 19.41 inches

New entries:

Exercise for Wednesday, December 14, 2011: Kyle and I had a nice, brisk walk around the shopping center after the debacle with the Denver Broncos fans. Now that we're no longer driving hundreds of miles a day, I expect to get better exercise.

Miles driven Wednesday, December 14, 2011: 521.1
Total miles driven: 1,724.9

Gas usage Wednesday, December 14, 2011: Filled up in Fort Collins, Colorado: 12.488 gallons at $3.0399 per gallon, for a total of $37.96. I then drove the 230.3 remaining miles to Cheyenne Wells, Colorado, so I will need a fill-up again if I do any significant driving while I am here.

What Kyle owes me for the music he purchased: nothing. He says he won't pay. If I were to press him for the money, he would owe me $231.

Addendum: Kyle has said four words to me so far today: "The TV here sucks." I am inclined to agree with him. Kyle has been able to tune in the over-the-air channels from Denver, and that's it. There is not even basic cable or satellite dish service here. I think I will go talk to the owner of this place.

She was surprised to see us come in last night. She came to the front desk in a robe and said, "I'm sorry for my appearance. Didn't expect anyone to come in. You'll be alone here tonight." She didn't make small talk, either, which I appreciated. She had me fill out a card with my information, and she took an imprint of my credit card, and she succinctly told us that continental breakfast would be served from 6:00 a.m. to 9:00 a.m. and that checkout was noon. When I told her we'd be staying two nights, she said, "Noon Saturday, then."

My plans for today:

1. *Look around Cheyenne Wells and see if it's familiar to me. I will do this on foot so I get some good exercise.*
2. *Drive out into the countryside and see if I can find any of the oil wells that my father's crew worked on.*

3. *Try to get Kyle to talk to me, or at least listen while I tell him that we are making a fresh start.*

I really want to keep going with my list, because I hate to end on an odd number, but Dr. Buckley is in my head. *Say what you need to say and be done.* I'm done. I throw the pen across the room and leave.

— • —

The woman who owns the motel is unimpressed with my complaint about the poor TV service.

"Do you know how many lodging nights I have a year?" she asks. I hope this is a rhetorical question, because I have no idea where I would get that kind of information. "Last year, it was 2,042. That means that on an average day, fewer than six rooms of this sixteen-room motel are occupied. Further, most of my guests stay one night, not the two that you're staying. It's only because the place is bought and paid for that I can afford to keep it running. Licenses for multiple cable or satellite dish receivers are expensive. People can do just fine with the over-the-air channels. People should watch less TV anyway."

She says this with such finality, and with such precision, that I am simultaneously eager to drop the subject and to ask her another question, because I'm fascinated with the way she speaks. She has blue eyes that seem to radiate intensity. I know that's just an optical illusion; eyes do not technically radiate anything. Eyes take in light that is reflected off an object. This light passes through the cornea, which refracts (I love the word "refracts") the rays that pass through the pupil, the round black hole in the middle of an eye. The colored part around the pupil is called the iris, and it opens and closes to regulate how much light passes into the eye. The lens of the eye then further refracts the rays and sends them to the retina, in the back of eye. The retina is full of things called rods and cones, which detect such things as colors and details. The cones and rods convert the light into electrical impulses, which are sent to the brain, producing an image. That's how eyes work. Everybody knows this.

What I'm saying is that her eyes make her look extra-alert, and that appeals to me. I cannot explain why.

Also, her dirty-blonde hair is pulled up into the kind of pony-tail that Donna Middleton (now Hays) often wears.

"How long have you owned this motel?" I ask.

"Groundbreaking was April eighteenth, nineteen sixty-seven. First room was rented on May first, nineteen sixty-eight."

"You owned it then?" I am flummoxed and again impressed with the precision. This woman cannot be much older than I am. "You would have been a little girl."

"I wasn't born yet, as a matter of fact. My mom and dad owned it. They're in the ground now, so it's mine."

I like the euphemism "in the ground." I may start describing my father this way. She and I have this in common, that our fathers are dead.

I start to ask another question but she cuts me off. "Can't talk. Lots to do. Enjoy your stay."

She walks past me, down the hallway into the main part of the motel, and disappears behind a closed door.

I guess I will talk to her later.

— • —

Kyle is still not speaking to me. That's his choice. I speak to him. This is my choice.

"Kyle, your debt is cleared. You don't owe me anything. I will not keep track of your bad deeds or your good deeds. You do what you think is right, and Saturday I will take you to Wyoming, and you can meet your parents and be free of me."

Kyle does not say anything. He keeps playing that bird game on my bitchin' iPhone.

"Also," I say, "the lady who owns this motel says this TV is the best she can do."

Kyle stops playing the game on the phone and tosses it onto my bed.

"What's that supposed to mean?"

"Well, Kyle, she says that it's expensive to put in cable television and—"

"No, douche, that's—" He stops talking, and he frowns like he has an ache somewhere. "I'm sorry. Really, Edward, I'm sorry. What I mean is, why aren't you keeping track of what I do anymore?"

I feel stung by what Kyle just said. He claims to be sorry, but he keeps calling me names. I want to give him what's called the benefit of the doubt, but how can I do that when there's so much doubt? I consider not answering him and letting him feel what it's like to get the silent treatment, but then I remember that the whole point of this conversation was to start fresh with him. Dueling silent treatments would not help the situation.

"You need to stop calling me names," I say.

"I said I was sorry."

"And I said you need to stop. Sorry won't work."

Dr. Buckley's words are again coming out of my mouth, and this continually astounds me. She used to say this very thing to me when I first started going to her office, when my condition was out of control and I said a lot of mean things to her. I think that's why I am so sensitive to such things now. I think that someday Kyle will look back on how he's acting now and be sorry for the things he has said to people. That's called regret, and regret hurts for a long time.

He looks down. "OK, I'll stop."

"OK," I say, and I sit down on my bed, keeping my distance but also trying to let him know that I will not hold a grudge. "I've decided to stop tracking your behavior because it's none of my business. I think you're a good young man, and I think no matter how hard things have been for you, you know what's right and what's wrong because your parents have raised you well."

Kyle nods. I keep talking. It's hard for me to believe these things are coming out of my mouth, because I don't sound like me. I sound like Dr. Buckley. Again.

"We were friends when you lived in Billings, and in my head and in my heart we will always be friends. But I don't know what kind of friends we'll be. A lot of it—most of it—will be up to you. I'm not going to make it hard on you by tracking your behavior. As far as I'm concerned, it's a new day."

I really can't believe I'm saying this, because it's such a stupid, self-evident phrase; every day is a new day no matter what, and it's silly to point it out.

Kyle sits on the edge of his bed quietly. I think this is the first time on this whole trip that he is actually listening to me. Not that thinking matters very much. It's the facts that count.

"Why did we come here?" Kyle asks. "This town is so small and boring."

I cannot argue with Kyle, even if I wanted to. When we drove into Cheyenne Wells, Colorado, last night, even though it was dark, I recognized this motel and the grain elevators in town, and that was it. It's funny—and not ha-ha funny—how something can appear to be so precise and vivid when you dream about it and then be so foreign and unrecognizable in the conscious world, when the cones and rods in your eyes are sending electrical impulses to your brain and showing you what things really look like.

The simplest answer to Kyle's question, the one Occam's razor would lead us to, is that I don't have a good reason for why we came here. But I don't tell Kyle that. I choose a different answer, one that is just as true.

"My father, before he became a politician in Billings, used to work for an oil company, and he was the boss of some crews that worked around here on the oil pumps. Those crews did some pretty neat things. Would you like to see the oil fields?"

"Sure," Kyle says.

We both stand up and grab our jackets and head for the door. Once we're in the hallway, the motel owner comes walking past us.

"Storm is coming," she says, her intense blue eyes looking straight at me. And then she is gone into the room two doors down and across the hallway from us.

She flummoxes me.

"That was weird," Kyle says.

It certainly was. I'm definitely going to talk to her later.

— • —

Kyle and I stand on the side of a dirt road, and I point out across a fallow (I love the word "fallow") field to an oil pump in the distance. The head of it slowly bobs up and down, like a bird pulling a worm out of the ground.

"That's an oil pump," I say.

"I know that."

Kyle thinks he's so smart.

"Do you know what cathodic protection is?" I ask.

"No."

"Do you want me to tell you?"

"Yeah."

I try to explain this simply, which means I leave out the most interesting parts, like electrochemical potential and cathodic disbonding.

"These oil pumps will corrode over time unless something is done to combat it. That's what my father's crew would do. They would attach a power source to the pump with cables that they buried underground, and these cables would also go to something called an anode, which would get corroded instead of the pump, so the pump could keep doing its business. Does that make sense?"

"Not really."

"You'll learn about it later in school."

"What's so special about it?"

"Nothing is special about it. It's just something my father did. The men who worked for him were very tough; you had to be, working with cathodic protection. Sometimes, the men would have to splice the cables together, which involved something called epoxy—a kind of glue. They would have these bags of liquid that were divided into two parts, and they would have to squeeze the bag repeatedly to heat up the liquid, then pull apart the divider to mix it, then cut open the bag of liquid, and pour it into a mold. My father said that epoxy, if it got on your skin, would be almost impossible to remove. He told me once when I was a little boy, 'Edward, I'm thirty-six years old, but my hands are eighty-four.' I don't think he meant that literally, because that would be impossible."

Kyle kneels down and picks up a small rock from the roadway. He throws it sidearm, and it thumps against a fence post.

"Good throw," I say.

"Can we go over there and look at the pump?" Kyle asks.

"Oh, no."

"Why not?"

"That would be trespassing."

My father warned me never to trespass. There was nothing he hated in the world more than disrespect of private-property rights. If you got him talking about those or the shenanigans of Democrats, he would get very angry. However, if you got him talking about tax cuts or Ronald Reagan, he would get very happy. To be honest, none of those subjects interests me very much.

Kyle spreads his arms wide and says, "Dude, there's nobody for miles. Let's go take a look."

"Kyle, no."

Kyle is not listening to me. He shimmies (I love the word "shimmies") under the barbed-wire fence while I say "No, no, no, no, no," and he takes off running across the field, his feet kicking up dust as he goes.

I am too large to shimmy under the fence. I grab a fencepost with my right hand and put my left foot on the bottom strand of barbed wire. The strand goes all the way to the ground as I put my weight on it. I look for Kyle, and he's now just a dot on the horizon, yards and yards away from me.

Slowly, I straddle the barbed wire, bringing my right leg over to the other side. I am in a precarious (I love the word "precarious") position now. My balls are hanging directly over the barbed wire. As I find the ground with my right foot, I start bringing my left foot over, and that's when it happens. I let go of the top strand of barbed wire too fast, and it springs upward, gouging me in my left hamstring. It tears my pants and cuts into my leg, and I fall down on the other side of the fence.

I pick myself up and dust off, and as I limp toward the oil pump, I see that Kyle has climbed up the back of it.

"Kyle, get down!" I scream. He can't hear me or doesn't want to hear me. The wind is blowing, and it's as if my words get scattered away from where I'm aiming them.

"Kyle, get off that right now!" I scream again, and this time I know he hears me, because I'm close enough to see his face.

He waves at me. "I'm a cowboy, Edward, and I'm riding the biggest horse there is!"

"Get down!"

"Make me!"

I am flummoxed. I'm not going to climb on the back of the pump to chase him; that is just asking for trouble and maybe even tragedy. I can't call his mother, because I left the bitchin' iPhone way back at the car. I can't get anyone to help me, because no one else is here.

I'm feeling helpless. I run several steps toward the oil pump and then I stop, because I have no idea what I'll do once I'm there.

"Get down," I yell again.

"No."

I pace back and forth and I run my hands through my hair and I get more and more frustrated. I want to scream.

"Kyle Middleton, you little fucking shitball, you get down off that right now! You're pretty high and far out, aren't you? Well, fuck you and the horse you're riding on."

Holy shit!

Kyle's face appears to lose all color. He climbs down off the back of the oil pump and walks over to me. He doesn't say anything. I'm breathing hard. I try to speak.

"I—"

"Wow, Edward."

"I—"

"'Little fucking shitball'?"

"I—"

"Wow."

"I—I don't know where that came from. I'm sorry," I say.

"Don't be sorry. That was cool."

"No, it wasn't. Also, Kyle, you shouldn't say 'fucking' or 'shitball.' I know I did just now, again, but it's not nice to say things like that."

"I know."

"I'm sorry again, Kyle."

"I'm sorry, too. What happened to your pants?" He points at the hole on the backside of my legs.

"That dumb fence," I say.

"It tore your pants up pretty good."

"I know, Kyle. It hurts, too. I'm lucky I didn't snag my balls."

We're making our way to the Cadillac DTS slowly, because I'm limping. I look to the sky now and I can see what the motel owner—why do I not know her name?—warned us about. It's not the bright blue it was this morning; instead, it's that gray color that forebodes (I love the word "forebodes") a storm. I think about R.E.M. and the song that was playing as we drove out of Cheyenne Wells, the one where Michael Stipe sings about a sky that looks like a Man Ray painting.

I also think about the awful thing I said to Kyle and where it must have come from. Actually, I know where it came from. When I called him a "little fucking shitball," that came from

Scott Shamwell the pressman. He usually said that about Elliott Overbay, the copy desk chief, but never when Elliott Overbay could hear him. When I said "you're pretty high and far out," I was quoting Sergeant Joe Friday from the first episode of *Dragnet 1967*, which originally aired on January 12, 1967. It's one of my favorites.

The last part, when I said "fuck you and the horse you're riding on" to Kyle, is easy. That's my father. Those are his words. I am flabbergasted (I love the word "flabbergasted") that they ended up on my tongue. Not literally, of course. That's a figure of speech.

Two things are clear. First, when it comes to yelling at people, I am derivative (I love the word "derivative"). Second, I have no business telling Kyle what he should or shouldn't say. I can't control my own mouth.

Kyle again shimmies under the fence, and then he steps on the middle strand and lifts the top one so I can dip my head and sneak through.

We get in the car, and I turn it on. Michael Stipe is singing about the flowers of Guatemala and how they cover everything. I make a U-turn on the dirt road and head back to the two-lane highway that will lead us to town, and that's when the first fat snowflake hits the windshield.

— • —

By the time we get back to the motel, it's an onslaught (I love the word "onslaught") of snow. The flakes are fat and wet, and they cling to the windshield almost as fast as I can use the wipers to get rid of them. The streets of Cheyenne Wells fill quickly with snow, and the Cadillac DTS fishtails as we pull into the parking lot.

Inside, the motel owner is waiting for us.

"I was watching for you," she says. "I told you a storm was coming."

I rub the top of my head with my hand, feeling the snow melt in my hair, and Kyle stomps on the entryway rug to get the snow off his shoes.

"It came on with no warning," I say.

"No," she says, "I warned you. I told you 'storm's coming.' I couldn't have been more clear than I was."

Again, her eyes are playing games with me. Every time she speaks they sparkle, or seem to. I know this is a trick of the light. And her mouth crinkles like she's holding something back—it flummoxes me that I can't tell if it's a grin or disdain for how stupid I was, getting caught in the storm like that.

"I don't believe I got your name," I say to her. Kyle tugs at my jacket and asks for the room key because "this is boring." I hand it to him, and he skips down the hallway.

"I don't believe I offered it to you," she says. "My name is Sheila Renfro."

She extends her right hand to me, and I take it in my right hand. Her fingers feel rough and chalky. She shakes my hand firmly, up and down three times, and then she lets go.

"I think I stayed in this motel when I was a little boy, with my father."

"It's the only motel in town. If you stayed in Cheyenne Wells, you stayed here."

"It was nineteen seventy-eight. I was nine years old."

"When in nineteen seventy-eight?"

"June."

"What day in June?"

"I don't remember."

"I was either two years old or three years old. I was born June fifteenth, nineteen seventy-five, so it depends on when you were here."

"When I was here, the motel was run by a big, fat guy who had white hair."

"That was my father. He wasn't fat. He was pleasantly plump. He's in the ground now."

"He and his wife had a little girl."

"That was me."

"That was you?"

She narrows her blue eyes at me. "Yes, silly. I just told you."

"So we've met before?"

"I guess we have."

"Do you remember me?"

"No, silly. I was just a little girl. Plus, you only have to remember a couple of people. Do you think I can remember everyone who has ever come to this motel? Sure, I could look at the register and see who's been here, but that doesn't mean I would remember them."

I'm really foundering (I love the word "foundering," but I hate to do it). I keep saying dumb things, and she keeps pointing out that they're dumb. And yet, I do not want to stop talking to Sheila Renfro. She fascinates me.

I decide to change the subject.

"Why do your hands feel so weird?"

She rubs her palms on the hips of her blue jeans twice. "They're not weird. I'm working. I'm doing drywall in room number eight."

"Papered or fiberglass?"

"Papered."

"Bathroom or living quarters?"

"Living quarters."

"I'm pretty handy with drywall. Do you need help?"

"Are you offering or do you expect to be paid?"

"I don't need to get paid. I'm fucking loaded."

"Don't curse around me. I would like your help, yes."

I excuse myself so I can go tell Kyle what I'm doing, and I tell Sheila Renfro that I will meet her in room number eight in a few minutes. She offers me another handshake. I happily accept, and this time, her hand doesn't feel weird at all.

As I'm walking down the hallway to the room I share with Kyle, room number four, I feel a little light-headed and funny in my stomach, like birds are flying around in it, which is of course impossible.

TECHNICALLY FRIDAY, DECEMBER 16, 2011

I cannot stop thinking about Sheila Renfro. At 9:47 p.m., Kyle and I left her cottage, which is attached to this motel, and came back to our room. We watched the 10:00 p.m. news out of Denver, although I must concede that I wasn't really paying attention because I kept thinking about Sheila Renfro. At 10:32, I shut off the light and listened as Kyle quickly fell asleep. That was three hours and nine minutes ago—it's 1:41 a.m. now—and I haven't closed my eyes even once, except when I blink. Kyle is snoring in the bed next to mine. He's lucky.

I've been lying here and thinking about Sheila Renfro. What an interesting lady. And a very no-nonsense woman, too.

The drywall work went well. As I told Sheila Renfro, I'm very handy with drywall. She needed help replacing a seven-foot-by-nine-foot section of the south wall in room number eight. By the time I got involved, she already had the old wall torn out, so I didn't get to see the original damage. Sheila Renfro said it was pretty bad, that the room had been "lived in hard" over the years. The final indignation occurred a week ago, when a young man and his girlfriend were staying in the room and got into a serious fight.

"I had a funny feeling about them when they checked in, but it was late and it was cold, so I ignored that feeling. An hour later, it's an awful racket in there. Yelling and hitting and the sound of things crashing. I called the cops. It was too late. I had a funny feeling about them when they checked in. I shouldn't have let them have the room."

Sheila Renfro was clearly holding onto regret about what happened, so I tried to be helpful as I nailed a section of drywall into place.

"Yes," I said, "but feelings are hard to quantify. What if they had been a nice couple and you had denied them a room based on a feeling? That wouldn't have been fair."

"They weren't a nice couple. They destroyed my room."

"I know. I'm just saying what if. You can't trust a feeling."

"I trust *my* feelings. I know what's what."

Sheila Renfro seemed to be getting annoyed with me, so I stopped talking about it. This is something I learned from Dr. Buckley, that it's not important to win every argument. The first time she told me that, I thought she was kidding, but she was serious. It took me a long time to see the wisdom in her contention, but as usual, she turned out to be correct. Her general principle is to fight hard for the things worth fighting for, like your family or your inalienable (I love the word "inalienable") rights. With a difference of opinion, why do damage to your relationship with someone by continuing to argue when there's no possibility of a resolution? I'm not saying that I always get this right. For example, I got it quite wrong when I was arguing with Kyle about Tim Tebow. But Dr. Buckley's words are never far from my mind, and in this case, with Sheila Renfro, I stopped the argument before it did damage. (I still don't know how anyone can trust feelings above facts, though.)

"How old is your son?" Sheila Renfro asked me.

I thought it was funny—interesting funny, not ha-ha funny—that she thought Kyle was my son, although I suppose I'm old enough to be his father.

"He's my nephew," I said, which was a fabrication and one I didn't feel good about. On the other hand, I could see where being too truthful about this might lead to more questions and suspicion, and I didn't need that. "We're on an adventure."

"In Cheyenne Wells?"

"Well, like I told you, I've been here before."

"Shouldn't he be in school?"

"He's home-schooled." Fabricating is getting easier for me.

"Do you have any children?" I ask her.

"Have you seen any around here?"

"No."

"Well, there you go. No children for me, at least not yet. I'm still young enough, though."

"Yes." It seems right to agree with her, although at thirty-six years old, her biological clock is ticking. That, too, is a figure of speech. There is no clock inside us. That's absurd.

"You're too old, though," she says to me. "Not biologically, but practically."

"No, I'm not."

"You have to be at least fifty-five years old, right?"

I am aghast. "I'm forty-two."

Sheila Renfro smiles at me. A real smile. "Gotcha," she says.

Sheila Renfro is pretty funny sometimes.

— • —

After we got the drywall in place, we had only the painting left. I told Sheila Renfro that I would help her do that tomorrow— technically today, now—and that Kyle and I would drag the old drywall and other detritus out to the garbage. That turned out to be harder than I figured. The snow continued to come down in big, heavy, wet flakes, and drifts had begun to form on the outside wall of the motel. It took us five trips into blowing wind and side-ways snow and walking through the drifts, but we got the garbage out. Kyle was a good helper.

When we got back inside and shook the snow off our shoes and jackets, Sheila Renfro asked us to join her for dinner.

— • —

Sheila Renfro and I are a lot alike.

She has lived her whole life in Cheyenne Wells, Colorado, where she was born. I have lived my whole life in Billings, Montana, where I was born. She likes routines and things she can rely on. I like the same. She's very smart—in one evening with her, I learned that she knows almost as much about pro-fessional football as I do, including offensive formations and defensive alignments. I even tested her by asking what a dime package is.

She said, "Don't be silly. It's when there are six defensive backs."

She was right.

She is even a Dallas Cowboys fan, just like I am. I asked her why she liked Dallas better than Denver, since Denver is much closer to Cheyenne Wells than Dallas is, and she said, "The Cow-boys are America's Team."

That kind of logic is impressive.

She received good grades in high school, and I did, too. She said she never felt like she fit in with her classmates, and I know exactly what that is like. I never fit in with my classmates at Billings West High School, either. Despite our good grades, neither of us felt prepared for college, so we didn't go. I asked her if she has regrets about not going to college—we agreed that regrets are not fun.

She said, "Heck no. I got to stay here and work for my daddy."

That's where Sheila Renfro's story turns sad. When she was twenty-two years old, on August 7, 1997, her parents were killed in a car crash just seven miles out of town as they were coming home from Denver. That left Sheila Renfro all alone.

"They're in the ground now," she told me. She took me around her living room and she showed me pictures of her parents. I vaguely remembered both of them from my time in Cheyenne Wells, but that was a long time ago and memories are faulty. In the pictures that were taken toward the end of their lives, when they were much older than when I met them, they look content. Contentedness is a hard thing to quantify—impossible, in fact—but the looks on their faces in the pictures tell a lot. The smiles are genuine and loving. I don't think you can fake something like that.

"Do you miss them?" I asked Sheila Renfro. I knew this was a silly question. Of course she misses them. It was all I could think of to say.

"Yes," she said, "but I can't do anything about it. They're in the ground now."

Sheila Renfro told me that she promised herself when her parents died that she would stay in Cheyenne Wells and make sure the motel they built together kept running. She said it has been hard sometimes, that her fortunes ebb and flow with oil activity and agriculture in southeastern Colorado. I knew what she meant. My father's mood often correlated (I love the word "correlated") with the price of oil, even long after he left the oil business and went into politics. Most people complain when the price of oil is high, because they know it will cost them more to fill their gas tanks. My father never saw that as a problem. Sheila Renfro doesn't, either.

"It's a great motel," I told her. "You've run it well."

"I'm glad I had the help today," she said. "I could use it on a full-time basis."

I told her that maybe things would pick up and she could hire someone. She sort of smiled at that. Then she said it was time to eat.

We had taco soup, which I'd never had before, and Jell-O brand strawberry gelatin. It was a good meal. Kyle liked it, too.

— • —

It's 2:59 a.m. now and I'm no closer to sleep.

I throw off the covers from the bed and limp-walk to the bathroom to get a drink of water. My mouth is dry.

The back of my leg still hurts from where the barbed wire snagged me. Sheila Renfro was nice enough to patch my pants after dinner. She said I could stay in the living room with her while she did her sewing, but I was embarrassed because I was down to my underwear and my shirt, so I went into the bathroom and closed the door, and Kyle stayed in the living room and talked to her.

After she was done with the pants, she came to the bathroom door and said, "Open up. I want to see that cut."

"No," I said. "I'm in my underwear."

"I have seen a man in his underwear before," she said.

This declaration from her brought to my mind several questions that I wanted to ask—the kind of questions Dr. Buckley has told me are inappropriate. So I kept my mouth closed, even though it was difficult.

I opened the door, and she barged in and knelt in front of me.

"Turn around," she said.

I did as I was told. Now my underwear-covered butt was in her face. I was so embarrassed.

"Looks like it nicked you," she said. "Have you had a tetanus shot?"

"November twenty-sixth, two thousand and eight, from Dr. Rex Helton," I said.

"OK, good. I'm going to put some peroxide on it. Stay where you are."

She stood and began looking through the cabinet drawers in the bathroom, which I couldn't see but could hear. Finally she said, "Aha," and the next thing I knew, the spot on the back of my leg was cold and tingly. Next she pressed hard on my injured spot as she affixed a strip bandage to it.

"Good as new," she said, and she left. I put on my pants. I had a boner, so they didn't fit right.

— • —

Kyle stirs as I'm heading back to bed.

"What time is it?" he asks. I left the light on in the bathroom by accident, and it is casting a yellow bar across his face.

"It's 3:03 a.m."

"Wow."

"Yes. Why are you awake?"

"I had a dream."

"About what?"

"I don't want to say."

I sit down on the edge of Kyle's bed, and he sits up and gathers his legs into his arms.

"Was it a bad dream?" I ask.

"Yes."

"You can tell me about it if you want."

Kyle sets his forehead on his knees. He speaks, but he doesn't look at me.

"I'm scared."

"Of what?"

"You know how you and that lady were talking about how your parents died?"

"Yes."

"I dreamed that my mom died. She was reaching out for me, and I was reaching out for her, and I couldn't reach her and she was gone."

Kyle looks up at me now. He's crying. I understand it. I feel like crying, too, when I consider such a dream. Donna is my good friend.

I tell Kyle something I've never discussed with him.

"Do you remember when we first met?" I ask.

"Yeah. You were painting your garage. I helped you."

"Did you know that a couple of days after that, I had a dream about you?"

"You did?"

"Yes. I dreamed that you were dangling off the rimrocks above Billings and that I was holding on to you, only I dropped you and you fell."

Kyle is looking directly at me. He uses the back of his hand to wipe his nose.

"I woke up and I drove to where your mom worked and I asked her to call your grandmother in Laurel and make sure you were OK. I was freaked out, and I freaked out your mom, and for a while she wouldn't even talk to me."

"Wow."

"That was as scared as I've ever been, Kyle. I don't keep statistics on such things, but I'm confident that's true. But here's the important thing: What I dreamed wasn't real. You didn't fall off the rimrocks. That's how I know your mom is fine."

"I want to go home."

This surprises me. Two days ago, Kyle couldn't wait to get away from Boise. Now he wants to go back. I'm flummoxed.

"We're meeting your mom and Victor in Wyoming on Saturday. Technically, that's tomorrow."

"Can we go early?"

I think of the plans I have for later today. I want to help Sheila Renfro paint the repaired wall in room number eight. I want to take a walk around Cheyenne Wells, if it stops snowing. I want to find out more about Sheila Renfro. I want to see if I can make her smile again.

"Aren't you having fun?" I ask.

Kyle leans across the bed and puts his hands on my head, which startles me a little bit, and then he musses my hair.

"Of course I'm having fun, douche." It's the first time he has called me a name and not meant it in a bad way.

I reach out and muss his hair back. "You're the douche."

"No, you are," he says.

"No, you are," I say.

"No, you are," he says again.

I lunge for Kyle, pretending that I'm a champion wrestler, and I knock him onto his back on the bed. I then lie gently across him and try to bundle his legs with my free arm. I'm going to count him out.

Kyle tries to throw me off. "What are you doing?" His voice is high. I lean into him so I can pin him.

"GET OFF!" he screams. "GET THE FUCK OFF ME!"

I let him go and I push myself off the bed and I run to the other side of the room. Kyle is screaming and crying and, oh God, maybe I hurt him. I clap my hands over my ears and I say "I'm sorry, I'm sorry, I'm sorry," and Kyle makes himself into a ball on the bed and he cries.

I hurt him. I hurt him really bad.

— • —

Twenty-three minutes go by. Twenty-three minutes of Kyle crying, a little less, and then a little less, and twenty-three minutes of me apologizing a little more, and then a little more.

When Kyle finally tells me what happened, after he makes me swear that I will not tell anyone, I am sick to my stomach.

I didn't hurt Kyle. Some big kids at his school did. They trapped him in the locker room, just him and the three of them, and they pinned him down, and they did bad things to him.

I have to get him home. I promised I would not tell anyone what he told me, but there are 267.5 miles between here and Cheyenne, the capital of Wyoming, that I can drive this morning, and during that time I can talk to him and convince him that he must tell his mother. We can get to Cheyenne and I can call Donna Middleton (now Hays) and tell her that we have to meet somewhere so she can have her boy back and they can figure out what to do.

It's 3:47 a.m. when I leave the handwritten note on the front desk for Sheila Renfro.

Sheila Renfro:

Something has come up, and we had to leave early. If there are any other charges, please add them to my bill. I'm sorry I won't be able to help you paint.
Thank you for mending my pants and for the taco soup and the Jell-O brand gelatin. Good luck with your motel. We enjoyed our stay.

With regards,
Edward Stanton

I leave the note and the room key, and then I go outside to the car, where Kyle is waiting for me.

It's dark and cold, and nobody is moving in Cheyenne Wells except for us. The Cadillac DTS skids in the deep snow as we turn onto Highway 40, headed west.

"I'm sorry, Edward," Kyle says.

"You never have to apologize to me," I say. "You're my best friend."

OFFICIALLY FRIDAY, DECEMBER 16, 2011

From the logbook of Edward Stanton, as recorded by Kyle Middleton:

Time Edward woke up today: Dont know. He was awake when I had that bad dream. He said it was 3:03. I guess 3:02.

High temperature for Thursday, December 15, 2011, Day 349: Dont know. Its weird that hes keeping temps in Billings while hes not there.

Low temperature for Thursday, December 15, 2011: Dont know.

Precipitation for Thursday, December 15, 2011: Dont know.

Precipitation for 2011: Dont know.

New entries:

Exercise for Thursday, December 15, 2011: Dont know. We saw that oil pump and stuff. He helped that lady at the motel I guess.

Miles driven Thursday, December 15, 2011: Dont know. We drove to the oil pump. That was like 20 miles or whatever. We tried to drive to Wyoming but hit the snowplow and Edward got hurt. That was like 50 miles or whatever. 70 I guess. Who cares.

Total miles driven: Who cares.

Gas usage Thursday, December 15, 2011: Who cares.

Addendum: I dont know what would have happened if that lady from the motel hadnt shown up. I told Edward he was going to fast in the snow but he was in a hurry and we hit the snowplow and he got hurt real bad. He couldnt talk and he didnt have any breath. The guy in the snowplow called an ambulance and while we waited Edward kept trying to talk and he couldnt breath and I was real scared and that lady from the motel drove up behind us just as the helicopter arrived.

Edward flew to Denver in the helicopter. I wanted to go but the lady took me here in her truck. Hes still in the operating room. Shes sitting here with me. She doesnt talk very much but Id be alone if she wasnt here and that would suck.

Mom and Victor are getting on a plane to come here.

The doctor people who took Edward on the helicopter said he was lucky.

I wish theyd come out and say something.

I hope hes okay. Im really scared. So is that lady.

I had the strangest dream.

In my head, I was a building. Only I wasn't a static building, rooted to one place like buildings are. I was a shape-shifting building. I would grow longer and longer and take up entire city blocks, then I would shoot up high into the sky and change color, and then I would double back the way I came on the other side of the block. It was a little like the old arcade game Centipede, the way the centipede would grow and grow, taking up more of the screen. The only difference, in this case, is that no one was shooting at me and trying to separate me.

I'm so thirsty.

I open my eyes, and sitting next to me is Sheila Renfro. She's looking into my face with her blue eyes. I must still be dreaming.

"Sheila Renfro."

"Hello, Edward."

"What are you doing here?"

"You had a wreck."

"Where's Kyle?"

"He went to the bathroom. He'll be back in a minute."

I look around the room. It's all white.

"You lied to me about Kyle," she says.

"What?"

"You lied to me. He's not your nephew. He's your friend, and his mom and dad are on the way."

I try to move my elbows behind me to push myself up, and the pain is so bad that I think I'm going to pass out. I don't keep statistics on such things, but it's the worst physical pain I've ever felt.

"Edward, be still," Sheila Renfro says. "You broke a couple of ribs."

I stop moving and wait as the pain recedes.

"Can I have some water?" I ask.

Sheila Renfro comes to the other side of my bed. I follow her with my eyes. I'm afraid to move again. She slips a big plastic cup of water with an oversize straw under my chin.

"Drink up," she says, and I do.

Every time I swallow, it hurts.

When I'm done, I say, "How did I break my ribs?"

"You drove into the back of a snowplow."

"Is Kyle all right?"

"He's fine. A little sore, but he wasn't hurt."

"Where is this?"

"St. Joseph Hospital in Denver."

"Is Kyle all right?"

"Yes. I said he is."

"How did you get here?"

"I drove. You left your phone and your medicine and I followed you."

"You brought us here?"

"I brought Kyle here. The helicopter brought you."

"Where's Kyle?"

"He went to the bathroom. I told you that."

"What happened?"

"I told you."

"I'm sorry I lied."

"Don't lie to me ever again."

"I'm sorry I lied."

"Close your eyes, Edward."

I close my eyes as Sheila Renfro tells me to do, and a new image fills my head. It's my father in the Cadillac DTS that used to belong to him and now belongs to me. It's midday and the sun is out, and my father is wearing sunglasses.

"Where shall we go, Teddy?" my father asks.

"You're driving, Father," I hear myself tell him.

"Damn right," he says, and we're off.

The dream blinks out of my head like a television being turned off. I open my eyes.

Sheila Renfro is stroking my forehead, pushing my hair back slowly and rhythmically, and she's looking at me. She's smiling at me.

— • —

When I wake up again, it is to the sound of multiple voices talking in my hospital room.

I open my eyes and wait for the adjustment to the light, for the retina and the iris and the rods and cones to do their jobs.

It's Donna and Victor and Kyle and Sheila Renfro and a young man in a white shirt and a black tie.

"Hi," I say. My ribs ache when I do.

My friends all jump as if they are surprised to hear my voice. Donna comes over and dips her head down to mine and kisses me on the cheek, and I feel suddenly warm. Sheila Renfro lingers behind her, watching. Victor shakes my hand gently; I think he sees me wince as I reach across my body with my right hand, and he spares me the vigorous shake I usually get from him. Kyle walks around to the other side of my bed, opposite the grown-ups, and says, "Hi, Edward."

"Hi, Kyle."

The young man in the white shirt steps forward.

"Hello, Mr. Stanton. I'm Dr. Ira Banning. Do you remember me?"

Even with all the activity in the room, some things are starting to return to me. I remember stopping for gas in Kit Carson, Colorado, after we left Sheila Renfro's motel in haste, when I looked down at the gas gauge and realized we were nearly empty. I remember the storm that kicked up between Kit Carson and Limon, where we got onto Interstate 70 and headed for Denver. I remember the snow flying sideways across the windshield and I remember not being able to see. I remember growing impatient at our pace and deciding to drive through the swirling flurries, thinking I could get ahead of them. I remember pulling into the passing lane.

"I remember you, Dr. Banning," I say.

I remember him because I remember not being able to breathe. I remember Kyle looking into my face and asking me what happened and what was wrong. I remember another man—I don't know where he came from—opening the door on my Cadillac DTS and saying "Oh, shit," and running off. I remember gasping for breath and not making any words come out. I remember the other man coming back and saying, "They're on the way, buddy, so just hold on." He grabbed my hand and held it, and Kyle cried, and I couldn't tell either of them that I couldn't breathe.

I remember waking up, my back stiff on a board, staring into yellow lights. I remember Dr. Banning—not in a white shirt but in a blue smock like the one Donna wears when she goes to work—telling me that they needed to take some scans to see how badly I was hurt inside. I remember being able to talk at last and saying that I needed a drink.

"Soon," the doctor said. "Let's see what's going on first."

I remember waking up. I remember Sheila Renfro talking to me and telling me to close my eyes and stroking my hair.

I don't remember anything else.

"What happened?" I ask.

"You drove into a snowplow," Sheila Renfro says. "Remember how I told you that? You broke your ribs."

"Three broken ribs on your left side, Mr. Stanton," Dr. Banning says. "Probably from the seat belt when you crashed. Your lung got punctured. We fixed that. The ribs will take a couple of weeks, maybe a bit longer, but they will heal. You have a concussion. Do you understand what that means?"

"My brain got hurt."

"Yes, that's it. You're very lucky, all things considered."

I turn to my friend. "Kyle, are you—"

"I'm fine," he says.

He squats beside the bed and he sets his head on my right shoulder. Donna reaches across me to stop him, but I shake my head to let her know it is all right, and my side hurts when I do. She pulls back. I pat Kyle on the head.

"What happened to my Cadillac DTS?"

Sheila Renfro makes a slashing motion across her throat, crossing her eyes and flopping her tongue out of her mouth. It's very funny, and I laugh, which hurts really bad, and I yell out in pain. Donna looks annoyed with Sheila Renfro.

As the pain diminishes, I regain my breath. "How am I supposed to get back to Billings so I can fly to Texas?" I ask.

"I don't want you on a plane for a while," Dr. Banning says. "It puts a lot of stress on a body, that pressurization at thirty-five thousand feet. You've been through a trauma."

"But I have to go to Texas on December twentieth. I'm going to see my mother."

"You're going to be here for a couple of days yet," the doctor says.

"Edward," Donna says, "don't you think maybe you should just concentrate on getting better?"

I have to concede that Donna is a very logical woman and that she's probably correct about this. And yet I am disappointed, because I was looking forward to going to Texas and seeing the Dallas Cowboys play in their new stadium.

"Does my mother know I'm in the hospital?" I ask.

Sheila Renfro holds out my bitchin' iPhone. "She's waiting for you to call," she says.

— • —

I have an audience as I make the call to my mother, with Kyle holding the bitchin' iPhone to my ear so I don't have to lift my arms and aggravate my broken ribs. It's not a fun phone call. Not too many phone calls are fun; I don't like to talk on the phone. This one is especially difficult. I'm happy to hear my mother's voice, but almost immediately she begins crying and telling me that her world would end if something bad happened to me, and that I must be more careful.

"Stop crying," I say, and that makes her cry even more. I look helplessly at Donna, and she's crying. I look at Sheila Renfro, and she's not crying. She's just watching me. Her look is intense, as if something bad will happen if she lets me out of her sight. I guess that's reasonable, even if it's not practical. Once I was out of her sight and out of her motel, something bad did happen to me.

I assure my mother that I will be careful and I apologize to her that I will be unable to make it to Texas for Christmas or to see the Dallas Cowboys.

"You just don't worry about that," she says. "When you're well, you can come down. Or I'll come see you."

"My car is destroyed, Mother. How am I supposed to get back to Billings?"

"I will call Jay. He'll make sure you have a car when the time comes."

"Thank you, Mother. I will see you soon, I hope." Hope is all I have in this instance. It's not much.

"I love you, Son."

I look around the room at everybody watching me. Only the doctor cleared out of the room. I don't like to say things like "I love you" in front of an audience. Or at all.

"Yes, Mother, I know."

"Good-bye," she says.

"Good-bye."

She hangs up. I'm glad that's over with.

— • —

Everybody stays in the room with me. I ask Sheila Renfro to track down my watch, which is set to the precise second, because the analog clock on the wall is the very definition of unreliable, and it begins to irritate me. We watch an episode of a show called *Everybody Loves Raymond*, which turns out to be funny even with the wildly overblown title. I highly doubt that there is anyone in the world whom everybody loves. I think even the unassailably wonderful people in the world probably have someone who doesn't like them. My father, for instance, often made jokes about Mother Teresa. (One I remember him telling: "Why did Mother Teresa stop eating buffalo wings? Because she kept dipping the chicken into the lepers' backs instead of the blue cheese dressing." To be honest, I'm not even sure what that means.) I am far from a perfect person—I am rude and self-absorbed, and Dr. Buckley would be happy to say so—but one thing I try not to do is make fun of people. When I was a boy, and even now, I was often made fun of, and it's hurtful. I've learned to forgive my father for many of the things he did, and it's not my place to stick up for Mother Teresa. Still, I think he was wrong to say those things. I don't know if I believe in God. Believing in God requires faith, and faith is difficult for me. But just the same, I would be inclined to not make fun of Mother Teresa, because if there is a God—especially the Judeo-Christian God—Mother Teresa has a lot more standing than my father does.

Leaving God out of it, I think that if someone who dedicates her life to caring for the poor and the sick can be an object of derision (I love the word "derision"), what chance do the rest of us have?

At 6:31 p.m., after the program ends, Donna and Victor say they're leaving, that they will be flying home to Boise with Kyle the next morning. Donna gives me another kiss, and this time Sheila Renfro looks angry, which flummoxes me. Victor again shakes my hand, gently, which I appreciate in my painful state.

The three of them are heading for the door when I say, "Can everybody else wait in the hall while I talk to Kyle?"

— • —

Kyle knows where I stand. I want him to tell his mother and father what he told me.

"But what if she hates me?" he says.

I'm pulled between the competing thoughts of how silly it is that Kyle would fear such a thing and a gentler realization that Dr. Buckley would be apt to make. She told me once that some people hold great shame for things that aren't their fault, awful things that were done to them by people who were stronger or more powerful than they were. Shame isn't something I've known in my life. Frustration, anger, wanting to be dead—I have known all of those things. But shame is difficult for me to understand. Dr. Buckley said it's a horribly destructive force, perhaps the most destructive force she has ever encountered.

I do not want Kyle to know what that's like.

"Donna will not hate you," I tell him. "She will know exactly what to do. Your mother is wise, and she loves you, and she can help you."

He doesn't want to cry, but one tear does spill down his cheek. He wipes it away.

"I just don't want to go back to that school. I hate it. I just want to forget it."

In ways that I don't think I could explain to Kyle—and even if I could, I don't have the time, because Donna and Victor are waiting outside the door—he and I are more alike than I ever noticed before. The kids who picked on me when I was in school made it miserable for me a lot of the time. I never tracked how often I disliked school, but it would be fair to say that the truly surprising days were the ones that I enjoyed. I liked the work; if I could have been alone at school, just me and my teachers, I might have had a fun time. I don't want that for Kyle. I don't want him to have to feel that way about school.

"Tell your mother," I say.

"Edward, can I ask you a question?"

"Yes."

Kyle isn't looking at me. "Did we have fun?"

"Kyle, you're my first and best friend. We always have fun."

"After you're better, will you come see me again?"

"I promise I will."

He covers the distance between us and hugs me, and it hurts terribly, so much that, at first, I think I'm going to pass out. But I don't pass out, and I hug him back, and it hurts again, and I don't care.

Finally he lets me go.

"Good-bye, Edward," he says, opening the door.

"Good-bye, Kyle," I say. "Tell your mother."

He's gone now, but I can hear Donna say, "Tell me what?"

I'm sneakily clever sometimes.

Sheila Renfro comes into my hospital room and closes the door behind her.

"Don't get comfortable, silly," she says. "You have to get up and walk. Doctor's orders."

— • —

It's amazing to me that it's nearly 2012 and the only cure for broken ribs is to let time heal them.

I don't find that approach altogether appealing when I'm made to get out of bed and walk. There is no other way to say it: it hurts like a motherfucker. That's not a precise statement. Of course there are other ways to say it, but why would I say it any differently? My way is direct and emphatic (I love the word "emphatic").

I swing my legs off the left side of the bed, a maneuver that hurts no matter how delicately I try to perform it. As my torso torques (that rhymes, sort of), I try to scoot my back along the bed so I don't have to aggravate my ribs. I manage this somewhat successfully, but then my feet are on the floor, I'm on my back, and my butt is sliding toward the edge of the bed. This isn't good.

Sheila Renfro and a nurse, whose name is Sally, reach for me.

"Give us your hands," Sally says.

I lift my arms, and my ribs scream. Not literally, of course. Ribs don't have mouths or voices.

They grip my hands and drop their rear ends like anchors.

"On three," Sally says. She counts it off: "One…two…three."

Sheila Renfro and Sally pull hard on my arms, and I try to shove myself up with my feet. The pain is the worst it has been, and I scream.

Sally, I guess, has seen a lot of people scream. She seems unconcerned. Sheila Renfro cups her palm on my face and tells me, "You did good, Edward."

— • —

Sheila and I make two laps around the hospital hallway. I tell her that I have to pee, and she says, "Go ahead. They put a catheter in you. What do you think this is?" She taps a bag that hangs from the monitor I'm pushing. It has yellow liquid in it.

"My pee?"

"Well," she says. "It's not mine." And then she laughs.

Sheila Renfro is pretty funny sometimes.

"What are you going to do when you get out of here?" she asks me.

"I don't know. Drive back to Billings, I guess."

"It's a long way when you're feeling bad. It's a long way under any circumstance."

"Yes. The distance is unchanged by my physical condition."

"That's what I'm saying."

"Dr. Banning told me he didn't want me to fly."

"You could come stay at my motel for a while."

"You'd let me?"

"Of course. You're going to pay, aren't you?"

"Yes."

Sheila Renfro laughs. "I was just kidding. You don't have to pay. You can be my guest."

Sheila Renfro is pretty funny sometimes.

"I could pay, you know," I say. "I'm fucking loaded."

She puts a hand on the small of my back. It feels warm, and for just a moment, I forget the pain.

"I know you are, Edward," she says. "Don't cuss around me."

— • —

Sheila Renfro says she's going to stay with me in the hospital. She doesn't put it in the form of a request. It's a declaration.

I tell her I don't know if they'll let her, that hospitals have rules about such things. When Sally comes into the room to give me my Percocet, which is a kind of painkiller, I ask her if Sheila Renfro can stay in my room.

Sally says, "Absolutely, we can set up a reclining chair for her in here, if you're OK with that."

Sheila Renfro says, "He is." And she's right, although I don't think Sally was asking her for the answer.

I eat a little bit of orange-flavored gelatin for my dinner, but, to be honest, I'm not very hungry. I ask Sally, when she comes by to change the bag I'm peeing into, if it's Jell-O brand gelatin, but she says she doesn't know, that those details are handled down in the kitchen. I suppose it doesn't matter.

There isn't much on TV, which surprises me. Unlike Sheila Renfro's motel, St. Joseph Hospital has an array (I love the word "array") of cable television channels. Maybe Sheila Renfro is correct and people shouldn't watch so much TV, if tonight's selection is any indication of the baseline level of quality offered on cable these days. Even if she is correct, what am I going to do? I have broken ribs. My options are limited.

"Do you want to watch *Adam-12* on my bitchin' iPhone?" I ask Sheila Renfro.

"That will be fine," she says. "Don't cuss around me. I keep telling you."

I queue up the twenty-third episode of the first season, "Log 12: He Was Trying to Kill Me." This episode originally aired on March 15, 1969. As the video comes up, I think of how much things have changed for me in just a few years. In my years of watching my favorite TV show, *Dragnet*, I never would have let so many days go between viewings, but here I am, watching *Adam-12* for the first time since the day I left Billings. If I'd known then what would happen to me on this trip—which was impossible, of course—would I have come? I don't know. I'm asking myself unanswerable questions lately, and that's not like me. Maybe I'm changing, or maybe I'm just off my game because I'm hurt and discombobulated. If I'm changing—and changing this profoundly—I have a big adjustment to make. If I'll be back to my old self eventually, I wonder if I will recognize the signs.

I'm watching Officer Pete Malloy and Officer Jim Reed, but I'm not paying attention; I'm more looking through them, beyond the bitchin' iPhone in my hands. Beyond this room and even beyond this day. I'm trying to see what's coming, but that is a silly pursuit. We never know. I don't, anyway. It's all a surprise, and I'm having to learn to live with surprises even though I prefer certainty. Certainty allows you to plan your life, and there are few things I like better than planning. Surprises make you adjust along the way, and I'm not very good at that.

Sheila Renfro has pulled her chair up tight against my bed, and her head is tilted to the right and resting on my pillow, next to my own head. I can smell her, and it pleases me.

I'm glad she stayed.

SATURDAY, DECEMBER 17, 2011

From the logbook of Edward Stanton, as recorded by Sheila Renfro:
Time Edward woke up today: Repeatedly. It's like he discovers all over again just how hurt he is every time he wakes up, and that's heartbreaking. I wish there was something more they could do for him, but the prescription is rest and exercise.

High temperature for Friday, December 16, 2011, Day 350: 44 in Billings. Also, Edward wants me to point out that although he appreciates Kyle's attempt to keep track of things yesterday, it's important that the temperatures be correct. I was able to find yesterday's paper down in the dining area, and it said that it was a high of 33 in Billings on Thursday, December 15. Edward was relieved that I was able to find this out. He is peculiar, but I like that about him.

Low temperature for Friday, December 16, 2011: 23. And the low was 18 on Thursday.

Precipitation for Friday, December 16, 2011: 0.00 inches. Same as Thursday.

Precipitation for 2011: 19.41 inches
New entries:
Exercise for Friday, December 16, 2011: We did three sets of two laps around this floor of the hospital. As Edward says, it's hard

to prove these things empirically, but he seemed to get better each time. The only bad part is that it hurts him so bad when we have to pull him out of the bed. It's heartbreaking.

Miles driven Friday, December 16, 2011: No mileage for Edward, I'm afraid. I was able to do some research and piece together how many miles he drove Thursday before the crash. It's 86.8 miles from Cheyenne Wells to Limon, where he got on Interstate 70. I came upon the wreck a little more than seven miles after that. It's not precise, but it's close enough. As far as gas usage goes, I have no idea. It doesn't matter.

Total miles driven: We're missing a chunk, including how far he and Kyle went Thursday while they were out looking at oil pumps, but let's just say, roughly, 1,838.7. That includes the 93.8 we know about from Thursday, plus another 20. It's close enough.

Gas usage for Friday, December 16, 2011: None. I'm with Kyle here. Who cares?

Addendum: I guess I get to decide what goes here.

Look, it's hard to see Edward hurting like this. I don't know him very well, but I've come to care about him, and I hate that I can't help him more.

Over the past day or so, I've been thinking about bad things and why they happen. When I was trying to catch up to Edward on that horrible night, I drove right past where my mommy and daddy died, and I didn't even think about it. That's the first time. I was fixated on someone else. That's the first time, too.

Very strange.

Edward is a gentle and good man, and yes, he's peculiar, but I'm peculiar, too. I think that's why we're friends.

Yesterday was a hard day. Today will be hard, too. I guess all we can hope for is that it's less hard.

Often, hope is all you have.

Unfortunately, Edward doesn't like to put his effort into hope. He's going to need to now.

I feel better today than I did yesterday, although it still hurts like a motherfucker when Sally and Sheila Renfro pull me to my feet for my first walk around the hallways. Sally tells me that three trips around the hallways yesterday was a good number but that she wants to see at least five today. I tell her I will do my best. She also says the catheter is coming out today and I'll have to get up to go pee from now on. Based on recent history since I went on my diabetic medicine, that means I'll be out of bed repeatedly today—and that, of course, means that Sheila Renfro and a nurse will be pulling me to my feet.

This sucks.

When Sheila Renfro and I get back to the room after the first set of laps, Dr. Ira Banning is waiting for us.

"Good news, Edward," he says. "I think you can go home tomorrow."

"Really?"

"Yep, you bet. The scans look good. You'll need to be careful for a while—with those ribs, for sure, but especially with your head. No boxing matches or football games, OK? I want your word."

I think Dr. Banning is having some fun with me.

"I promise. Can I still watch the Dallas Cowboys, if I promise not to play?" I'm having fun with Dr. Banning now.

"Hey, Edward, I can't stop you, buddy. Wouldn't you rather watch Tim Tebow?"

Everybody in this town is brainwashed about Tim Tebow. I laugh, and laughing hurts. So I stop laughing and let myself fall into the chair that Sheila Renfro slept in. Sally told me she wants me to spend some time out of bed today, that the only way my ribs are going to heal is if I make them do what they're designed to do.

I wait till my breath slows down. "That's a good one, Dr. Banning."

He looks at me funny. "Tim Tebow is a big deal around here."

So I've heard.

I'm pretty funny sometimes.

— • —

"Do you remember what I said yesterday about coming back to the motel with me?" Sheila Renfro asks.

I'm dipping baked, breaded chicken chunks into low-fat ranch dressing and eating them. My appetite has returned. Dr. Banning says that I'm going to be amazed at how quickly I start feeling better now, and for the first time I'm inclined to believe him. Still, it's barely past noon, and I've already been up four times to pee, each one an exercise in extreme pain as Sheila Renfro and the nurses pulled on my arms to get me on my feet. So despite my obvious improvement from yesterday and Dr. Banning's proclamations (I love the word "proclamations") of imminent health, I'm not ready to say that it's going to be smooth sailing from here, to use a well-known idiom.

"Yes, I remember," I say.

"Have you thought about it some more?"

"Since you brought it up yesterday?"

"Yes."

"No, I haven't."

"Oh."

"What's there to think about? I'm going."

"Oh!"

She smiles at me, and I don't take it for granted. I remember when I first met Sheila Renfro and I wanted to see her smile and she hid it from me. She's not hiding it anymore, and I'm glad. It's a friendly smile. She has her hair drawn into a blonde ponytail, which makes her face look sleek and pretty. I don't see any makeup on Sheila Renfro, but I'm not sure anyone could tell whether she wore it or not. She has what the TV commercials call a "fresh look."

"May I ask you something?" I say.

"Yes."

"Are you going to take care of me?"

"Yes."

"Will you make me Jell-O brand gelatin?"

"Brand-name gelatin is expensive, but if that's what you want, I will make it for you."

"I could help buy the groceries," I say. "I'm fucking loaded."

"I know you are. Don't cuss around me."

"Can I ask you something else?" I say.

"Yes."

"Will you take walks with me?"

"Every day."

"Will you watch *Adam-12* with me?"

"Any time you want, unless there's a guest needing my help."

"Will you put in cable television?"

"Yes...I mean, no, I mean...Edward, are you being serious now?"

A big grin comes to my face. "Yes."

She looks at me really closely, and her eyelids narrow to little slits. "Are you sure?"

I can't help it. My grin begins to collapse into a giggle, and that makes my ribs hurt, and so I grab my side and say "Ohohohoh." This must be a funny sight, because now Sheila Renfro is starting to laugh. It's the first full-throated laugh I've ever heard from her, and it's so high-pitched that I'm amused all over again, so I begin to laugh again, and it's really bad because it's uncontrollable. I laugh, and then I say "Ohohohohoh," and then I grab my ribs, and then Sheila Renfro laughs some more, which makes me laugh. This is what they call a vicious circle, although I think I would amend that to a hilariously vicious circle.

"Get out," I say between gasps for air, and I say it with such emphasis (I love the word "emphasis") that my ribs really hurt, and I say "WOWowowowow," and Sheila Renfro falls out of her chair onto the floor on all fours, laughing.

"Get out," I say again, meekly this time.

Sheila Renfro crawls on her hands and knees to the door, only it's not a fluid movement. She's going in spurts, and these spurts are interrupted by her failing attempts to keep from laughing out loud. So she is, essentially, sputtering across the floor, and as she finally reaches the opening, she lets go of a laugh that sounds like someone spitting out water, and at the same time, she farts.

Now I'm really laughing and really hurting, and I can hear Sheila Renfro in the hallway, laughing with abandon. I also hear the quick pat-pat-pat of feet, and then I hear Sally scolding Sheila and telling her that she can't laugh uncontrollably in the hallways here at St. Joseph Hospital.

My ribs throb in pain. I want my Percocet and I want it now, but Sally isn't yet ready to bring it to me.

I can hear Sheila Renfro in the hallway, trying to smother her giggles, and I'm here in the room, still laughing despite the incredible pain.

Holy shit!

— • —

At 3:03 p.m., my mother calls. I know this because Sheila Renfro picks up my bitchin' iPhone and looks at the number and then hands it to me, saying, "It's your mom."

"Hello, Mother."

"Wow. You sound a lot better today."

"That stands to reason. Dr. Ira Banning said I can leave tomorrow."

"Well, then, it's good that I called. Listen, Son, your car is ready. I hope it's OK that Jay got you another Cadillac. You know, I figured you'd want the familiarity. He even got the same color."

"That's fine."

"Wonderful! Hey, can someone there write something down for you?"

I look at Sheila Renfro, who is listening intently. "Will you get my notebook and pen?" She pulls them off the table beside the bed.

"OK, Mother, go ahead."

"It's at seven-seven-seven Broadway in Denver. You're to ask for Glenn."

"Seven-seven-seven Broadway. Glenn. Got it." Sheila Renfro writes this down. "Mother, is it OK if I don't pick the car up for a few days?"

"But I thought you—"

"I'm going back to Cheyenne Wells to rest up before I drive home."

"Back to Cheyenne Wells? Whatever in the world for?"

"My friend invited me to stay at her motel while I recuperate."

"Her? Who?"

"Sheila Renfro." At this, Sheila Renfro's eyebrows go up and her forehead crinkles.

"Who's Sheila Renfro?"

"You talked to her."

"I did?"

"She's the woman who called you to say that I'd been in a wreck."

"I thought that was a nurse."

"No, that was Sheila Renfro of Cheyenne Wells, Colorado."

Crinkly-headed Sheila Renfro continues to look at me. She mouths the words "What's going on?" I shrug my shoulders, and it hurts. I won't do that again.

"Well, who is she?"

"She owns the motel I stayed in while I was in Cheyenne Wells."

"Is she there now?"

"Yes."

"I want to talk to her."

I hand the phone to Sheila Renfro, who shakes her head. I purse my lips and push the phone toward her with insistency. Finally she takes it, and soon I'm left to bemoan (I love the word "bemoan") the fact that I can hear only one side of their brief conversation. That must have been frustrating for Sheila Renfro when I was the one on the phone.

The side of the conversation I hear goes like this:

"Hello, Mrs. Stanton."

(Pause.)

"I'm thirty-six."

(Pause.)

"It was my mother and father's motel. Now it's mine. They're in the ground."

(Pause.)

"I don't think that's any of your business, with all due respect."

(Pause.)

"He wants to come."

(Pause.)

"But—"

(Pause.)

"Tell him, not me."

(Pause.)

She hands the phone back to me.

"Yes, Mother?"

"I don't like this, Edward. I think you should go home before you get into any more trouble."

"Trouble? I'm not in trouble. Did Jay L. Lamb say something?"

"No, no, that's not what I meant. You're not in trouble, trouble. It's just that you've been through a lot. It's time to go back home. That's all I'm saying."

"Why?"

"I think people are taking advantage of you."

"Which people?"

"That woman, for one."

"But she's my friend."

"I know you think she is, and maybe she is, but given what you've been through, I think it's best that you just go back to where you live and she goes back to where she lives. I don't trust her."

"I do."

"I think you should go home."

My mother flummoxes me. I've never seen her act this way.

"I'm going to Cheyenne Wells, Mother. It's just for a few days. Then Sheila Renfro will bring me back to Denver, I'll pick up the car, and I'll go home."

My mother sighs into the phone. She's not happy.

"I think you're making a mistake."

"I think we should see what the facts bear out."

"Fine. But I want you to call me every day, OK?"

"Yes."

"Good-bye, Son. Be careful."

"Good-bye, Mother. I will."

I hang up and I look at Sheila Renfro, who is biting at her bottom lip.

"You don't have to come," she says.

"I want to."

"It's going to cause trouble for you with your mom."

"I'm forty-two years old. I can do what I want."

Sheila Renfro smiles just a bit at this, the kind of hidden smile she would give me back at the motel in Cheyenne Wells.

"She's bossy," she says.

— • —

I pee four more times throughout the afternoon. Twice I'm sitting in Sheila Renfro's chair while she sits on the end of my bed, and those instances make it easier for me to stand, although I still need help getting to my feet. I've learned to anticipate the pain from my broken ribs, and at the moment I'm being pulled up I blow out my breath as hard as I can, which seems to help with the discomfort. It doesn't cause all of the pain to go away, of course. Only when the ribs are fully healed will that happen. Dr. Banning, who comes and sees me one more time before dinner, assures me that will happen within the next few weeks.

After dinner—grilled chicken breast, rice, and cauliflower, which I despise and thus do not eat—Sheila and I watch another episode of *Adam-12* on my bitchin' iPhone. This one is called "Log 172: Boy, the Things You Do for the Job." It's the twenty-fourth episode of the first season, and it originally aired on March 22, 1969.

Sheila Renfro again puts her head next to mine as we watch on the tiny screen. In this episode, Officer Pete Malloy and Officer Jim Reed pull over a blonde who is driving recklessly in a foreign sports car. Officer Pete Malloy tells her that in addition to her considerable driving violations, she also has an expired driver's license. This kind of flagrant disregard for the law flummoxes me, even on a TV show. As Officer Pete Malloy is writing the ticket, the blonde puts on her feminine wiles (I love the word "wiles") and suggests that they have a date instead. Officer Pete Malloy, being a good, upstanding cop, declines her offer.

Sheila Renfro sits up and looks at me and says, "I bet your mom thinks all women act like that."

I start to say something, but Sheila Renfro waves me off. "I'm sorry," she says. "Listen, I'm not really up for watching this show. I'm just going to go to sleep, OK?"

I nod and leave it be, which is difficult.

"Good night, Edward," Sheila Renfro says as she pulls the hospital blanket over herself.

"Good night, Sheila Renfro."

TECHNICALLY SUNDAY, DECEMBER 18, 2011

I wake up at 1:33 a.m., as if I've been jolted. Usually, it's a dream that causes an abrupt wake-up like this, but I can't recall any dream. If I was having one, the visions associated with it have left my head.

But, in this case, I do not require a dream to be preoccupied. I'm worried about what my mother said to Sheila Renfro. I tried to get Sheila Renfro to talk about it as she was falling asleep, but she was having none of that conversation.

She said, "Forget it, Edward. It's not important. Just get some rest, OK? Big day tomorrow."

It is, indeed, a big day, and technically tomorrow is here. I'm leaving the hospital, first of all. Second of all, I'm going back to Cheyenne Wells to stay at Sheila Renfro's motel while I recuperate (I love the word "recuperate") for a few days. Sheila Renfro says she will feed me good food and make sure I exercise and even let me help her with some small repairs at the motel, or at least talk her through some repairs if my injuries don't allow me to do them myself.

I have to be honest about this: the idea that someone would find me useful for small jobs is making me excited about going to Cheyenne Wells. After I was involuntarily separated from the *Billings Herald-Gleaner*, having something to do is what I missed most. Not the money. Not even hanging around with Scott Shamwell and listening to his creative cursing, which now I'll have to curtail because Sheila Renfro does not like it. Once I was consigned (I love the word "consigned") to my house after being involuntarily separated, I found that I had little interest in doing the household chores and repairs that filled my day before I had the job at the *Herald-Gleaner*. They no longer seemed important for a man who had been entrusted with painting parking lot lines and repairing inserter equipment and unplugging spray bars on the press. I suppose it's haughty (I love the word "haughty") of me to say that, but that's how I felt.

As long as I'm being honest, I have to carry it over—I'm excited about spending more time with Sheila Renfro. I do not make friends easily, and the ones I have moved away from me in this shitburger of a year. To be able to make a new friend as easily as I have with Sheila Renfro—and under such difficult circumstances—makes me happy. I've also noticed that she's a lot like me in that she's no-nonsense and doesn't spend a lot of time talking around things. If something needs to be done, she does it. She doesn't talk about doing it. I appreciate that.

On the negative side, she does put more energy into conjecture and generalities than I am comfortable with. Take what she said about my mother as an example. I'm reasonably certain, from what I heard of their phone conversation, that my mother said something that upset Sheila Renfro. I don't like that, but I cannot control what my mother says. Whatever my mother might have said, it's no excuse for Sheila Renfro to extrapolate (I love the word "extrapolate") that statement into a much broader assumption about my mother. Sheila Renfro said, "I bet she thinks all women are like that," in reference to the Penny Lang character from *Adam-12*. I don't know if Sheila Renfro was being serious about wanting to lay down a bet; if she was, she's doubling down—that's a gambling term—on assumption, and I think that's a risky thing to do.

I also think it's odd that I'm suddenly being fought over by women in my life. That's never happened before. By the time my mother found out about Donna Middleton (now Hays) a few years ago, we had already been through some tough situations, like dealing with her mean ex-boyfriend Mike and learning how to be friends with each other, and my mother was just happy I'd found someone who liked me. Now I've made another friend, and my mother isn't so happy, apparently. That's not consistent behavior, and I think my mother owes me an explanation. She might even owe Sheila Renfro an apology, although it would be wrong to assume anything at this point.

I've decided what I am going to do. Tomorrow, I'm going to take advantage of being in a truck with Sheila Renfro to try to get her to tell me what happened between her and my mother. Later, after we're in Cheyenne Wells, I will call my mother on my bitchin' iPhone, as I said I would, and I will try to learn her side of things.

I may have to broker some sort of agreement between my mother and Sheila Renfro, and I feel a little bit devious when I realize that I'm hoping this is the case. It's the kind of grown-up problem that I'm not often allowed to help solve.

This could be a breakthrough for me.

And now, suddenly, I realize I have to pee really, really badly. I find the nurse call button and I push it four times. But I'm too late. Holy shit!

OFFICIALLY SUNDAY, DECEMBER 18, 2011

From the logbook of Edward Stanton, as recorded by Sheila Renfro:
Time Edward woke up today: He's still awfully embarrassed,
so I'll try to piece this together. He says he woke up at 1:33 a.m.
and did some thinking, which he must have done quietly because
I didn't wake up and this chair is killing my back. (Edward wants
me to point out that "killing my back" isn't meant to be taken
literally. I am in no danger of dying.) This thinking went on for
maybe 10 minutes, until Edward realized he had to pee. He didn't
make it.

High temperature for Saturday, December 17, 2011, Day 351:
44 in Billings, the same temperature as the day before. (Edward
wants me to point out that this is a remarkably seasonable Decem-
ber, and that he will do some in-depth calculations when he gets
back to Billings and has access to his full dossier—Edward loves the
word "dossier"—of weather data.)

Low temperature for Saturday, December 17, 2011: 29. That's
six degrees warmer than the low from the day before.

Precipitation for Saturday, December 17, 2011: 0.00 inches.
Same as Friday.

Precipitation for 2011: 19.41 inches

New entries:

Exercise for Saturday, December 17, 2011: As Sally directed, we did five sets of laps around this floor, and we also had Edward sit upright in my chair three times for an hour at each stretch. Edward wants me to point out that it remains difficult to quantify the degree of his physical improvement but that he definitely feels better than he did the day before. He also says he's getting antsy to stop walking with the monitor he has to push, and that he's eager to wear regular clothes again.

Miles driven Saturday, December 17, 2011: Not a one. (Edward wants me to point out that "not a one" is a weird way of saying "none," that it uses more words than is necessary. I point out to him that my daddy used to say that and I don't care how many words it takes.)

Total miles driven: Edward wants me to point out that he's reviewed the past entries and that we're way off on the mileage, so we'll correct it here. He says that he and Kyle drove 27.4 miles while looking at oil pumps, so the grand total is 1,846.1 miles, not 1,838.7. Edward also wants me to point out that we don't know exactly how far he had traveled on Interstate 70 before the wreck, so even this number is suspect. He says we'll try to find the wreck site on the way home. I don't understand what the big deal is, but he says that's what we're going to do. So there.

Gas usage Saturday, December 17, 2011: None.

Addendum: Edward is trying to lean over and see what I'm writing, but every time he does, his ribs hurt. That's why I am sitting on his left. I'm not dumb.

He needs to get over the fact that he peed the bed. Yeah, under normal circumstances, a 42-year-old man should not wet the bed, but he should know by now that these are not normal circumstances.

I'm antsy to get back to the motel. I don't make much money there, but even so, a three-day shutdown is going to affect my bottom line in a bad way. Edward pointed out to me again last night that he's "fucking loaded," and I really wish he'd stop saying that. He said he will compensate me for my losses. That made me really mad. He doesn't get it sometimes.

EDWARD, I KNOW YOU'LL BE READING THIS EVENTU-ALLY SO STOP LEANING IN AND HURTING YOURSELF!!!!

Dr. Banning said it probably won't be till noon or later that Edward will be discharged. I'm going to leave for a little while and get ready to go.

I'm really nervous about this. EDWARD, JUST WAIT!!!!!!

OK, I'm going to go now.

I can't believe I peed in the overnight nurse's shoes.

I know she was mad about it, too. She tried not to let me see that she was. She said, "It's OK, Edward. This isn't even close to the worst thing that's ever happened here," but after she left my room to go get new shoes and socks and the outfit that the nurses call "scrubs," I could hear her tell her supervisor at the desk what happened, and she sounded really disgusted by it.

Sheila Renfro tells me that I need to forgive myself for doing what I did. It would be different, she says, if I'd intended to do it, but it most definitely wasn't my intent. ("You didn't mean to do it, did you?" she asked after asserting that I did not, as if she needed verification. That flummoxed me.) She says that accidents happen, especially in a health care environment. She actually said that: "Especially in a health care environment." I think I'm start-ing to rub off on Sheila Renfro a little bit.

She's probably correct. It's just really embarrassing, and I'm not someone who deals well with embarrassment. I'm not sure I'd want to know someone who deals well with embarrassment. That would suggest a person who regularly messes up on a grand scale. I think those people are best avoided.

I'm also embarrassed about something else—the Dallas Cowboys played last night, and I completely forgot about it. If you had told me before this trip that I would forget about a Dallas Cowboys game, I would have politely but firmly disagreed with you. But now there's proof. The one plus, I guess, is that the Dallas Cowboys won against the Tampa Bay Buccaneers. That's good, but it's not surprising. The Tampa Bay Buccaneers are terrible.

— • —

Sheila Renfro is acting weird. She seems annoyed at me because I was trying to make sure all the data got recorded properly in my notebook. She kept telling me "I know how to do it," which was completely beside the point. I know she knows how to do it. My point is that I've been doing it longer than she has, and thus I know better.

Finally, Sheila Renfro left. She didn't say where she was going, just that she would be back in time to get me loaded into her truck after I am released from the hospital. But she did take my notebook with her, which is damned dirty pool. (When I say "pool," I'm speaking of billiards, not a swimming pool. Besides, if I were speaking of a swimming pool, that sentence would have required the indefinite article "a," as in "That is a damned dirty pool." The absence of the "a" is a giveaway as to the nature of the noun "pool." I hear people say that grammar is difficult to understand, but it's really not if you just pay attention.)

— • —

When I awake from my nap at 10:37 a.m., a uniformed police officer is standing at the side of my bed. This alarms me. I'm not a fugitive from the law, so I have no reason to fear cops, but my past interactions with them have not been good. This is another instance of what Dr. Buckley would call a conditioned response.

"Are you Edward Stanton?" he asks me. This is a dumb question. My name is written on the dry-erase board over my bed. Still, I am self-aware enough to not tell the officer that he's being dumb. Nobody likes to hear that. Policemen take it particularly personally.

"Yes," I say.

"This is for you."

He hands me a slip of paper, which I take in my right hand— I'm learning to avoid using my left arm, which will aggravate my broken ribs—and hold close to my face so I can read it.

I'm being ticketed for my crash on the interstate. The ticket says I was traveling too fast for the conditions and that I was driving recklessly when I ran into the back of the snowplow. The ticket also says I owe the state of Colorado $562. I'd never received a traffic ticket before this trip, so I don't have the means of comparison, but this seems like a lot of money. I'm fucking loaded, so I can afford it, but that doesn't mean I can just blithely (I love the word "blithely") part with $562.

"This is a lot of money," I say to the policeman, who introduces himself as Officer Jonathon Hunter of the Colorado Highway Patrol.

"It is," he agrees. "We like to make speeding and reckless driving unpopular violations."

I giggle, and Officer Jonathon Hunter looks at me quizzically, so I stop. I do not want any more trouble. Policemen also do not appreciate being laughed at. I know this from experience.

It's just that Officer Jonathon Hunter's statement reminds me of something Sergeant Joe Friday said in an episode of *Dragnet*. It's called "The Bank Jobs," and it's the fourth episode from the second season, and it originally aired on October 5, 1967. In this episode, Sergeant Joe Friday and Officer Bill Gannon are investigating a series of bank robberies in which a man makes random women help him with his crimes. After Sergeant Joe Friday and Officer Bill Gannon clear one woman of wrongdoing, she has a question. She has red hair and inspires sultry (I love the word "sultry") music on this episode of *Dragnet*, but no-nonsense Sergeant Joe Friday doesn't seem to notice that. When she asks what the penalty is for bank robbery, Sergeant Joe Friday tells her it's twenty-five years for each offense. She says it hardly seems worth it for a few hundred dollars.

"That's the idea. They want to make it an unpopular crime," Sergeant Joe Friday tells her. Sergeant Joe Friday is a very logical man.

And now you can see why I giggled.

Officer Jonathon Hunter puts his sunglasses on and says, "You can pay that at the DMV, or you can mail it in, or you can appear on the court date and contest it."

Officer Jonathon Hunter is very businesslike. I appreciate that. Maybe he learned something from watching Sergeant Joe Friday, like I did.

"Thank you, Officer Jonathon Hunter," I say, and he again looks at me quizzically. Then he leaves.

I wanted to ask him what he thinks of Sergeant Joe Friday, but in the end, I'm glad that's over with.

— • —

When Sheila Renfro comes back to the hospital room, she is wearing clean clothes and she looks as though she has had a shower. I guess I hadn't noticed that she had been wearing the same clothes and pulling her hair back into the same ponytail while I've been in this place. I'll go ahead and admit it, as there's no denying the situation: I got preoccupied with my own problems, and I didn't pay as much attention to my friend as I should have. That was wrong. I decide I need to rectify this.

"You look nice, Sheila Renfro," I tell her, and she smiles again. I am getting better at making Sheila Renfro smile. I'm proud of myself and happy for her. After what I've been through on this trip, I'm starting to appreciate the value of happiness.

"Are you ready to go, Edward?" she asks me. "I got some nice bedding material for you to ride in the backseat of my Suburban, and I got some clothes for me, and then I gassed up at a truck stop and took a shower."

"You smell like Irish Spring," I say.

"I like Irish Spring," she says.

"So do I."

Sheila Renfro smiles again.

I'm pretty talented sometimes.

— • —

Sally makes me ride in a wheelchair all the way to the loading area, which is silly. I didn't break my legs. They still work, and I tell her this.

"Sorry, Edward. Regulations," she says.

That, of course, changes everything. A society can't function unless its members obey the rules. It seems to me that we have a nation full of people who think rules are for other people. This is not an idle observation on my part; I've been watching closely. Despite my better judgment, I continue to try to understand politics in America, since I live here and have been entrusted with a vote for more than twenty-four years. I'll point out here that I'm emphasizing the word "try." I've begun to think that no one understands politics in America except the politicians. I have a fact-loving brain. I think that's well-established by now. Politics, it seems to me, celebrates the absence of facts rather than the existence of them. I cannot comprehend that. We're going to elect a president in a little less than a year, and I expect facts to be so marginalized (I love the word "marginalized") by then that we'll have to rename our country the United States of Happy Horseshit.

I could say more about this, but I'm done now. I didn't mean to go off on a political tangent. My point is, I don't fight Sally about the wheelchair. I follow the rules.

— • —

Sheila Renfro has made me a paradise in the back bench seat of her old Suburban. I have a foam bedlike base to sit on and a big beanbag wedged into the corner, where the seat meets the door, so I can remain in a reclined position and ease the stress on my ribs. I have lots of blankets. It's perfect.

From where I sit, I can see the back of Sheila Renfro's head, and it's very easy to talk with her, so I don't feel left out of the action at all. The Suburban is really old—"It's my daddy's nineteen seventy-two model," she tells me—and thus doesn't even have a CD player, much less an adaptor that will play songs from my bitchin' iPhone. As we work our way through Denver, Sheila Renfro sings along with Merle Haggard on an old-time country music station. Sheila Renfro seemingly has good taste in country music. She prefers the era before Garth Brooks ruined it.

"Why do you keep such an old vehicle?" I ask her. "If you had an adaptor, we could be listening to R.E.M. right now."

"It's my daddy's. I don't have him anymore, because he's in the ground with my mother. So I have his Suburban. Besides, I like this music."

This seems to be a plausible answer, so I don't intend to ask another question. Sheila Renfro looks in the rearview mirror and makes eye contact with me.

"My daddy bought this before he and Mom started thinking about a family," she says. "Daddy always wanted a big family, with lots of kids. That's why they built the motel. It was the kind of place where you could raise a family and bring them into a business."

She stops talking. I want to ask her questions, but I get the sense that she's not done, so I wait.

"But Mom found out that she couldn't have kids—"

"But—"

"At least, that's what the doctors told her. When she got pregnant with me, I guess it surprised everyone. When I was born, though, she nearly bled to death, and the doctors were saying, 'OK, you got your miracle baby, so now, no more.'"

"You're a miracle baby!" I say. This makes me indescribably happy.

"I guess. Daddy just couldn't bear to part with the Suburban, even though it was way more truck than we ever needed. It's like it reminded him of what he dreamed about but couldn't do."

"He said that?"

"Well, no, not like that. But the way he'd talk about things, I'd kind of know. You know, Edward, I wasn't very popular in school.

I didn't have a lot of friends, or any, sometimes. That's hard on a kid. My daddy was my best friend."

Sheila Renfro's story makes me as sad as it does happy. First, it *is* a sad story. Even if she was a miracle baby, her mother and father clearly wanted more children. It's also sad on a personal level. Sheila Renfro had a relationship with her father while he was alive that I've been forced to try to find with mine since he's been dead. I know for a fact that once my parents found out that there was something different about me—I'm speaking here of my developmental disorder and my obsessive-compulsive tendencies—they decided that they didn't want any more children. This is not conjecture. My father told me this during the height of the "Garth Brooks incident," when he and I were fighting all the time. He was drunk; he had been drinking all day. He came into my bedroom after one of our battles and said, "You're such a fucking idiot, boy. I wish you'd never been born so you wouldn't fuck everything up."

That devastated me. First, I'm not a fucking idiot. I have a developmental disorder, but I'm not stupid. Second, it upset my mother terribly. It's the first and only time I ever saw her really stand up to my father. She told him that he was a cruel and awful man and that he should apologize to me. He never did, at least not while he was alive. Four days later he bought the house where I now live, and I was made to leave my parents' home and begin seeing Dr. Buckley. I was thirty-one years old, so maybe it was time. I think my parents wanted to keep me close to protect me; that's what Dr. Buckley said when she diagnosed me. But as my condition worsened, my father came to resent me (and I came to dislike him). I was certainly happier on Clark Avenue than I was in my parents' house, but it was hard to forget what my father said to me in those last days at his house. The truth is, I've never forgotten it. From time to time, my mother tried to explain my father's behavior when he was mean to me, telling me that he was struggling at his job on the county commission and that he was under a lot of stress. I think she gave him too much credit, and to be fair, my mother would agree with that. After my father died, and after she saw the way he controlled me through Jay L. Lamb, she made a break with him. She scarcely talks about him anymore.

I don't like remembering that story about my father, and I don't like telling it. I've never told anyone except Dr. Buckley, not even Donna Middleton (now Hays). I think I would like to tell Sheila Renfro, however, and this surprises me.

I will have to think about it a while before committing to telling her. Instead, I say something else, because it occurs to me that as Sheila Renfro describes her parents to me, she's telling me about people I never got a chance to know even though I met both of them in the summer of 1978. That's odd. It's like they're more than an anecdote and less than a robust memory.

"I wish I'd gotten to know your parents," I say. "I'm sorry they're in the ground."

"You'd have liked them," Sheila Renfro says. "And I think they'd have liked you."

I'm trying to formulate my next question when I actually hear the words coming out of my mouth.

"How did you find out when your parents died?" I can't believe I just asked it like that. I was too abrupt, but Sheila Renfro doesn't seem to mind.

"It happened in the middle of a hot summer day, seven miles from home," she says. "The sheriff and a deputy got there fast, and one of them came to the motel to get me. I was making dinner for us. Grilled chicken. It was too hot to cook inside, so I was on the patio. He said, 'Sheila, you've got to put that chicken away and come.' By the time we got there, it was over with. Daddy and Mom were in bags on the side of the road. The guy who hit them was, too. I guess he had a heart attack and lost control of his pickup. He hit their pickup on my daddy's side at seventy miles per hour. Sheriff said there were no skid marks."

Sheila tells me all of this matter-of-factly. I am mesmerized.

"How did you find out about your daddy?" she asks me.

"My mother called and woke me up and told me to come to St. Vincent Healthcare right away. He died after I got there."

"What happened?"

"He had a heart attack in the parking lot of his favorite golf course."

"I'm sorry."

I haven't thought about the actual day that my father died in a long time. It's been three years, one month, and eighteen days, and most of my effort where my father is concerned has been focused on making peace with every day other than the one on which he died.

"After the doctor told us he'd died, we got to go into the hospital room and see him. It was weird. It was clearly his face, but his hair was mussed, and the qualities that made him who he was—things like his loud voice and his mannerisms—were gone. The only thing that I really thought was odd was how peaceful he looked. He looked much more peaceful than he did the last time I saw him alive."

"They wouldn't let me see my daddy," Sheila Renfro says. "They said it was really bad and that it wouldn't be something I'd want to see. My mom didn't have a scratch on her, though—she died because of how shook up her insides were in the wreck. They let me see her. It looked like she was sleeping."

"What was your mother like?"

"She was a good person. My daddy was my best friend; he had the mind of a child, and so I related to him. My mom didn't make a lot of time for fun. She was too busy trying to keep things going. I think I'm more like she was."

It's interesting to me that Sheila Renfro has thought all of this out. I've never considered whether I'm more like my father or my mother. I don't think I'm like either one of them. That's been the problem.

— • —

When we leave the interstate at Limon, I ask Sheila Renfro if we can turn around and go find the place where I ran into the snowplow. I would like to see it, now that the sun is out and it's not snowing. Also, it will give me a chance to correct this mileage discrepancy.

"The gauge says 268,443.4," she says as we merge onto Interstate 70 westbound.

I try to reconcile what I'm seeing now with what it looked like two days ago, when Kyle and I were driving through a blinding snowstorm in the middle of the night. It's impossible to do.

"Here it is," Sheila Renfro says, and she slows down so she can pull over on the shoulder of the interstate.

Broken pieces of my turn signal are on the side of the asphalt. I see them now, and I guess that's how Sheila Renfro knew to stop here. You're not supposed to stop here, but she doesn't seem concerned. It's her business if she wants to risk a traffic ticket.

"What does the mileage say?" I ask.

"Let's see…it's 268,449.2."

"So that's 5.8 miles from Limon."

"Looks like it."

I do the calculations in my head. "So that means I've driven 1,844.9 miles on this trip, not 1,846.1."

"If you say so."

"That's clearly what the math indicates."

"What difference does it make?"

This flummoxes me. "I don't know. I like to track things."

"Are you going to include the miles we've gone today in your total?"

"That's a silly question, Sheila Renfro," I say. "Of course I am."

"Do you know how far we've gone today?"

"No, but I can look up the distance from St. Joseph Hospital to Cheyenne Wells, and I can account for this detour."

"Can you account for the different route I took through Denver?"

I don't like where this conversation is headed.

"You took a different route?"

"Yes. There was road construction and bad traffic, so I went a different way."

"Which way did you go?" This situation, while not ideal, is not irretrievable (I love the word "irretrievable"). I can still use the Internet to figure out the mileage.

"I don't remember."

This situation has become irretrievable.

"Shit," I say.

"It's no big deal, Edward. Also, don't cuss around me."

— • —

I try to stay miffed at Sheila Renfro, but it's not possible. I like her too much. I remember how much she has done and is doing for

me, taking care of me at the hospital and now bringing me back
to Cheyenne Wells so I can recuperate.

"Sheila Renfro," I ask, "what did—"

"Why do you say that?"

"Say what?"

"Sheila Renfro. You say my first and last name every time you
talk to me."

"I don't know."

"It's weird."

"No, it isn't."

"It's a little weird."

"What do you want me to call you?"

"Just Sheila. Or you could call me 'She-Pumpkin,' which is
what my daddy used to call me."

"I don't think I could call you that."

"I know, silly. I was making a joke."

Sheila Renfro is pretty funny sometimes.

"She-ster?" I say.

"What was that? A nickname?"

"I thought I'd try it."

"Don't. Nicknames should come naturally. It sounds like
you're trying."

I'm growing flummoxed and frustrated.

"OK, can I just ask you the question I've been trying to ask?"

"Sure, E-Dog."

"E-Dog?"

"Yes, that's your nickname."

"It sounds like you're the one trying now."

"I'm not trying at all. It came perfectly naturally."

"I don't like it."

"OK, how about Eddie Smoochiekins?"

"E-Dog is fine, I think."

Sheila Renfro laughs and bobs her head left and right.

She's having a good time.

Here's a secret: I'm having a good time, too.

— • —

We pass through the town of Kit Carson and Sheila Renfro says, "We're close now. Twenty-five miles."

I like the countryside here. It's stark and hard, not the lush and mountainous beauty that one tends to associate with Colorado. In that way, it reminds me of the part of Montana I'm from.

I remember being in the eastern Montana town of Terry with my father when I was a teenager and him pointing out the buttes in the distance, which he called "badlands." He said that whole part of Montana was homesteaded and that a lot of people couldn't make a go of it, because the weather and the terrain were so unforgiving. He said we should admire the people who still lived there, because they had beaten the odds and the land and whittled a life into that bleak landscape. My father was big on defeating things, be they political opponents or systems or landscapes. It was all a competition for him.

I haven't read up on the history of homesteading in this part of Colorado, but I bet that the people who have made this area home would draw my father's admiration for their tenacity (I love the word "tenacity"). Maybe that's why he enjoyed working here. Maybe that's why he's been in my dreams, urging me to come here.

I must be careful. That's a lot of maybes and projections, and those are unreliable things, as I know all too well.

— • —

Sheila Renfro slows down and eases her Suburban to the shoulder of the road. We're on a flat, straight stretch of the highway, with fallow farmland on both sides of us.

"How are you feeling, E-Dog?" she says. "Can you get up and walk a little bit?"

"Here?"

"I want to show you something."

"OK, S-Money."

"Another nickname?"

"Yes."

"I like that one."

I put my hands on the bench seat and push myself to the full sitting position while Sheila Renfro gets out of the Suburban and walks to the other side to let me out. My ribs ache, but it's not the screaming pain I've come to expect. With the door now open, I scrunch along on the seat until my feet are nearly out the door.

"Do you need some help?" she asks.

"No, I think I have it."

Slowly, I reach for the pavement with my toes, until at last they find it. I grab the door frame with my hands and push myself to my feet. Again, the pain is slight rather than over-whelming.

"You did great, E-Dog!" she says.

"Thank you, S-Money."

Sheila Renfro laughs and so do I.

"Follow me," she says.

She leads me behind the Suburban, and then she looks both ways on the two-lane highway to ensure it's safe to cross. There's nobody out here.

We walk across the road to a grassy area on the other side. Sheila Renfro points to a spot about ten feet off the road.

"My daddy and my mom died right there." Again, she says this matter-of-factly, as if she's passing along esoterica (I love the word "esoterica") rather than something deeply personal and painful. Dr. Buckley calls this "compartmentalization." Dr. Buckley often told me that people develop strategies for keeping themselves from being harmed by others. Compartmentalizing pain helps with this. Compartmentalization was a difficult concept for me to master. I'm not good at developing strategies for pain. If something hurts me, I'm hurt, and I don't hide it well. I hope Sheila Renfro knows that I don't wish to hurt her.

"I drive by here all the time," she says. "Unless I want to go to Kansas, it's the only route that leads anywhere I want to go. Every time I pass by, I think 'Bam. They're dead.' People tell you life is short. They have no idea."

I finally understand how deep Sheila Renfro's loss is. As I think about it now, I realize that in the three years, one month, and eighteen days that my father has been dead, I have never driven past the golf course where he had his heart attack. I don't think I have consciously thought "I can't go by there," but I have avoided it just the same. Before I left on this trip, when I was coming home from Rimrock Mall (after getting my bitchin' iPhone) and taking a circuitous (I love the word "circuitous") route home to avoid left turns, I went all the way to Shiloh Road instead of Zimmerman Trail, because Zimmerman Trail runs right by the parking lot where my father was stricken.

In a big city like Billings, I can compartmentalize my pain. Where Sheila Renfro lives, she must confront it all the time. I feel sad for my friend. She continues to stare at the spot, her hands jammed in her pockets, saying nothing.

"Sheila Renfro?" I say.

"Yes?"

"I would like to give you a hug."

I have accepted hugs from people before, and I've even learned to like them from some people, like Donna Middleton (now Hays). I don't remember ever asking to give somebody a hug. I'm going with a feeling, as Dr. Buckley would say.

Sheila Renfro takes her hands from her pockets and steps toward me, closing the distance between us and pressing against me gently. She is being mindful of my ribs. I close my arms around her back. I smell Irish Spring. I miss my father. I miss certainty. I've begun to wonder if I ever had it. If I didn't, I miss the illusion of certainty.

I could stand here with her forever. That's intentional over-statement. Obviously, I can't stand here forever. Eventually, we'll have to eat. Our muscles will get tired. The weather will turn poor sometime.

A pickup headed toward Kit Carson passes, and the stirred-up wind stings us. I hug Sheila Renfro again. It won't be forever, but I'll hang on for as long as I can.

TECHNICALLY MONDAY, DECEMBER 19, 2011

My father came back.

It's 2:11 a.m., and I'm breathing heavily again. The dream that knocked me out of sleep was a strange one. I was viewing my father's body in the hospital, only it didn't look like the antiseptic room where I saw him at St. Vincent Healthcare. This looked more like a church, with wooden seats and dark-colored carpeting. Carpeting, of course, would be totally impractical for a hospital.

The scene was different from what happened in the conscious world in other ways, too. My mother was there, and she was crying, and that was the same. But Jay L. Lamb wasn't there, like he was the day my father died. Sheila Renfro was there in my dream. She said, "He's going into the ground now, Edward."

That's when I woke up.

I lean to my left and flip on the light in my room. I'm back in room number four. Sheila Renfro told me I could stay in her little cottage, but I declined. I told her that if I stayed there, she wouldn't have anywhere to sleep. She said we could share her bed—not that we'd do anything, she said, just that we could share it. I didn't feel comfortable with that. I also told her that I would just as soon pay her for the time I spend here, and she got angry about that, which flummoxed me. She said I was her guest. I said that she had already lost a lot of money by closing down while I was in the hospital. She said she would think about it. So that's where we are now. She's in her cottage, I'm in room number four, and she's thinking about it.

Sheila Renfro wrote down her direct home number on a piece of paper. If I have any distress at all, I'm to pick up the in-room phone, dial nine, and then dial that number. So far, there has been no distress, only a perplexing dream.

Slowly, I rotate my legs to the side of the bed and sit up. The pain is considerable, much worse than it was just a few hours ago. According to the clock, I can have another pain pill, and I think it's wise that I take advantage.

The pain hits me again as I stand. I walk, blinking, to the bathroom and get a Percocet and fill a cup with water, and then I wash the pill down. With that done, I head back to bed and turn on the TV. Given the limited selection of channels, there's not much on, just a late-night movie on one of the Denver stations. Jim Carrey, who used to be funny, is in it. I decide I'm not interested and turn it off.

When Sheila Renfro was driving me back here from Denver, I tried once to ask her about what my mother said to her the night before, but all that business with nicknames made me forget the question. At dinner, I remembered.

"What did my mother say to you?" I asked.

"She asked what my intentions are."

"About what?"

"You, I guess."

"You have intentions?"

"Yes. I intend for you to eat that dinner I put in front of you. It's getting cold."

I laughed, but Sheila Renfro didn't laugh in return. She was serious.

"What did you say?"

"You know what I said. You were there. I told her it was none of her business."

"What did she say?"

"She asked to talk to you again. Look, Edward—"

"Call me E-Dog."

Sheila Renfro did not smile.

"Look, I get it. She cares about you and she doesn't know me. I'm a grown woman. I don't care to be talked to like that by anyone."

"She hasn't had a chance to know you."

"That's not what I mean."

"What do you mean?"

"I mean, if she knew anything about me, she'd know that you and I are more alike than we are different."

"What do you mean?"

Sheila Renfro stood up and collected the dishes, hers and mine. "I wish you'd eat more," she said. She carried the dishes into the kitchen.

"What do you mean?" I asked again.

"I'm too tired tonight, Edward. Let's talk about it tomorrow."

After dinner, I stepped outside to call my mother in private, because my questions for her were similar to the ones I asked Sheila Renfro. I didn't get any better answers.

"I'll just be glad when you're home, where you belong," my mother said. After that, there wasn't much left to talk about, so we said our good-byes and I went back inside.

I didn't see Sheila Renfro for very long after that. She suggested that we both turn in early and get some rest after the stress of the past few days, and that seemed logical to me.

She walked me to room number four and let me in, and she reiterated (I love the word "reiterated") that I was to call her if I had any trouble at all.

"I will, Sheila Renfro."

Next, something extraordinary happened. She took one step toward me and stood on her tiptoes and she kissed me on the mouth. It was quick—she kissed like a bird pecks—but it was a real kiss-on-the-lips kiss, my first real one. A girl in high school let me kiss her once, but that was just so she could embarrass me in front of her friends.

This was the real thing.

It made me feel warm and happy and flummoxed, flummoxed, flummoxed.

OFFICIALLY MONDAY, DECEMBER 19, 2011

From the logbook of Edward Stanton, as recorded by Edward Stanton again:

Time I woke up today: 2:11 a.m. and then again at 7:13 a.m. Sheila Renfro and I had continental breakfast together, since there's no one else in the motel. She said she'd been up at 4:37 a.m. She said she always sets her alarm for 4:37 a.m. so she can prepare breakfast and attend to the motel. I think that is neat.

High temperature for Sunday, December 18, 2011, Day 352: 50 in Billings. (Holy shit!) That's six degrees warmer than the day before.

Low temperature for Sunday, December 18, 2011: 35. That's also six degrees warmer than the low from the day before.

Precipitation for Sunday, December 18, 2011: 0.00 inches. Same as the previous three days.

Precipitation for 2011: 19.41 inches

New entries:

Exercise for Sunday, December 18, 2011: Not much, since we were traveling part of the day. However, I am getting up and sitting down much more easily, except when I haven't had my pain pill and it hurts. Sheila Renfro says we're going to take a long walk today. I'm looking forward to that.

Miles driven Sunday, December 18, 2011: Sheila Renfro threw a kink into my program by taking an alternate route out of Denver (and she seems gleeful about having done so, which is damned dirty pool). So I've decided that the only miles that count on this trip are the ones driven by me. Sheila Renfro thinks she outsmarted me, but she didn't.

Total miles driven: Given my decision, I'm holding steady at 1,844.9, now that I've determined how far from Limon I drove before hitting the snowplow.

Gas usage Sunday, December 18, 2011: None by me.

Addendum: I just now read what Sheila Renfro wrote in this space yesterday. I think it's pretty funny how she was yelling at me in writing for trying to see her words. I guess she doesn't understand that this is my logbook and my data, so of course I would be proprietary (I love the word "proprietary") about it.

I should also say one other thing. She wrote that I need to get over the fact that I peed the bed. I could get past that. But I also peed in the overnight nurse's shoes. It's much worse than Sheila Renfro made it out to be. But I'm trying to get past that, too. In general, Sheila Renfro makes a good point. She just didn't make it with the level of precision I would prefer.

At 10:24 a.m., after Sheila Renfro has put away the breakfast food, collected the mail, and done a sweep of the rooms, she tells me that she would like to take me on a walk through Cheyenne Wells. Snow still sits deep on the ground, but the sun is out and there is little wind.

"How far do you think you can go?" she asks. "A couple of blocks?"

"I think so," I say.

I'm walking all right, but I do get short of breath. One of my lungs collapsed in the accident, and while the doctors did manage to repair it, I'll have to keep exercising to get my wind back.

Sheila Renfro leaves a note on the door to tell prospective lodgers that she will be back in an hour. We set out across the highway into the middle of the small town. At South First Street, we turn left, and Sheila points to a large redbrick building in front of us.

"That's the county courthouse," she says. "Let's go over there."

Cheyenne Wells seems like a pleasant town, and Sheila Renfro seems like a well-regarded resident. She is greeted by name at the lumberyard and outside a bar. Three cars honk at her, and she waves to all of them.

"You know everybody," I say.

"I should. I've lived here all my life. There's only a little more than a thousand people here. It's not hard to know them."

"There are more than a hundred thousand people in Billings," I say.

"Too many."

"I don't know them all."

"I should think not."

"My father might have, though. He was very popular."

"Really? You made him sound kind of mean."

"He was sometimes." I feel defensive about my father, even though Sheila Renfro is only reacting to what I've told her. "He was a complicated person. But people loved him."

"Edward, let's sit down," Sheila Renfro says. She guides us to a bench outside the courthouse. "I'd like to talk to you."

I ease myself onto the wooden bench. It has a sturdy back, which is good, as that allows me to keep from putting too much stress on my ribs.

"Do you like me?" Sheila Renfro asks me.

"Of course I do."

"Why do you like me?"

This question flummoxes me. Where do I start? "You're nice, and you've been friendly to me."

"That's true."

"You've been very helpful since I got hurt."

"That's also true. Do you like anything else?"

"You're pretty." My cheeks flush with warmth, and I'm embarrassed.

"Thank you. Anything else?"

"You smell good."

"Thank you again."

"That's about it," I say. That's not even close to it. I don't like to lie, but I'm too embarrassed to say anything more.

Sheila Renfro takes my left hand in her right hand. She is wearing gloves. I am not.

"I want to tell you something," she says.

"OK."

"Do you remember last night when I said that you and I are more alike than your mother knows?"

"Yes."

"I want to tell you what I meant."

"OK."

"When I was in school, a lot of the other kids didn't like me. They called me names like 'tard.' Do you know what that means?"

"Retard."

"Yes."

"You're not a retard, Sheila Renfro."

"No, I'm not. And neither are you."

"No one has ever called me a tard. I got called a spaz a lot."

"Well," she says, "you're not one of those, either. What I'm trying to say is that I didn't have any friends, and that was hard when I was a kid. My daddy used to tell me all the time that I was a special girl, and it would take a special person to see me for who I am."

I like Sheila Renfro's daddy, even if he is in the ground. "That's nice," I say.

"Yes. But I've been waiting a long time, and I haven't found that person. I don't like to think that my daddy was wrong about something, but so far, he is."

"Yes. I understand." I keep looking down at my hand in Sheila Renfro's. She notices this.

"Does this bother you?"

"Yes."

"Do you want me to stop?"

I have an answer that flummoxes us both. "No."

I don't make sense anymore.

"I'm sorry about fighting with your mother," Sheila Renfro says, and she grips my hand tight. "I know she loves you, like my daddy loved me. I know she's worried about my intentions. I like you, Edward. I want to learn more about you. I want to see where this goes."

My mind is scattered. I put my other hand over the top of hers and squeeze, and when she looks at me, I smile and look away.

"Why do you like me?" I ask.

"Because you have good taste in football teams." She laughs, but when I don't, she stops.

"You're kind," she says. "You give to other people. You were so good with Kyle, and he worships you. I think you can tell a lot about a person from how he treats children. You're a special man, Edward. That's why I like you."

I like her, too, and it makes me feel warm inside to hear her say these things. But I'm flummoxed by the idea of this going somewhere. In a few days, I will have to go back to Billings, where my life is. This isn't going somewhere. I'm going somewhere.

And I'm not ready to do that yet.

— • —

Sheila Renfro asks me to keep holding her hand as we walk back to the motel. I do as she requests.

"Have you ever had a girlfriend?" she asks.

"No."

"Never?"

"No."

"Why not?"

That's an unanswerable question. I tell her about my one disastrous venture into online dating, when Joy Annette wigged out (I love the slang phrase "wigged out") on me after I told her we couldn't have sex on our first date. She ended up writing me a series of increasingly bizarre e-mails, until I unplugged my account. Since then, I've been fearful of trying to date someone again.

"Have you ever had sex?" Sheila Renfro asks. I'm taken aback by this.

"No."

"Really?"

"How could I have sex if I didn't have a girlfriend?"

Sheila Renfro laughs. "There are people in the world who don't consider a boyfriend or a girlfriend a necessity for sex, Edward."

This perplexes me, until I remember Kyle and *Jersey Shore*. Those guidos would have sex at the drop of their pants.

I just made a joke where I take a common phrase—"the drop of a hat"—and turn it into something fresh and new by referencing the droopy trousers of the guidos on *Jersey Shore*.

I'm pretty funny sometimes.

— • —

We have a lunch of spaghetti—my favorite—in Sheila Renfro's cottage.

After her interrogation of me earlier, I feel bold enough to ask my own questions.

"Have you ever had a boyfriend?"

"Yes."

"You have?"

"Why are you surprised?"

"I'm not, I guess. Did he live around here?"

Sheila Renfro goes to the refrigerator to pour some more cold water into her glass.

"Yes. Still does. His name is Bradley Sutherland. He owns one of the bars in town."

"Did you have sex with him?"

"Yes."

I don't make my earlier mistake of suggesting surprise. I just pick a saucer off the table and smash it. It shatters. Sheila Renfro, at the refrigerator and with her back to me, turns around.

"What happened?"

"I accidentally dropped it." This is a lie.

"Well, don't hurt yourself." She comes to the table with the trash can and sweeps the shattered pieces of the saucer into it.

"Why isn't he your boyfriend anymore?" I ask.

"I told you, my daddy said it would take a special person to see how special I am."

"I remember that."

"Bradley Sutherland is not special enough."

— • —

Before Sheila Renfro leaves for the grocery store to stock up on supplies, she shows me how the guest register and the credit card machine work. She says she'll be gone for about an hour and doesn't want to close the motel. She asks me to run things, if there's anything to run.

I am happy to do this. And sure enough, four minutes after she leaves, a man and a woman who look to be in their twenties come through the door.

"Any vacancies?" the man asks.

"Sixteen of them," I say. "Wait. Fifteen."

"We just need one."

I consult the list of questions Sheila Renfro wrote down for me.

"How many nights?" I ask.

"We're not sure yet."

"Business or pleasure?"

The man looks at the woman—I almost said wife, but that would be an imprudent (I love the word "imprudent") assumption on my part—and shrugs his shoulders.

"Business, I guess," she says.

"One king bed or two queens?"

"Two is fine," he says, and this intrigues me.

"We'll put you in room number sixteen, upstairs."

"Do you have anything on the ground floor?"

I consult the motel layout. I'm in room number four, which has two beds. Room number eight does, too, but that room is under repair. Everything else is one bed.

"No, I'm sorry, I don't."

"OK, one bed is fine."

I consult the layout again. "We'll put you in room number six."

"Fine."

"I'll just need you to fill this out"—I push a registration card across the desk to him—"and I'll need your credit card."

"I'll pay in cash."

I consult Sheila Renfro's instructions again.

"I need to know how many days you're staying. And there will be a three-hundred-dollar deposit for damage, which will be refunded after—"

"We're not going to damage your room, man."

"I'm just telling you the rules."

"Oh, yes, the rules. We must obey the rules."

I agree with what this man is saying, but I don't think he does. He's saying it in a mocking manner.

"OK, buddy, let's call it three days, and I'll add more if I need them. What's that plus the deposit come to?"

I start punching numbers into the calculator, using the base room rental fee and the state sales tax and local lodging tax.

"It comes to $491.21, sir."

The man reaches into his back pocket and pulls out a thick roll of bills. He peels them off one by one and puts them in my hand.

"One hundred…two hundred…three hundred…" He says this and I hear the voice of U2's lead singer Bono in my head. "Four hundred…five hundred."

"Let me get your change."

"Keep it," he says. He swipes the key off the desk, and he and the woman turn and walk down the hall. I don't even get a chance to tell him about our continental breakfast.

Still, that was fun. It made me feel responsible again. Also, I made Sheila Renfro $8.79 extra. Cha-ching! That's how the saying goes, right? Cha-ching? I'm feeling a little whimsical (I love the word "whimsical") today.

— • —

When Sheila Renfro comes home, she's not as happy about the extra $8.79 as I assumed she would be. Once again, the danger of assumptions is made clear to me.

"Let me see the registration card," she says. I hand it to her.

"Steve and Sandy Smith," she says. "I'll bet." She carries the card outside and then returns perhaps fifteen seconds later.

"The license number matches. Probably figured we'd check that."

"What's going on?" I ask.

"I don't have a good feeling," Sheila Renfro says. "I don't like cash payers."

Sheila Renfro clearly is more willing to trust gut feelings than I am. I prefer to let the facts of a situation bear out.

"Keep manning the front desk, Edward. I'll be back."

— • —

Sheila Renfro's motel is jumping today. Again while she's gone, another lodger shows up. This time, it's just a single man, and he says he needs one night.

"Gotta be in Denver in the morning," he says.

I put him in room number seven, across the hall from our other guests. He pays with a credit card. He writes down his name as "Ed Piewicz," which matches the card. I tell him about breakfast, and he says he knows. I can't imagine that Sheila Renfro will have a problem with him. She should be thrilled. She needs the money.

— • —

Sheila Renfro returns and I fill her in on the new guest. She knows him.

"Oh, sure, Ed," she says. "He drives a run between Salina and Denver. Must have had a delivery in Oakley. He stays here a few times a year."

"Where did you go?"

"Sheriff."

"Why?"

"Told him about our mystery guests."

"You think Steve and Sandy Smith are criminals?"

"No, Edward, I don't. At least, I hope they're not. But I've had trouble here before and I know what trouble looks like. I can't be too careful. If they're trouble, the law will know what to do."

"What did the sheriff say?"

"He thanked me for the information and told me to run the place like I normally would. So that's what I'm going to do. Do you want to help me replace the hand soap in the rooms?"

This is a silly question. Of course I do.

— • —

Perhaps I should not have been so eager to help Sheila Renfro with her chores around the motel. When we made it upstairs to replace the soap in those rooms, I was so out of breath that I had to sit down on the bed in room number fifteen and wait for my heartbeat to slow. Dr. Ira Banning warned me about this, that my freshly repaired lung would need some time to work itself back to capacity. The way to do that, he said, is through exercise, which is what I just did.

"You can wait for me downstairs," Sheila Renfro says.

"I'm OK."

"After I'm done here, we can take a break. I'll make some hot tea."

"That sounds nice."

"I'm glad you're here, Edward."

"So am I."

— • —

Sheila Renfro asks me a question that causes me to spit my tea back into my cup.

"Edward, have you ever kissed a girl?"

I wipe my mouth with the back of my hand. "Yes."

"When?"

"Last night."

"What—"

"Remember, I kissed you right before you went to bed. You were there."

Sheila Renfro smiles and grips her teacup with both hands.

"That was more me kissing you than you kissing me. Have you ever kissed a girl besides me?"

"No, not with my mouth. Donna Middleton—she's now Donna Hays—has kissed me on the cheek, but I've never kissed her back. This girl in high school let me kiss her, but it was just so she could embarrass me in front of her friends."

"I hate that girl."

"She was pretty mean."

"Tell me about Donna Middleton."

"Donna Hays."

"Yes. Tell me about her."

This is one of my favorite subjects. I tell Sheila Renfro about how Donna didn't trust me initially because men had been mean to her, but that Kyle and I were friends first, and then Donna and I became friends. I tell her about how we threw snowballs at each other and had pizza, and how bad things kept happening but we hung in there together and remained friends. I tell her about Donna marrying Victor and moving away. I also tell her what happened with Kyle.

"She sounds like a wonderful friend," Sheila Renfro says, and she is correct about that. "I wish I had a friend like that here."

"Donna Middleton has been very good to me. I mean, Donna Hays. I always forget to use her married name."

"I don't think she liked me."

I was hurt when I was in the hospital, so I don't remember all of Sheila Renfro's interactions with Donna.

"It was a tense situation," I say, and Sheila Renfro nods.

"Did you ever want to kiss Donna?" she asks.

I consider this for a moment. It's true that I developed strong feelings for Donna as we were becoming friends, but I don't think those feelings were romantic. At the time, I was much more interested in Joy Annette, my blind date, and that turned out to be a disaster.

"No," I say. "She was just my friend."

"Would you like to kiss me?" Sheila Renfro asks.

I look down at my cup. I don't like making eye contact with people when I'm uncomfortable, or at all.

"I don't know," I say.

"That's not how you talk confidently to a girl."

"I'm afraid I won't be good at it. Also, mouths are gross."

"I could teach you. And we could brush our teeth first."

"Can we also floss and use mouthwash?"

Sheila Renfro laughs. "Yes."

"Because mouths are gross."

"I know, Edward."

— • —

Sheila Renfro gives me my own new toothbrush and a tiny tube of Crest brand toothpaste, along with a tiny bottle of Oral-B brand mouthwash and Johnson & Johnson brand dental floss. She says she keeps these small items on hand for lodgers who forget to bring their own supplies.

We stand together at the mirror in Sheila Renfro's bathroom and we floss, brush, and swig mouthwash. In the reflection in the mirror, it looks like we choreographed it. I have to give Sheila Renfro credit. She is a very competent steward of her dental health. She brushes with at least one hundred strokes, just like I do. Some people rush through things like brushing their teeth, but they shouldn't. It's important to take the time to do the most important things the proper way.

— • —

We sit facing each other at an angle on Sheila Renfro's couch.

"I'm nervous," I say.

She puts her hands on my thighs and leans in.

"It's going to be all right. Now, stop leaning away from me, or this won't work."

I return to an upright sitting position. Sheila Renfro leans in again. Her breath smells good.

Her eyes are closed when her lips touch mine. My eyes are open, which is how I know hers are closed. She moves her head in small, tight circles, and I try to move mine in the same direction along with her. Her lips feel warm against mine.

It's not that I don't enjoy what we're doing. I do. It's that I don't know what to do. I'm trying to do what I've seen in movies, but it feels weird.

Sheila Renfro, her mouth now removed from mine but still very close, gives me instructions.

"Put your hands on my hips," she says.

I do that, and she slides her hands farther up my thighs as she leans in again. This time I lean toward her, even though my ribs ache a little bit, and we kiss again.

I can feel her tongue trying to get between my lips. I pull back and look at her.

"Open your mouth," she says. "Move your hands up."

Both of these things sound inadvisable to me—mouths, even freshly brushed mouths, are gross—but I do as I'm told.

Sheila Renfro's tongue goes into my mouth, and it's the strangest thing, because I expect to be grossed out, but I'm not. I like it. She uses her tongue to touch mine, and then she pulls back again.

"Use your tongue, Edward."

Again I do as I'm told, and my tongue and hers flop around inside our mouths. I move my hands from her hips and up her side. Through her plaid work shirt, I can feel her ribs. As I do this, her hands again move up my thigh, almost to where my legs meet my tallywhacker.

Then she touches my hard tallywhacker through my pants. Holy shit!

"Do you want to go to the bedroom?" she asks.

"I want to keep kissing," I say.

She smiles at me, the biggest smile I've seen yet from her, and I realize that I'm smiling big, too. She leans into me and I meet her with my mouth open.

This is so great.

— • —

After we're done kissing, Sheila Renfro sits close to me and rests her left hand on my right knee.

"When I put my hand on your knee," she says, "you should put your arm around me and make me feel safe."

I lean to my left, and I feel the dull ache in my ribs. I lift my right arm and clip her under the chin.

"Ouch."

"I'm sorry, Sheila Renfro."

"When are you going to call me just Sheila?"

She holds her jaw between her thumb and first two fingers and moves it back and forth.

"What about S-Money? You liked that."

"That was just for fun. I don't like that one anymore, and it's not warm and sexy to hear my full name."

"I'm sorry, Sheila Renfro."

"Edward, put your arm around me."

I set my arm where her back meets her neck.

"Like this?"

"Don't hold it so stiff. Wrap me up and pull me in."

I do as she describes. It feels weird.

"Like this?"

She nestles her head into my shoulder.

"Perfect."

Her hair smells like strawberries.

"What do you know about sex, Edward?"

I did not expect this question. Expectations are just a way to be disappointed with what you get anyway.

"Just what I read," I say.

"Have you ever masturbated?"

"Yes."

"You're awfully honest about it."

"I read 'Dear Abby' every day. 'Dear Abby' says that half of men practice self-satisfaction and the other half lie when they say don't. I figure with those odds, why lie?"

"Do you want to have sex with me?"

This question is one I expected, given the direction of things.

"I don't know," I say.

"You keep saying that. Why?"

"It makes me nervous."

"What are you afraid of?"

"I didn't say I was afraid. I said I was nervous. But, yes, I'm afraid, too."

"Why?"

"What if I'm not good at it? What if I can't do it? What if I have sex with you and I think it's great, and then I have to go home? What if I miss it when I'm gone?"

I hate what-if questions, because they almost never have answers.

Sheila Renfro sits up, removing her head from my shoulder. She makes a half-turn on the couch and faces me.

"You don't have to go home. My daddy left a full shed of tools here when he died. You could have them. You could stay here. You could help me run this motel."

"I live in Billings, Montana," I say. "Not here."

"Well, I live here," she says.

"I'm sorry," I say.

"Don't you like me?"

"Yes."

"Didn't you like kissing me?"

"Yes."

"I liked kissing you, too. We could kiss every day if you were here. We could have lunch and work on the motel and go have a beer at the tavern—"

"It's better that I don't drink alcohol with my type two diabetes."

"The alcohol isn't the point. We could be together. That's what I mean. Don't you want that?"

"I live in Billings, Montana," I say again.

At that, Sheila Renfro stands up and walks away. I call after her, but she doesn't turn around. She goes into her bedroom and closes the door.

— • —

I stay away from Sheila Renfro for the rest of the afternoon and stick to my room. I sat in her living room for sixty-eight minutes after she closed herself in her bedroom, but she never came out. So I left.

I wish I could explain myself to Sheila Renfro. She is asking me to take a leap of faith, and I have a lifetime's worth of experience that suggests a keen attention to the facts is the more advisable course. My house is in Billings, Montana. My job was there, and while Jay L. Lamb seems to believe that I can make it through the remainder of my days without working, I know I'll need something else to do. Returning to the *Billings Herald-Gleaner* is not an option. But it's a big city, and I will find something.

I know where all the right turns are in Billings. My memories are there. My routines are there waiting for me to reestablish them.

When I embarked on this trip, I thought that perhaps the road would hold some answers for me, but it doesn't. It's just a bunch of concrete and asphalt connecting one town to another. Seven hundred and twenty miles of it stand between me and home. Tomorrow, I think, it will be time for me to head that way. I hope I can make amends with Sheila Renfro before I do.

TECHNICALLY TUESDAY, DECEMBER 20, 2011

It's 3:18 and I'm awake. Again. This keeps happening to me. There was a time, one that seems long ago, when my hours were heavily regimented and I went to sleep at the same time every night, slept through until morning, and then woke up, usually at the same time. Those days are in my past, and if my present circumstances are any clue, they're not likely to return. This, however, is conjecture, and conjecture is not for me. I prefer facts.

I think this bed has something to do with it, too. As Sheila Renfro and I came back from Denver, I told her that the bed in room number four, where I'm staying, was too hard. She switched it out with the mattress from room number one, which she said was older and fluffier. She was correct about that. It's too fluffy. I would rather have the first mattress back.

But if I were forced to make a determination about why I'm distracted in these wee hours, I would have to say that it's because of Sheila Renfro, who is asleep next to me on this bed and has her right arm flopped across my lap.

How this came to be is an odd story.

Given our protracted (I love the word "protracted") silence, I was prepared to skip dinner at Sheila Renfro's cottage and instead walk into Cheyenne Wells and find a restaurant. It seemed prudent to prepare for such an eventuality. The last I'd seen of Sheila Renfro, she had walked away from me and disregarded my pleas for her to stop and talk.

As it turned out, she intercepted me in the lobby as I headed for dinner and said, "Edward, come on in and have some grilled cheese sandwiches with me. I'd like to talk with you."

I'll concede that I was wary of talking with Sheila Renfro, but I do love grilled cheese sandwiches. It seemed that the risk-reward gamble of getting bawled out versus having something good to eat was worth taking.

Sheila Renfro had no intention of bawling me out. Her voice was really quiet—not at all excited like it was when we were kissing and touching on her couch. She asked me when I wanted to go to Denver to pick up my new car, and I told her tomorrow—now today—if she didn't mind. She said that would be fine, that she needed to get some bulk supplies in Denver anyway.

I decided that I should try to explain to her what I was feeling.

"It isn't that I don't like you," I began, and she cut me off.

"I know, Edward. You don't have to tell me. I thought you were the special man who would understand my specialness. But you're not. It's not your fault."

Those words hurt me more than I can describe, because I'm not good at describing anything. I think I do understand her specialness. It's just that I don't see where I fit here. I want to tell her these things, but I don't. I hear Dr. Buckley's voice in my head again, telling me that when two people see the same set of facts but disagree in their interpretation of them, one of the most

destructive actions one can take is to attempt to convince someone of his or her errant view. *Some facts have no room for interpretation*, she once told me. *The freezing point of water. The sum
of two numbers. But when it comes to the human heart, variables
always exist.* I think Dr. Buckley was trying to tell me that a fact-
loving brain can carry me only so far and that empathy would
have to do the rest.

I did not contradict Sheila Renfro. I ate my grilled cheese.
Sheila Renfro ate hers.

That's when my mother called my bitchin' iPhone. I asked
Sheila Renfro if I could answer there in her kitchen, and she said
I could.

"Hello, Mother. I was going to call you in about an hour."

"I have a concert tonight, dear. I didn't want to miss you. How
are things in Cheyenne Wells?"

"Great."

"Are they really?"

My mother sounded skeptical, and she was not incorrect in
her feeling. At that moment, things weren't so great, but I thought
it would only create more friction with my mother if I told her
how difficult the situation with Sheila Renfro had become. I
focused on something positive instead.

"Yes, they really are. Today, Sheila Renfro and I practiced
kissing—"

"You practiced *what*?" my mother asked in a loud voice.

Sheila Renfro stood up like she had a rocket in her badonkadonk, which is of course absurd, and she slapped my bitchin'
iPhone and knocked it from my ear.

"Hey!" I yelled.

"What are you doing?" Sheila Renfro said. "That's between
us. Nobody else."

"You hurt my bitchin' iPhone and my ear! What the fucking fuck, Sheila Renfro?"

Sheila Renfro began to cry. "Don't cuss around me, Edward! Just get out of here. Go! I don't want to see you until tomorrow morning."

Sheila Renfro ended up back in her bedroom. Again. And I ended up back here in room number four. Again. And my ear still kind of hurts.

— • —

At 8:57 p.m., I heard a loud thump, and then there were all these voices—all men, all loud—coming from the hallway.

I pushed myself off the bed, walked to the door and opened it.

Next door, outside room number six, stood a uniformed man in a cowboy hat. He carried a rifle, and he heard me open my door.

He headed toward me.

"Sir, get back in your room, please."

"What's going on?"

"Back in your room, sir."

I closed the door fast.

The loud voices continued for some time, an imprecise measure, but I was so spooked that I forgot to look at my watch. After that, it was a continual clomp of boots walking past my door in both directions. I pulled back the curtains that covered the exterior window of my room and saw the sheriff's squad car. At 9:46, two uniformed officers walked out with the young man and young woman I'd checked into the motel earlier that day. The officers put them into different cars and then drove away. Other people, not in uniform, emerged in the parking lot carrying banker's boxes and guns. Three more cars left the parking lot.

Someone knocked on my door.

I closed the curtain and made my way back across the room. I opened the door, and Sheila Renfro stood there in her nightgown.

"I knew there was something about those two," she said.

"What happened?"

She walked past me into the room. I closed the door.

Sheila Renfro sat at the foot of my bed and invited me to sit down with her.

"They were selling crank."

"What?"

"Meth."

"Meth is bad. And illegal."

"Very, very bad. And totally illegal."

"Totally illegal" is redundant; something is illegal or it's not, subject of course to the vagaries (I love the word "vagaries") of the local ordinances. Meth is illegal everywhere.

Sheila Renfro put her hand on her chest and fluttered it.

"That's a lot of excitement," she said.

I was flummoxed by that. I felt only fear, especially when the deputy sheriff was walking toward me with his gun.

"Edward, I'm sorry, but I'm not going to be able to take you to Denver in the morning. I mean, I know you want to go, but the cops are going to be in and out of here tomorrow, and I really need to stay."

"It's OK."

"I can ask around town, see if anybody's going to Denver tomorrow. Maybe we can find you a ride."

"No, I want to ride with you. I can wait."

Sheila Renfro reached for my hand, and I let her have it.

"I was hoping you would," she said. "I know you have to go home eventually. But it would be nice to have a little more time."

"Yes."

Sheila Renfro looked down at the floor. Her left foot was thumping up and down.

"Can I ask a favor?" she said.

"Yes."

"Can I stay here with you tonight?"

"I—"

"No kissing or funny business," she said. "I just don't want to be alone."

Her eyes, normally fixed and unblinking, were looking around the room with uncertainty. She looked scared, not excited, and that made sense to me.

"OK, Sheila Renfro."

— • —

She had no trouble falling asleep. We watched the late news, and then we subdivided the blankets so she would have hers and I would have mine. By 11:27 p.m., she was lightly snoring, a tendency I did not notice when she slept next to me at St. Joseph Hospital. I suppose I was preoccupied with my own problems then.

At 12:14 a.m., she rolled toward me and set her arm across my lap, which was in her path because I continue to sleep—or try to, anyway—in a sitting position. She has violated our agreement to segregate (I love the word "segregate") the bed, but I am not going to call a penalty. I'm going to let her sleep. One of us should.

I keep looking down at her resting head. In my mind, I draw patterns by connecting the small freckles on her nose. I think about the R.E.M. song where Michael Stipe sings about secretly counting his lover's eyelashes, and I wonder where Michael Stipe must have been sitting when he did that. I cannot count Sheila Renfro's eyelashes from here.

She stirs just a bit. I hold my breath. She falls back into slumber, and she grips me tighter across my hips.

She looks peaceful.

She is beautiful.

OFFICIALLY TUESDAY, DECEMBER 20, 2011

From the logbook of Edward Stanton:
   Time I woke up today: 3:18 a.m. and then again at 8:37 a.m. Sheila Renfro was already up and gone, which did not surprise me. She has to wake up early to get this motel moving. I threw on yesterday's clothes and hustled out to the lobby for breakfast. The deputy who walked toward me with a gun last night was there, eating a muffin.
   "How's it going?" he said.
   "Fine. I'm sorry I left the room."
   "No harm, no foul." That's a sports euphemism.
   High temperature for Monday, December 19, 2011, Day 353: 35 in Billings, a 15-degree drop from the high the day before. Might we finally be seeing some seasonable weather? Let's see what the facts bear out.
   Low temperature for Monday, December 19, 2011: 18. That's a 17-degree drop from the day before.
   Precipitation for Monday, December 19, 2011: 0.07 inches
   Precipitation for 2011: 19.48 inches
   New entries:

Exercise for Monday, December 19, 2011: I took a long walk with Sheila Renfro during which she suggested that she struggles with an affliction similar to mine. She did not go into specifics, and I did not ask, because I don't like people asking me what's wrong with me. There's nothing wrong with me, and there's nothing wrong with Sheila Renfro.

Miles driven Monday, December 19, 2011: None.

Total miles driven: Holding steady at 1,844.9.

Gas usage Monday, December 19, 2011: None.

Addendum: It's strange how just the passage of a few hours can change things so profoundly. When I retired to my room last night, it was with the full expectation that I would be going to Denver today to pick up my new Cadillac DTS and begin the drive back to Billings, Montana. Now, because of the meth bust in Sheila Renfro's motel, I am going to be staying at least another day. Sheila Renfro said she thinks we can leave tomorrow. To be honest, that makes me happy and sad at the same time. I've been gone from Billings, Montana, for more than a week, and that's the longest I've ever been away as an adult. But I also want to enjoy my remaining time with Sheila Renfro.

After I shower and change clothes, I see Sheila Renfro for the first time today. She is laundering bed linens. Ed Piewicz has checked out, she says, and of course the cops ended the stay of her other two guests. She says there are no reservations for today.

"Do you want to take a walk?" she says.

"Yes."

"Let me get this last load into the wash and we'll go."

— • —

Before we leave, Sheila Renfro checks in with the sheriff in room number six and makes sure he doesn't need her. He asks her to bring him back a cup "of that good coffee from the Kwik Korner and not this instant swill you serve here."

This makes Sheila Renfro super-mad, as well she should be, I think.

"You listen to me, Pete. You're lucky I don't bill the county for all the coffee and food you and your men have been drinking and eating. You're a lot more solvent than I am, that's for sure. If you want a different kind of coffee, you can go get it yourself."

The sheriff holds up his hands in a surrender pose.

"All right, all right. Jesus."

"And don't you cuss around me."

She turns and walks toward the door in short, choppy steps, and I notice that she walks exactly the same way that Donna does when she's mad. I like this.

In the parking lot, I put a hand on her shoulder to slow her down. With my achy ribs and recovering lung, I cannot keep up.

"You really told him," I say.

"That paternal son of a…doo-doo head!"

The last syllable emerges from Sheila Renfro in a squeak, and I begin to laugh but throw my hand over my mouth. I don't want to join Sheriff Pete on Sheila Renfro's bad side.

"Come on," she says. "Let's go for a walk."

We take much the same route we followed the day before, past the lumberyard and across the brown courthouse lawn, which is mottled with bits of snow that hasn't melted in the past couple of days.

"How is your endurance?" Sheila Renfro asks.

"Good."

"Want to go farther?"

"Yes."

We leave the business district and head into the residential streets, and I see Cheyenne Wells as I've never seen it before, not even when I was here as a little boy in 1978. Most of the houses sit on generous lots, as if the original builders figured that, yes, they were part of a town but there was no reason to be too close to one's neighbors. That's an ethic I can appreciate.

The houses are not much different from the ones on my street. Most of them are wooden, built in a bungalow style. Yards are a patchwork of well-tended lawns and weed farms. The overwhelming characteristic of Cheyenne Wells, in my memories and in my vision now, is the sky. Nothing intrudes on it. This terrain is flat in all directions.

Sheila Renfro points at a small, tidy, brown stucco house on Fourth Street.

"My parents lived there while the motel was being built," she says.

"It's nice."

"Yeah. I like to walk past it and think of what their life must have been like at that time, before I came along. They never talked much about those days, so it's left to my imagination."

Up ahead, on the corner, she points out Cheyenne Wells High School, her alma mater. She says she doesn't have much school spirit, and I understand completely. I went to Billings West High School, and aside from Mr. Withers, who was my wood shop teacher there before he became my boss at the newspaper years later, I didn't have any friends.

"We had a fifteen-year reunion a couple of years ago. Some of the people who moved away came back and stayed in my motel and had parties. It took me a week to clean it all up," she says.

"People can be really rude," I say.

"Amen to that. Well, come on, Edward. Let's head back."

She offers her hand for me to hold.

"Just as friends," she says.

I take her hand in mine and off we go, the way we came.

— • —

I'm watching daytime TV—some kind of reality-style, in-the-court-room show—when the in-room telephone rings, startling me.

I pick it up, and before I can say hello, Sheila Renfro's voice is in my ear, urgent.

"You'd better come up here," she says.

I turn off the TV and push myself off the bed with little pain, just a twinge (I love the word "twinge").

As I step into the hallway, I can see that someone is at the front desk, but she—the shape looks like a she—is leaning over the ledge and I cannot see her face.

Then I hear the voice and I know.

"Mother?"

My mother faces me. Her appearance, as always, is immaculate. She is clearly not happy to be here. This signal is unmistakable in her face and in her voice when she speaks.

"Get your things. I'm taking you home."

"But—"

"Your things, Edward. I have your car. We're going back to Billings today, you and me."

"But—"

"Now."

Hers is the voice of finality. I've heard it before. It's the voice she used to tell Jay L. Lamb that he was never to contact me again without her approval.

I walk back down the hall toward room number four. Behind me, Sheila Renfro's voice is saying, "I was going to take him to Denver tomorrow. You didn't—"

"I don't want to hear it," my mother replies.

I open the door to my room and get inside so I don't have to listen to anything else.

— • —

I need two trips to get everything to the car. I still have six water bottles left from the case I started with.

"Do you want these?" I ask Sheila Renfro.

"I guess."

She walks with me to the car. My mother is standing in the door frame, one foot on the floorboard, the other on the asphalt.

"I guess I'm leaving now," I tell Sheila Renfro.

"I guess."

"I'm sorry we got only part of today together."

Sheila Renfro is tearing up. I hate that.

"Me, too," she says.

"Edward…" my mother implores.

Sheila Renfro reaches around my neck and pulls herself in tight to me. My mother begins to say something, and I hold out my left hand, and she stops.

Sheila Renfro lets me go. I ease into the passenger seat of my new Cadillac, and my mother also gets in. I look out the window at Sheila, her eyes all red-rimmed and translucent (I love the word "translucent," but I hate it right now), and I put my hand against the glass.

My mother backs out of the parking space and turns toward the highway. I watch in my side-view mirror, and Sheila Renfro follows us for a few steps until we're on the highway and my mother steps on the gas.

In 6.8 seconds, I can't see Sheila Renfro anymore.

— • —

We're nearly to Limon before my mother says anything. For miles, we have been glancing at each other, sometimes opening our mouths, but no words have come. When the silence ends, it's as if someone has pumped oxygen back into the car.

"I was worried about you," she says.

"I was all right."

"It's just…you know, the whole trip seemed like it was turning into a disaster. You've been doing so well. I didn't want you to land in any trouble."

I am flummoxed by my mother's assessment of how I'm doing. It's been a shitburger of a year. I haven't been doing well for weeks. For months. But I was doing fine with Sheila Renfro.

"I wasn't in any trouble."

"That woman, she's trouble."

"No, Mother, she's not."

She says nothing to this, and I'm not going to explain it. I remember what Dr. Buckley said about how people make up their mind about things by processing information through their biases and experiences. I will not idly accept my mother's pronouncements about Sheila Renfro, but neither can I force her to see things my way.

"You were going home anyway," she says.

"Yes."

"So it doesn't matter if it's a day early."

"If it makes you feel better to think so."

My mother's face scrunches up.

"You look like you've lost weight."

"I was in a bad car wreck, Mother."

She holds tight to the steering wheel up top with both hands.

"I'm trying to talk to you, Son."

"I know," I say. "I don't feel like talking."

I plug my bitchin' iPhone into the adaptor and turn the receiver on. I shuffle the songs. Michael Stipe begins to sing about how he found a way to make someone smile.

I turn my body to the right. My ribs scream. I face the window. I don't want my mother to see me like this.

— • —

We eat dinner at Hathaway's restaurant in the Little America Hotel near Cheyenne, Wyoming. I've slept most of the way—a fitful, in-and-out sleep during which I lurch awake and take in the passing landscape before drifting off again. Now I pick at my roasted chicken and I try to bring myself out of my stupor.

"You're not mad at me, are you?" my mother asks.

I learned from Dr. Buckley that this is a passive-aggressive question. My mother knows that I should be and am angry with her. She knows she overstepped her boundaries. Now she's asking me to tell her it was OK.

"You shouldn't have done what you did," I say.

"You needed my help."

Now my mother is bargaining.

"No, I didn't. I had the situation under control."

"I still say it doesn't really matter because you were going home anyway and now we get to spend some time together."

My mother is still bargaining.

I don't say anything.

"What's wrong? It seems like there's something you're not telling me," she says.

I rub my eyes with the heels of my hands.

"I don't have a job anymore. My best friends are gone. I have type two diabetes—"

"You have diabetes?"

"Yes, I told you that."

"No, you didn't."

"I didn't?"

"No. When did you find out?"

"Dr. Rex Helton told me on December eighth."

"What are you doing about it?"

"I'm eating roasted chicken and vegetables," I say, passing my hand over my plate.

"How can I know what's going on in your life if you don't tell me, Edward?"

"How can you pretend to know if you don't ask?"

This is probably the most acidic (I love the word "acidic") thing I have ever said to my mother, and instantly I wish I hadn't.

Her mouth puckers up like a chicken's asshole.

"Let's just eat," she says.

— • —

My mother asks me to drive for a while. She says it's been a long day, what with the early flight from Dallas/Fort Worth, the drive down to Cheyenne Wells from Denver, and now the drive back across Colorado to Wyoming, the entirety of which still stands between us and Billings. She says all of this as if she had no choice in the matter, which tells me that my mother still thinks she did the right thing. This flummoxes me. It's not like her to be so obtuse (I love the word "obtuse").

The full night is upon us now, and only Michael Stipe's voice is fighting against the silence as he sings about the imitation of life. I've turned the volume down to where only someone who knows the songs as well as I do can make out the words.

"Losing your job really threw you for a loop, didn't it?" my mother says.

"Yes."

"I'm sure it was nothing personal. Mr. Withers always liked you."

"It's not the insult. It's the timing."

"Edward," she says, "you are so fortunate. You don't have to work if you don't want to."

I laugh. It's not a ha-ha-funny laugh. It's bitter and hard.

"Jay L. Lamb said the same thing," I say.

My mother sits up.

"I'm going to call Jay in the morning. I bet he can help you find a job. Would that be all right?"

I consider this. When it comes to talking to Jay L. Lamb, I'm always in favor of someone else doing it. And I do need a job. Somehow, I have to start rebuilding a life in Billings, Montana, which seems odd to say since it's the only life I've ever known. I might as well start the rebuilding project with a new job.

It can only get better from there.

— • —

I stop for gas in Casper, Wyoming, and fill the tank with 15.464 gallons of unleaded at $3.0399 per gallon, for a total of $47.01.

My mother asks me if I'm getting weary. It's 8:31 p.m. now, and I probably could use a break from driving.

As we get back on the road my mother says, "I want to show you something."

Instead of heading back to the interstate, she drives in the other direction, through Casper, and soon I am unsure where we are. We pass a building emblazoned with TOWN OF MILLS, and we ride on from there. About a mile up the road, my mother turns left into a patch of 1950s-era ranch-style homes.

"Where are we?" I say.

"I'll tell you when we get there."

She takes a left turn (bad), then a right turn (good), then another left (bad). She rolls the Cadillac up to a small box of a home.

"Your father and I used to live in that house," she says.

I have never heard about this.

"When?"

"Right after we got out of school. He went to work for the oil company, and they put us here in Casper. God, I hated it. I'd grown up in Texas—your father had, too, of course, but at least he had something to do here. The wind blew all the time. We'd get buried in drifts of snow in winter, way worse than anything we ever saw in Billings. Anyway, that was our first house together."

I stare at the structure. It looks too small, even for just two people. However, I have to concede that whoever lives here now takes pride in it. The yard is neat and tended. The chain link fence doesn't sag. It's small, but it's nice.

"Was it red like this?" I ask.

"No, it was white. The red looks better. It also had a garage, but it looks like they've turned that into a room. Good idea. It was a tiny, tiny place. Your father and I had to turn our backs to the wall to pass each other in the hallway."

"How long were you here?"

"Fourteen months. I counted every day." My mother laughs. "Getting to go to Billings was like paradise. We built a good life there, too. You came along."

"It's weird to think of any place other than Billings being home to you and Father."

My mother puts the car back in drive and leaves her past behind. I'm still struck by the fact that there's something I could learn about my parents this late in my life.

"I'll tell you something, Edward. It's becoming weird for me to think of Billings as home. I'm a little nervous about seeing it again."

"Why?"

"Oh, I don't know. I'm getting ingrained in Texas. It's like I rediscovered where home is. Now that your father has been gone awhile, there's not so much for me to do in Billings anymore."

TECHNICALLY WEDNESDAY, DECEMBER 21, 2011

We make it to Billings at 12:07 a.m. My mother drives through the quiet dark to her downtown condo and then turns the car over to me. She says she will call Jay L. Lamb first thing in the morning and let me know what he says. She gives me a kiss on the cheek and says good-bye. Four minutes and twenty-eight seconds later, I come home to 639 Clark Avenue.

The house is as I left it eleven days ago. And yet, it feels foreign to me. That doesn't make sense, but then a lot of what I'm feeling lately doesn't seem logical. I'm going to have to hang on until things sort out.

I'll have to go to the post office later today and retrieve my mail. I'll call the *Billings Herald-Gleaner*, too, and get my paper going again. I've been thinking about it during the entire drive from Cheyenne Wells, and figuring out how my life works here—what Scott Shamwell calls "sorting out the shithouse"—is going to take discipline. Throughout this shitburger of a year, I've been letting routine get away from me. Routine, I've decided, is my way back to happiness, if happiness is anything I can aspire to. At this point, I'd take normalcy, whatever that is.

My ribs ache. The constant motion and the getting out of and into the car have sapped me physically.

I need to make a list of things to do when I wake up, so I can begin to round my life back into shape. A list represents discipline, and discipline is what I need.

EDWARD'S TO-DO LIST

1. *Go to the post office and get my mail, and reinstate delivery.*
2. *Call the Billings Herald-Gleaner and restart home delivery of the paper.*
3. *Go to the grocery store. Think lean meats, whole grains, and fruits and vegetables.*
4. *Go to Rimrock Mall and get something for Mother for Christmas.*
5. *Before going to Rimrock Mall, see if a good item can be found online and delivered before Christmas. Rimrock Mall four days before Christmas? What was I thinking?*
6. *Arrange to see Dr. Rex Helton and Dr. Bryan Thomsen. A good life means good health. I need to get on top of this.*
7. *Stop writing this list.*
8. *Stop now.*
9. *Dammit.*
10. *Go to sleep.*
11. *Shit.*
12. *STOP IT!*

I break another pen in half to keep from writing another item. It's 12:49 a.m. I'm tired.

Since we left Casper, I've been thinking about my mother and my father and their life together—the way it was before I came along and the way it was after. I was surprised to learn that they had lived in Wyoming when they first got married, and after that, I was happy to have heard the story. My mother doesn't talk much about my father anymore, and I struggle with that, because I think about him more than I ever have and would like to talk with her about him. I don't measure such things as the amount of time spent thinking about my father, of course, and that's not really my point. My point is that my father is often on my mind.

When we drove into Montana, I reminded my mother about my father's crashing into a deer, and she scoffed.

"That was up by Little Bighorn," she said. "He was drunk, you know."

"No," I said. "I didn't know that."

"Yes, he was drunk. The whole thing scared me to death. That deer, he bounced off the front of the car and into the windshield, and I swear, I thought he was going to come through and land in the backseat. Your father there, prattling on, not paying attention. We're lucky we weren't killed. That's when I told him, 'Ted, never again. I'm never riding with you again when you've been drinking.'"

I could tell from the look on my mother's face that she wasn't sure whether she had anything left to say.

"I miss him," I said.

"He was one of a kind, that's for sure."

"Do you miss him?"

My mother drummed her fingers on the steering wheel. After that, she licked her lips a couple of times.

"No. I'm sorry, Edward, but no, I don't."

I didn't even know what to say or think about that.

OFFICIALLY WEDNESDAY, DECEMBER 21, 2011

From the logbook of Edward Stanton:

Time I woke up today: 8:48 a.m. My face was in a puddle of my own drool.

High temperature for Tuesday, December 20, 2011, Day 354: 42, according to the Billings Herald-Gleaner website. I don't have a paper yet. That's a 7-degree improvement from the high a day before. These are just highly unusual December temperatures.

Low temperature for Tuesday, December 20, 2011: 28, a 10-degree improvement. Remarkable.

Precipitation for Tuesday, December 20, 2011: 0.00 inches

Precipitation for 2011: 19.48 inches

New entries:

Exercise for Tuesday, December 20, 2011: I took an even longer walk with Sheila Renfro, before my mother showed up and short-circuited my stay in Cheyenne Wells.

I told my mother yesterday that I wasn't mad at her. That was a lie. I'm pissed off.

Also, I wonder if Sheila Renfro will walk without me. I hope so. I'm going to try to walk here, without Sheila Renfro.

Miles driven Tuesday, December 20, 2011: I refuse to recognize any miles driven by my mother or by me yesterday. I shouldn't have been in that car.

Total miles driven: Holding steady at 1,844.9, because of the technicality I just outlined.

Gas usage Tuesday, December 20, 2011: I also refuse to recognize any gas I put in my new Cadillac DTS, although I will be unable to persuade my bank to disregard the money I spent on it. That sucks.

Addendum: OK, I still intend to embark on my new program to get my life into shape. That's just good common sense. But I'm pissed off that I'm here right now, and I'm pissed off at my mother for butting into my business the way she did. Sovereignty. That's a word. I love that word. It means that I have the right to make the decisions that affect the course of my life. My mother infringed (I also love the word "infringed") on my sovereignty by doing what she did. What's more, she doesn't even recognize that she did anything wrong. She doesn't think it's a big deal! That makes things even worse.

Something else that pisses me off is the way my mother talked about my father, saying she doesn't miss him. How can she not? He was her husband. This is difficult for me, because I believe that a person has a right to feel the way he or she wants to, but my mother is acting irrationally on several levels.

I am so pissed off at my mother right now. I want to call her and tell her off, and maybe I will, but even as I wig out, I can hear Dr. Buckley talking in my head about this. She told me once that it's never a bad move to wait until anger passes before having a confrontation. She said that doesn't mean you overlook a transgression, but rather that you allow yourself to be in the proper frame of mind to achieve the best possible solution from a necessary confrontation. If I call my mother right now, I am going to yell at her and probably make her cry (I've done it before). That might make me feel good for a little while, but it won't solve the problem between us. I will wait for my anger to recede. In fact, I think I will call Dr. Bryan Thomsen and see if he can fit me into his schedule today. It's not ideal, as today is Wednesday and not Tuesday, but my need for the help outweighs my need to stick to my schedule.

Can Dr. Bryan Thomsen help me? I have my doubts. But doubt is in the realm of conjecture. I need facts. I need them as badly as I ever have.

Also, I don't think I should keep referring to Sheila Renfro in these notes. It didn't happen ideally, but I'm gone from there. It's over. It's just too painful to think about her.

(Who am I kidding? I can't not think about her. But I can try not to write about her, which makes the thinking much more intense and painful.)

My morning is being dominated by phone calls. That's not how I'd prefer to spend my morning, but life doesn't always unfold for us the way we would like. Obviously.

It starts with good news: Dr. Bryan Thomsen can see me at 1:00 p.m. today, which is three hours and twenty-two minutes from right now. He says he's eager to hear about my trip, and, as it turns out, I have plenty to tell him.

I am in no mood for inefficiency today, and I make this clear to Dr. Bryan Thomsen. "Will you be ready promptly at one p.m.?" I ask him.

"Yes, indeed. One p.m. I've written it on my schedule right here."

"I know you've written it down. You always write it down. What I'm asking is if you're going to be ready at the appointed time."

"Yes."

"Because you've missed it before."

"I have? I guess I don't recall that."

"Seven times," I say. "I am supposed to see you at ten a.m., and yet we started our session on those seven occasions at 10:01 twice, 10:03, 10:04 three times and, perhaps most egregiously, 10:11." (I love the word "egregiously.")

"Well, I'm terribly sorry about that, Edward. You're clearly on a mission today."

"I'm just trying to sort out the shithouse, Dr. Bryan Thomsen."

"I will be ready at one p.m. I give you my solemn word. I'm looking forward to talking about this issue—"

"Maybe next time. I'm controlling the agenda today. See you at one p.m."

I hang up.

— • —

I've just crossed Dr. Bryan Thomsen off my to-do list when the phone rings.

I pick it up. "Yes."

"Is that any way to answer the phone?"

It's my mother. I wonder if she's calling to take another chunk of my sovereignty.

"It's the way I'm doing it today, Mother. What do you want?"

"Be nice."

"I'm busy, Mother. What do you want?"

"I just talked to Jay, and he thinks he has a lead on a job for you. Can you swing by his office this afternoon?"

"No."

"It will only take a few minutes."

"No. I'm busy. Tell him I'll come by tomorrow."

"He's really sticking his neck out for you."

"Tell him I appreciate it. Tell him I will come by tomorrow."

"Why are you being so huffy?"

"I told you. I'm busy. Is there anything else?"

"Well, then, perhaps you're too busy to come by for lunch."

"Yes, I am."

"Good-bye, then."

"Good-bye, Mother."

I return to my list. Time is wasting.

— • —

By 11:48 a.m., my list is whittled to a single item: go get my mail from the post office. I can do that one after my appointment with Dr. Bryan Thomsen.

Gifts for my mother and Kyle will be here in two days. Kyle's gift was easy—it's a Tim Tebow jersey, which I promised him. My mother's gift is something that seems pedestrian (I love the word "pedestrian"), but I read several online gift guides, and apparently this thing is the hot gift for this year—it's a single-cup coffee brewer called a Keurig. It seems to be an ingenious product. You put something called a K-Cup—this can be virtually any flavor of coffee or tea—into this compartment, close it, and hit a button on the machine. Sharp needles puncture the K-Cup, and hot water is sent coursing through it and into your cup.

I hope my mother likes it. Just in case, I'll keep the receipt and tell her how she can ship it back if it doesn't meet with her approval. Some people take gift-giving personally and become despondent if a gift isn't enjoyed. I've never been that way. It's just a silly inanimate object. Why should I let it bother me, when so many other things make me legitimately upset?

I'll be seeing Dr. Rex Helton tomorrow at 10:00 a.m. I got lucky there; the appointment desk said someone else canceled on him—a common occurrence around the holidays, according to the woman who answered my call—and I was able to slip into the open spot. Otherwise, I'd have had to wait a couple of weeks, the appointment clerk said.

I can't imagine that I've lost much weight, as infrequent as my exercise has been, but I do want to fill him in on my injuries from the car wreck, as he is my primary care physician. I also want to tell him that he shouldn't soft-peddle the significant effects of diabetic medicine on a patient's urinary rate. Yes, Dr. Rex Helton told me that I would pee a lot, but he should know as well as anyone that "a lot" is an imprecise measurement that leaves far too much room for individual interpretation. He needs to give people the facts.

Now I've just come in from the grocery store with a few days' rations. I bought two packages of chicken breasts for grilling, a pork loin that I can roast in my oven, a bag of carrots, two heads of iceberg lettuce, four cans of green beans, and a big tub of oatmeal for my regular morning dose.

In just a few hours of being awake, I've made positive steps toward a healthy mind and a healthy body. So far, my plan to reset my life is playing out the way I want. To celebrate, I treat myself to a Lean Cuisine lasagna.

— • —

Dr. Bryan Thomsen deserves credit, and I'm giving it to him.

At 12:59:45, he opens his door and beckons me to join him in his office. I walk down the hallway, stopping to shake hands with him, and then I settle into my regular chair. I look down at my watch, and it says 1:00:00.

This day just keeps getting better.

The first thing I do is give Dr. Bryan Thomsen a rundown on what happened on my trip. I know we have only an hour and a half—he was nice enough to block out a little extra time for me—so I try to tell my story in a straight line and without embellishments. This is harder than it seems. I make sure I bring in the major points: Kyle's insolence, our adventure together in the car, meeting Sheila Renfro, Kyle's revelation to me about how he'd been hurt by the bullies in his school, the car accident, the return to Cheyenne Wells, kissing Sheila Renfro (I leave out the part where she touched my boner; that's none of Dr. Bryan Thomsen's business), deciding to leave Sheila Renfro, my mother's unexpected appearance.

It's this last point that I wish to address in depth, and I put it to Dr. Bryan Thomsen.

"Did my mother take my sovereignty?"

Dr. Bryan Thomsen considers this for a while.

"You want my opinion?"

"Yes, I do."

"I would say it's a qualified yes. Yes, your mother overstepped. But she overstepped in the service of protecting you. I think you need to account for that in your decision about how severely to confront her."

"But you're saying I should confront her?"

"Edward, yes. It's obvious how much this bothers you. She needs to know that. The question, for you, becomes what you want the message to be. Do you want her to be punished or do you want her to be informed?"

"Informed."

I'm angry at my mother—as angry at her as I can ever remember being—but I do not want her to be hurt.

"Let that answer guide you. That's my advice."

Dr. Bryan Thomsen is making a good deal of sense.

"Edward, I'd like to ask you something."

"Yes."

"I would like for you to tell me about your thought processes when bad things happened on this trip. You've had a remarkable stretch in a short amount of time, and it's covered quite a lot of the human spectrum."

"What do you mean?"

"I mean, you've dealt with a child's hostility, violence, the emergence of secrets, romance. How did you cope with all of that? You certainly could have called me, but you didn't. How did you get through it?"

I look down at the floor and rotate my ankles back and forth.

"You might not like the answer."

"Try me."

I sit up straight. My ribs still hurt.

"Sometimes I asked myself what Dr. Buckley would say if she were there with me," I say. "Sometimes, I didn't have to ask myself. It was like Dr. Buckley's voice was right there with me, helping me see my path out of the situation. Dr. Buckley liked to talk to me about pathways."

"Why did you think I wouldn't like that answer?"

"Because I miss Dr. Buckley. I wish she were still my counselor. I think you're a nice man, Dr. Bryan Thomsen, but you haven't put in the work with me that she did. You don't know me like she did. It's been hard dealing with you since she's been gone, and I wish I didn't have to."

He leans forward in his chair, cupping his hands together, and I'm afraid he's going to yell at me.

"I'm going to tell you a secret, Edward. That doesn't bother me at all."

"It doesn't?"

"No. Do you want to know why?"

"Yes."

"Because it means Dr. Buckley and you were successful in your work together. This might surprise you, Edward, but I've read your notes dating to the first time you came here, in 2000. I've read every word. And the entire time, Dr. Buckley was imparting life skills to you. She was helping you find a way within yourself to live well and to live safely in a world that doesn't always move the way you move. What you did out on the road simply proves that her approach worked. She didn't try to change you. Instead, she helped you find the best way to live that works for you."

I'm listening to what Dr. Bryan Thomsen is saying, and I'm regretting ever saying anything bad about him. All this time, I thought that he didn't know me or care to know me, and it turns out that the opposite was true.

"So here is what I propose," Dr. Bryan Thomsen says. "I propose that we go forward with you not expecting me to be Dr. Buckley, because I'm not and will never be, and I will go forward respecting what you need. If you want to keep coming every week, great. I will see you then. If you want to check in a few times a year, fine. If you want to move to Spain and do this on Skype, we can make that happen."

"I'm not moving to Spain," I say.

"Wherever," he says. "The point is, it's your life to live, and you have the skills to live it in the way you choose. When you talk to your mother, Edward, that's what I suggest you tell her."

— • —

I'm pretty smart sometimes.

Because my bills are paid by my lawyer, Jay L. Lamb, and because I don't sign up for things that cause me to be put on mailing lists, I have only two pieces of mail waiting for me at the post office.

The first, postmarked December 14, is from the human resources department at the *Billings Herald-Gleaner*. I'm both flummoxed and excited. Although Mr. Withers called me personally and said there would be no returning to my job, this letter at least holds out the possibility that someone at the *Herald-Gleaner* has considered my request. There is only one way to find out, as they say, and that's to open the letter. (And "they," whoever they are, are wrong when they say that. For example, I could just call the *Herald-Gleaner* directly and ask someone in human resources to tell me my status. I'll grant you that's not an efficient way of finding out, as this letter is here in my hand, but at least it's plausible. That means there is more than one way of finding out.)

I tear off the corner of the envelope, stick my index finger inside, and rip open one end.

December 14, 2011
Mr. Edward Stanton:

Thank you for your interest in the Herald-Gleaner. At this time, we have no job openings that fit your stated areas of interest, but we will keep your information on file and will contact you in the future if you're a good match for an available position.

We wish you the best in your endeavors.

Sincerely,
The Billings Herald-Gleaner

If there is such a thing as being flummoxed to the power of ten, that's what I am. Mr. Withers told me on December 9 that I could not have my job back. He stated this with clarity. I had come to accept this state of affairs, even though it hurt me badly to see my job gone forever.

So what is the point of this letter? To tell me five days after Mr. Withers's direct phone call telling me I could not work at the *Herald-Gleaner* that, in fact, I cannot work at the *Herald-Gleaner*. That seems redundant and cruel.

I realize I was involuntarily separated. Must I also be involuntarily mocked?

This letter has real potential to derail what has been an outstanding day so far.

I open the other letter.

December 18, 2011
Dear Edward,

I'm sorry we haven't checked in on you. As you can probably imagine, it's been a difficult time around here since we brought Kyle home.

I want to thank you for whatever you did to get him to talk. I never in a million years would have wished to hear what he told us, but I also cannot imagine the horror his life might have been if we'd never found out the truth. He is going to get all the help he needs to get past this, and we're going to get all the help we need as a family. And you, as a member of our family, helped us reach this point. We love you. You will always be one of us.

I can tell you that Kyle is doing well. We just started seeing a counselor—together as a family, and also Kyle alone—and have begun the work of repairing what has been done. I have spoken with the administration at Kyle's school, and to their credit, they are taking this issue seriously. I would destroy them if they didn't.

We're eager to talk to you again very, very soon and to have you come out here and have the vacation we never managed to give you (I'm so sorry about that!). One of the keys to moving beyond this is finding a way to live normally again. We look forward to that.

All our love,
Donna

I was wrong about the letter from the *Herald-Gleaner*. It can't ruin my day. Kyle is getting the help he needs. Nothing can ruin my day now.

— • —

I've returned from a post-dinner walk around my neighborhood when my phone rings. I pick up the receiver.

"Hello?"

"Hello, Edward."

It's my mother.

It's funny—not ha-ha funny, but just funny—how a few hours and some good news can change things. I'm still angry that my mother intruded on my sovereignty and spoke poorly of my father, but I'm no longer angry at her. One tiny preposition is removed, and everything changes. I still intend to make sure she understands that she cannot do that to me again. I simply have no intention of being mean about it, and I was a bit mean earlier today.

"Hi, Mother."

"I know you're angry at me, but I'm hoping that you'll come for dinner tomorrow. I didn't expect to be in Billings for the holidays, but since I am, let's try to make the best of it, OK?"

"Yes. I understand."

"I want us to get back to where we were. I don't want to be feuding."

"I don't want that, either, Mother. We can talk about that when we see each other tomorrow."

"That sounds good. Good night."

"Good night, Mother."

— • —

I've made another important decision. My effort to renew routine in my life is going so well that I realize I've been missing my most important routine for far too long. It's time for me to get back to watching *Dragnet* every night. *Adam-12* was fine, a perfectly worthy show, but it's not the gold standard. If it were, I wouldn't have gotten off-track with it. That's clear now.

As today is the 355th day of the year and there were ninety-eight color episodes of *Dragnet*, if I had been on my old routine all year, where I start with the very first episode on the very first day of the year and watch the episodes in order, one a day, I would be watching the sixty-first episode of the series, "Narcotics: DR 21." This is the sixteenth episode of the third season and it originally aired on January 30, 1969. It is one of my favorites.

I queue this episode up on my bitchin' iPhone and settle into the couch to watch it.

In this episode, Sergeant Joe Friday and Officer Bill Gannon are flummoxed because drug cartels are moving large amounts of contraband through the airport and the police are having trouble stopping it because they cannot develop probable cause. It's an offhand comment from Officer Bill Gannon about not being a dog who's able to sniff out the drugs that gives Sergeant Joe Friday an idea—the police department should train a dog to identify packages containing marijuana.

This seems like a no-brainer, and I remember when I watched it for the first time wondering whether Sergeant Joe Friday and Officer Bill Gannon were idiots for not thinking of it earlier, but it turns out that training a dog to sniff out drugs is not easy. In fact, I get stressed out watching the episode for fear that the dog, Ginger, won't be up to the task. This is silly, of course; I know how the episode goes. Ginger ends up joining the police force, and she's so good at what she does that the drug cartels put a price on her head. Drug cartels are assweeds, and it's a testament to Jack Webb's filmmaking ability that I stress out every time I see this episode.

But regardless of the stress, today has made this much clear: I'm on the right track. I'm on the right track. I'm on the right track.

TECHNICALLY THURSDAY, DECEMBER 22, 2011

It's 3:06 a.m.

I am not on the right track.

I did not give Sheila Renfro permission to be in my dreams. I guess she didn't need permission, because there she was, in the nightgown she wore the night she slept in my bed, following me in the night through a wooded area. She would let me see her, but she would not look at me and would not respond when I called for her. For hours, we walked through the woods, a place I did not recognize. It could not have been Cheyenne Wells, Colorado, as there are no woods there. Sheila Renfro has no context in my life here in Montana. It was a confusing dream, and when I finally decided to run for her—in the dream—she vanished.

That's when I woke up, scared and screaming "Sheila!" Not "Sheila Renfro," which always bemused (I love the word "bemused") Sheila Renfro, but just "Sheila." What does it mean?

That's a rhetorical question, of course. For as long as I've had vivid dreams, I've been reading what I can about the science of dreaming, and I'm afraid the oneirologists are not much help when it comes to definitively diagnosing what we see when we sleep. Some believe that deeper meaning underlies our dreams and that interpreting them can lead us to greater understanding of our conscious selves. Others think that dreams are nothing more than images we've stashed away in consciousness that are then unfurled and combined in nonsensical and psychedelic ways by our deep brain as we sleep.

In my reading, I've learned about authentic dreaming and illusory dreaming. I've experienced both. The dream I had about being on the barstool with my father in Cheyenne Wells, Colorado, was an authentic dream. It really happened. This one tonight, with Sheila in her nightgown and following me through the woods, that was illusory. The nightgown stemmed from something real; everything else did not.

It's all very baffling, the mixture of the known and the unknown, and it's a burden on this fact-loving brain of mine, so I find that I must be practical about this.

It will be very hard to get a decent night's sleep if I'm going to be regularly dreaming about Sheila Renfro.

It's a practical impossibility not to think of Sheila Renfro when I'm awake. When I was speaking with Dr. Bryan Thomsen yesterday, my favorite part was when I got to talk about Sheila Renfro.

I have to deal with things as they are. I'm here and she's there, and so I have to build the best life I can. This shitburger of a year has taken so much from me, and it took Sheila Renfro, too. I have to accept that. I'm not the special man to recognize her specialness. She said that herself, and she should know.

I hate that she said it, but she did, and I must get on with things.

OFFICIALLY THURSDAY,
DECEMBER 22, 2011

From the logbook of Edward Stanton:

Time I woke up today: 3:06 a.m. from my terrible dream. After I calmed down, I set an alarm for 8:45 a.m. so I could attend to my data and make my appointment with Dr. Rex Helton.

High temperature for Wednesday, December 21, 2011, Day 355: 35, a seven-degree drop from the high the day before. It's still a very reasonable late-December temperature.

Low temperature for Wednesday, December 21, 2011: 28, the same as the day before.

Precipitation for Wednesday, December 21, 2011: a trace amount.

Precipitation for 2011: 19.48 inches

New entries:

Exercise for Tuesday, December 21, 2011: I took a 45-minute walk around my neighborhood, my longest walk since the accident. I stuck to the sidewalks of Lewis, Clark, and Yellowstone avenues. I really enjoyed the route and the scenery. I think I will do it again today.

Miles driven Wednesday, December 21, 2011: It will be a while before I take another long driving trip. Let's retire this category.

Total miles driven: Let's retire this one, too.

Gas usage Wednesday, December 21, 2011: Let's retire this one, too.

Addendum: I'm nervous about a lot of things today. I'm nervous about seeing Dr. Rex Helton. I'm nervous about going to see Jay L. Lamb about a job. I don't like Jay L. Lamb very much, which may be unfair of me now that he is treating me well, but I can't help it. I don't like the idea of his finding a job for me, but I have to balance that against the certainty that I need something to occupy my time if this new program of mine is going to work. I will stifle my concerns and see what Jay L. Lamb has to say.

My mother called this morning and told me to come by her condo at 5:00 p.m., that we would have dinner and talk. I'm ready for this discussion now. My destructive anger is gone. I still wish to make her acknowledge what she did to me, but I can do so in a constructive way, thanks to Dr. Bryan Thomsen.

I can barely believe I wrote those last five words, but there they are, right above these words. Nobody else did that.

Astoundingly—adverbs are not my favorite things, but "astoundingly" is a good one—Dr. Rex Helton says I'm on the right track.

"Blood pressure is down. You're at two hundred and eighty-four pounds, so you're losing it steadily but not too quickly. And, of course, the car wreck probably has something to do with that. As for the diabetes, it's too early to do the full blood work again, but let's see what a test strip says."

He puts on rubber gloves and brings out a glucose reader. I set my hand palm up on the counter, and he says, "Little prick," which I assume is in reference to the needle and not my character.

I just made a joke. I'm pretty funny sometimes.

"It's a hundred and twenty-three. Not bad, Edward. Not bad at all. Keep up the fine work."

— • —

The delightfulness of Dr. Rex Helton's office is offset by the intimidation of Jay L. Lamb's. For the first time since just after my father died, I'm made to sit in this uncomfortable modern furniture that Jay L. Lamb insists on buying. I'm sitting in front of the desk of his impossibly beautiful secretary, who has now just said, for the fourth time, "He'll be with you shortly."

Jay L. Lamb also has a magazine problem. In Dr. Buckley's office, now Dr. Bryan Thomsen's office, there are women's magazines, sports magazines, car magazines, outdoor magazines—in other words, pretty much every kind of magazine you can imagine, except pornography. It speaks to Dr. Buckley and Dr. Bryan Thomsen's willingness to make a range of clients feel welcome and at ease.

Jay L. Lamb has only investor magazines. I'm his client, and yet I feel neither welcome nor at ease. Excuse me for saying so, but that's pretty shitty of Jay L. Lamb.

"He'll be with you shortly," the impossibly beautiful secretary says.

I look at my watch. It's 1:17 p.m., seventeen minutes past our appointed meeting time. We passed "shortly" a long time ago.

— • —

At 1:21 p.m., I'm finally shown into Jay L. Lamb's office. He directs me to sit in a chair in front of his desk, one only slightly more comfortable than the seat I just extricated (I love the word "extricated") myself from.

"Edward, how have you been?"

"Well, Mr. Lamb, I've been in a car wreck and forcibly removed from Colorado. Things have been better."

Jay L. Lamb smiles uncomfortably, which is the only sort of smile he's ever given me.

"Yes, well, your mother has filled me in on things, which is why we're here today. I have found you a job, if you want it."

"What is it?"

"It's a courier position."

"You mean, a delivery boy?"

"No, not quite. This is actually a very trustworthy position. This law office—there are three partners, plus six associates—generates a lot of paperwork, and that paperwork needs to find its way to various places, be it the courthouse or a regulatory agency or a client or another law office. We need someone who is highly organized, who knows the city and the region, and who is reliable. It's actually the perfect position for you, because you're all of those things. In fact, I'm a little stumped that I didn't think of it before."

"Would I report to you?"

The position sounds pretty good, but his answer to this question could be a deal breaker for me.

"Ordinarily, you would, yes. Me and the other two partners. But this is a different kind of situation, for two reasons. First, I'm your lawyer and a family friend, so it wouldn't be right for me to be your supervisor. Second, I'm retiring early next year."

"You are?"

"I'm sixty-three years old, Edward. It's time. I've been working nonstop since Clea died two years ago. It's time to relax and enjoy the time I have left. So, anyway, I've talked it over with Mr. Slaughter and Mr. Lambert, and one of those men will be designated as your supervisor. You and I will be coworkers, for a few weeks anyway. If we have to discuss your employment as partners, I will recuse myself from that discussion. Does that sound fair?"

It sounds more than fair. I think now that perhaps I have not given Jay L. Lamb enough credit.

"Yes, it does," I say. "I have two more questions."

"I figured you would."

"Who will be our lawyer now?"

Jay L. Lamb laughs, and he stands up and sits on the edge of his glass desk.

"I'm becoming something called 'partner emeritus.' That means I'll still have a role here. I'll keep an office. And I'm taking two clients with me into retirement—your mother and you. So in that regard, nothing changes. Now, you had a second question?"

"Yes. What does the position pay?"

"It pays thirteen dollars an hour to start. I know that's less than you were making at the *Herald-Gleaner*, but on the plus side, your health benefits will be entirely paid for, you'll get three weeks of paid vacation to start, which I believe is better than you were getting at the newspaper, and we also do a 401(k) match. It's a good package, and I think we both know that in your financial condition, this paycheck isn't going to make much of a difference."

I think Jay L. Lamb just said, in a nice way, that I'm fucking loaded.

"I accept the position," I say. "When do I start?"

"Let's say January second, the Monday after the new year. It's going to be a ghost town around here between now and then. Be here at eight a.m. and we'll get you started. Welcome aboard, Edward."

We shake on it. This astounds me.

— • —

I'm home by 2:42 p.m. While I'm grilling chicken for lunch, I watch the next *Dragnet* episode on my bitchin' iPhone, since I may be late at my mother's tonight. I wouldn't want to miss *Dragnet* so early in my return to it.

"Administrative Vice: DR-29" is the seventeenth episode of the third season of the *Dragnet* color episodes, which ran from 1967 to 1970. This episode originally aired on February 6, 1969, and it's one of my favorites.

One of the things I appreciate about *Dragnet* is its authenticity. Unlike television shows today that are monuments to falsehood, *Dragnet* shows you how police work actually takes place. In addition, Sergeant Joe Friday (played by Jack Webb) often provides a history lesson on Los Angeles in the intro. I will not hold my breath waiting for *Jersey Shore* to do something similar.

— • —

My mother's condo is in a place called the Stapleton Building downtown. When it was built in 1904, it was the tallest and most glorious building in Billings, Montana. It held the city's finest department store, Hart-Albin; offices; and even a men's overnight club. For much of my life, however, it was empty and dilapidated (I love the word "dilapidated"), until some local developers turned it into something new, with the condo units and restaurants and shops. My mother moved here after my father died, and now she splits her time between here and Texas—with an increasingly larger share of the time being spent away from here.

My mother rings me in from the lobby, and I ride the elevator to the third floor, where her condo is. She has a view of the downtown streets. It's a very nice place, although I still prefer my bungalow on Clark Avenue.

My mother opens the door and sweeps me into her condo. Jay L. Lamb is standing in the living room.

"Hello, Edward," he says.

"Hello, Mr. Lamb."

My mother, having closed the door, has walked up behind me and wrapped an arm around me.

"Jay was just telling me about your new job. I'm so glad this worked out."

I wrench myself out of my mother's arm.

"My ribs still hurt," I say, and she quickly apologizes.

"Why don't you two chat?" she says. "I'll finish with the dip."

Jay sits down and invites me to take a spot on the couch opposite him. Instead, I follow my mother into the kitchen.

"Do you need something to drink?" she asks.

"No, Mother. Why is Jay L. Lamb here?"

"I invited him."

"Why?"

"He's our friend, and he just did something very nice for you."

"And I appreciate that. I thought you and I were going to talk."

"We are."

"With Jay L. Lamb here? I have some things I need to say to you."

"Go right ahead."

My mother is being obtuse. I leave her and go back into the living room. Jay L. Lamb is stirring his drink. I go to the window and look down on Broadway, with my back to Jay L. Lamb and my mother so they don't see how flummoxed I am.

"What's new, Edward?" Jay asks me.

"Since you saw me four hours ago? Not much."

My mother comes into the room carrying a tray of crackers. I can see her reflection in the glass.

"Edward, are you ready to talk? We have some time before the roast comes out of the oven."

"No."

"Could you come sit down, dear? We'd like to chat."

I turn from the window and walk to the couch across from Jay L. Lamb and my mother, who are sitting together. I sit on the far end, as far from them as I can. I'm not hungry. I thought I was, but I'm not.

"Edward," Jay L. Lamb says, "you remember how I told you I'm retiring."

"Yes."

"Your mother has asked me to come with her to Texas, and that's what I'm going to do—if it's all right with you."

I look at my mother. She's nodding, smiling at me.

"Why?"

"Because we care about each other."

He reaches into my mother's lap and takes her hand in his.

Holy shit!

"You mean, like, you're her boyfriend?" I ask.

"Something like that."

"Something exactly like that," my mother says.

I look at them sitting there, holding hands. They look so happy, and that makes me angry. Two days ago, I was holding hands with someone, too. Now look what has happened.

"How come you didn't tell me?"

"Until recently, there wasn't a lot to tell," Jay says. "I know you're surprised, Edward. We were, too."

I want him to shut up and never say another word to me. I don't look at him. I look only at my mother.

"We're selling the condo," my mother says. "We're going to live full time in Texas."

I cannot even believe what I'm hearing.

"But Jay L. Lamb just told me 'if it's all right with you.' Does that mean I have veto power over this?"

My mother squeezes Jay L. Lamb's hand tightly.

"Not exactly veto power. What Jay wants is your blessing. It's important to him, and to me, too. I think he's showing a lot of respect for you by asking."

I am dimensions beyond flummoxed.

"You told me you didn't want a smelly old man living with you!"

Jay L. Lamb coughs some of his drink back into his glass, and then he looks at my mother incredulously.

"That's what I thought when I said it. And by the way, Jay, you're not smelly at all. Things change, Son."

"How long have things been changing?"

I sound shrill and angry, and I realize that I *am* shrill and angry and that, furthermore, Dr. Bryan Thomsen's best advice is not going to help me now.

"It's been gradual," Jay L. Lamb says. "Imperceptible. We've spent time together these past couple of years, gone to a lot of the same functions, shared our hearts. It just happened."

"You should be happy," my mother says. "For me, you should be happy."

I stand up again and return to the window.

"I'm not happy, Mother. Not just about this, but about a lot of things."

"Let's talk about it," she says.

"No."

"I should go," Jay L. Lamb says. "You two should talk first."

"No," my mother says.

"Yes," I say.

Jay L. Lamb looks like a trapped animal. I take bitter pleasure in this.

"Jay, please sit down," my mother says, and he does.

I turn around and face them.

"I'm leaving. I'm going home. I can't believe you are just going to leave here. And with Jay L. Lamb! What would Father think? No wonder you said you don't miss him."

My mother's face has lost color.

"I think he would be happy for me, unlike you. But it doesn't matter. He's gone, and I'm here. I found someone I want to be with. You're selfish to be against that."

"It's selfish of you!"

I leave the condo, and once I'm in the hallway, I run for the elevator. My ribs scream out their objection to this, and I don't care.

On the street, I find my new Cadillac DTS. The one Jay L. Lamb bought for me. The one my mother drove to take me away from Cheyenne Wells. The one parked next to Jay L. Lamb's Volvo.

I go around to the driver's side door of the Volvo, rear back my right foot, and kick hard against the door, leaving a size-fourteen impression.

I return to my car, open the driver's side door, and climb in. I'm tired. I'm hurt. I'm flummoxed. I wonder how many shitburgers I can be expected to eat.

FRIDAY, DECEMBER 23, 2011

From the logbook of Edward Stanton:

Time I woke up today: What difference does it make?

High temperature for Thursday, December 22, 2011, Day 356: Who cares?

Low temperature for Thursday, December 22, 2011: What does it matter?

Precipitation for Thursday, December 22, 2011: It doesn't matter.

Precipitation for 2011: This doesn't matter, either.

New entries:

Fuck new entries.

My mother's Keurig arrived today, brought to my door by the UPS delivery man.

I walked it through the house, out the back door, across the yard, into the alley, and tossed it into the garbage bin.

Merry Christmas, Mother.

SATURDAY, DECEMBER 24, 2011

From the logbook of Edward Stanton:
  Time I woke up today:
  High temperature for Friday, December 23, 2011, Day 357:
  Low temperature for Friday, December 23, 2011:
  Precipitation for Friday, December 23, 2011:
  Precipitation for 2011:
  New entries:
  Fuck new entries. (This still stands.)

The phone starts ringing at 7:38 a.m. today. By 8:56, I've had fourteen calls. I remove the line from the back of the phone.

At 9:04, my bitchin' iPhone rings. Kyle has changed my ringtone to "Honky Tonk Badonkadonk," and even in my sour mood, I have to concede that's funny. The phone call is from my mother. I turn the ringtone to silent. She calls thirty-six more times by 2:00 p.m. Every time the bitchin' iPhone lights up, I hear "Honky Tonk Badonkadonk" playing in my head. It's not funny anymore. I shut the phone completely off.

Now I'm watching the Dallas Cowboys play against the Philadelphia Eagles. The New York Giants have already beaten the New

York Jets, so no matter what happens in this game, the whole season comes down to January first, in New York against the Giants.

It's weird to be sitting in my living room in Billings, Montana, and watching a game that I was supposed to attend in person. It makes me think about how little things can change big things. If Kyle hadn't stowed away in my car when I left Boise, I probably would have gone to Cheyenne Wells, spent a couple of days, driven home, and been aboard my scheduled flight to Texas. If I take Kyle out of the equation, I eliminate that awful moment when I found out what had happened to him, the frantic drive through the darkness to get him back with his family, the impact when I drove into the snowplow. If I take those things away, I take away Sheila Renfro finding my pills and my phone and chasing me down the highway. I take away her staying with me in the hospital and then bringing me back to Cheyenne Wells. I take away kissing on the couch, and holding her sleeping body in my arms after the drug raid at her motel. I take away my mother showing up the next day and bringing me back here. OK, that one I would like to take away, but I can't without affecting everything else.

If I take away all those things, I'm in Texas. I'm at my mother's house in North Richland Hills, which would have been decked out for Christmas, the way her houses always are. I would be sipping eggnog with my mother and Aunt Corinne and meeting all the Texas ladies she always talks about.

We would ride in her car to Cowboys Stadium, just the two of us, for this game. Maybe my mother would introduce me to Jerry Jones, the Cowboys' owner, because she knows him. I would have to restrain myself from telling him what I really think about his stewardship (I love the word "stewardship") of the team.

Now, I'm thinking maybe it's just as well that I didn't end up at Cowboys Stadium. The Philadelphia Eagles just drove quarterback Tony Romo into the ground, and he has hurt his hand. The TV announcers are saying that they don't expect to see him return, since the Cowboys have nothing to gain.

On the other hand (not Tony Romo's other hand; that's a joke, because I'm pretty funny), maybe I would like to change everything. I can't, of course. I'm speaking only hypothetically. I'm thinking now of the butterfly effect, which holds that one small change in a nonlinear system can cause massive changes in later situations. In other words, even if I could change something in my past—and, to be clear, I cannot—that single alteration would change many other things, perhaps in ways I didn't like.

I have to wonder what the difference would be. It seems to me that everything changes anyway and that God or the universe or whoever's in charge doesn't give a damn what I think about it.

— • —

My mother knocks on my door at 6:11 p.m. I know it's her because she says so.

"Edward, I know you're in there. Let me come in so we can talk."

I walk to the door and put my cheek against it.

"Please leave me alone, Mother."

"It's Christmas Eve. Let's talk about this."

"Your present is in the alley in the garbage bin. You can go get it if you want. Other than that, I don't want to talk to you, Mother."

"Edward!"

"Please go away."

"Will you ever talk to me again?"

"When I'm ready. It's my sovereign right to choose when that is."

"I love you, Edward."

My mother is crying. I can hear it.

"I know you do. I love you, too. Please go away."

I hear her climbing down the steps of my porch. I go to the window and open the curtain just enough to see into the yard. My mother crosses the street and climbs into Jay L. Lamb's Volvo, which has the impression of my foot on the driver's side door. He drives her away from me, just as he'll soon do forever.

SUNDAY, DECEMBER 25, 2011

From the logbook of Edward Stanton:
Time I woke up today: 7:38 a.m. The 211th time this year I've awakened at this time, if you count yesterday, when the phone started ringing.
High temperature for Saturday, December 24, 2011, Day 358: 51. Holy shit!
Low temperature for Saturday, December 24, 2011: 23. I have no idea what the highs and lows were for December 23rd. I threw that newspaper away without looking at it.
Precipitation for Saturday, December 24, 2011: 0.00 inches
Precipitation for 2011: 19.49 inches, which means we picked up a hundredth of an inch Friday.

Two days ago, I wrote in my logbook "Who cares?" about my regularly charted data. I care.

Merry Christmas.

— • —

At 9:03 a.m., someone knocks at my front door. I walk over and press my face against it.

"Mother?"

"Edward, it's Bryan Thomsen. Can you let me in, please?"

Holy shit!

I open the door.

— • —

Dr. Bryan Thomsen sits on my small loveseat and clasps his hands on his lap.

"A lot of people are worried about you, Edward."

"My mother."

"Yes, your mother. Your friend Donna, who tried to call you last night after your mother called her. Your mother's friend Jay—"

"He's an asshole."

"Look, Edward, I'm not here to take sides. I'm your counselor. People who care about you asked me to come make sure you're all right, and because I care about you, too, I'm here and I'm making my wife and kids wait on Christmas morning. So how about we forget who's an asshole and who isn't and talk about things. OK?"

"Yes. OK."

"Good. Now, do you want to tell me what happened?"

I tell him, starting with our talk just two days ago and how invigorated I was by it. I came home, and I made a commitment to living my life fully and responsibly.

"Then I went to my mother's place and found out she's in love with Jay L. Lamb, and everything crumbled."

"Do you still have an issue with this man that leads you to believe he won't be a good partner for your mother?"

I have to think about that one. There was a time in my life when Jay L. Lamb was the person I hated to hear from most, other than my father. But with my father, there was a history of love, which in a strange way made the anger between us much more powerful and personal. I tell Dr. Bryan Thomsen this, and he nods as if he knows exactly what I'm talking about. But his question is if I have an issue with Jay L. Lamb today that I believe puts my mother in some sort of jeopardy for being involved with him.

I have to be honest; I do not. Jay L. Lamb has been dealing with me respectfully for more than three years. My mother clearly has fondness for him, although I cannot imagine why.

"I would have liked to have known that he was courting my mother," I tell Dr. Bryan Thomsen. "But aside from that, no, I have no issues with him."

"Is the issue with your mother?" he asks. "Did you ever talk to her about what we discussed?"

"No. I didn't have a chance."

"I want to make sure I have the sequence right," Dr. Bryan Thomsen says. "You went to her place to talk with her, this Jay Lamb was there, and so you didn't want to talk about it in front of him, and then your mother and Jay spring the news on you that they're a romantic item and they'll be living in Texas full time? Is that how it went?"

"Yes."

"May I tell you what I think?"

"Yes."

"First, I think you continue to have a good reason to talk to your mother. She needs to know how her actions have affected you. If you'd felt comfortable enough to do so, this thing might not have gone as far as it has."

"Why do you say that?"

Dr. Bryan Thomsen sits forward and looks me in the eye, which makes me uncomfortable.

"What was the word you used to describe how your mother had transgressed against you?"

"Sovereignty. She invaded my sovereignty by making me leave Colorado before I was ready to go."

"She took a decision that should have been yours and made it hers," Dr. Bryan Thomsen says.

"That's correct."

"OK, good. Now, let me ask you something. If you're angry at your mother for leaving Montana for good and becoming romantically involved with Jay Lamb, and you're punishing her for that with your silence, what are you trying to do?"

Dr. Bryan Thomsen doesn't have to try to draw a picture for me. I see it.

"I've been dumb," I say.

"No, you've been emotional. You've been human. And so has your mother. Each of you thinks he or she knows what's best for the other, and you've both been behaving badly in an effort to exert that control. If your mother wants to move to Texas with Jay Lamb, you have to let her do that. You can't change her decision. You can only decide how you're going to live with it. Do you think you can?"

"Yes. But I have to be honest. It bothers me to imagine her loving another man after my father. I don't think that's rational."

"Emotions often aren't," Dr. Bryan Thomsen says.

"It's just that my mother told me she doesn't miss my father, and that flummoxes me. I miss him all the time. In some ways, I miss him more now than I ever have."

"Why do you think that is?"

"I don't know."

"Think about it."

This is one of those areas where Dr. Bryan Thomsen bothers me. I've been thinking about it for days, months, and years. I don't know.

"I don't know," I say.

"It sounds to me like your mother has made her peace with him," Dr. Bryan Thomsen says. "Perhaps you should ask yourself if you have. You might better understand her point of view when you do. Failing that, maybe it's time to ask her. You have a lot to talk about, don't you?"

"Yes."

"Are you going to do it?"

"Yes."

"Good. Merry Christmas, Edward."

MONDAY, DECEMBER 26, 2011

From the logbook of Edward Stanton:

Time I woke up today: 7:38 a.m. The 212th time this year I've awakened at this time. A sign of normalcy, I guess.

High temperature for Sunday, December 25, 2011, Day 359: 47. Four degrees lower than the high the day before, but still very warm for this time of year.

Low temperature for Sunday, December 25, 2011: 29. Six degrees warmer than the low from the day before.

Precipitation for Sunday, December 25, 2011: 0.00 inches

Precipitation for 2011: 19.49 inches

I have been thinking about what Dr. Bryan Thomsen said about my mother and her sovereignty, and I think it makes sense. I suppose that I will have to talk to her again sometime, and I do feel bad that Christmas has come and gone, but I'm just not ready. We have a lot of topics to cover, more than we've ever had before. When I am ready, I will talk to her.

This morning, I went to the garage and retrieved the boxes of old letters of complaint that I removed from the house on Wednesday, November 5, 2008. For three years, one month, and twenty-two days, I have resisted the urge to resume my daily letters of complaint, and I'm pretty sure I can keep resisting. Of course, "pretty sure" is a far cry from a verified fact, but it's all I have.

Before my father died, my daily, unsent letters of complaint were how I dealt with the uncertainty and frustration in my world. If someone was mean to me (often my father, but not always), or I grew irritated with a situation, I would write a letter of complaint and then file it away. Dr. Buckley had me do that. She said there was something therapeutic in writing the letter and letting my emotions out, but that I might get in trouble with people if I actually sent them. She is a very logical woman. For example, I can't imagine that Dallas Cowboys owner Jerry Jones would be happy if he received a letter from me calling him the biggest numbskull in the history of the NFL. I actually wrote six letters in which I called him that. That would hurt anybody's feelings.

After my father died, I began to question the value of my letters. I wanted to see how things went if I just tried to deal with my frustrations as they emerged. And I have to say, I've been pretty good at it. What I want to do now is reread all of these old complaints and remember the incidents that set me off and see if there is a pattern to them. If there's a pattern, perhaps I can learn from it. If there's no pattern, at least I can reminisce (I love the word "reminisce").

— • —

At 12:16 p.m., the doorbell rings. I put down a letter of complaint dated April 3, 2001, in which I scold my father for making my mother cry during dinner. I'm retroactively annoyed with myself for writing a letter I never sent. I should have just told my father right there, over dinner, that he was being mean. He needed to hear it.

I go to the door and lean into it.

"Who's there?" I shout.

"Dr. Asskicker and his band of merry men."

That can be only one person. I open the door, and sure enough, Scott Shamwell is standing on my front porch wearing a T-shirt that says "You're Welcome to Join Me at My Intervention."

"Ed!" he says. "What the hell is up, dude?"

"Scott Shamwell, what are you doing here?"

"I told you, man. I said after Christmas we'd get together and do some radical shit. Well, it's after Christmas, hoss."

"But you told me to call you," I say.

"Come on, man. I knew you wouldn't. Now check this out."

Scott Shamwell stands aside and sweeps his arm toward the street, like one of the pretty women on *The Price Is Right* showing off a prize. Parked in front of my house is a black motorcycle with a sidecar.

"Come on, dude," Scott Shamwell says. "You can be my side-kick. Let's go get stupid."

— • —

Getting stupid is not what I do.

Scott Shamwell stretches his arms out as he holds the steering wheel of my Cadillac DTS, locking his elbows.

"A frickin' Cadillac," he says. "God, I hope none of my friends see me in this thing."

"I'm sorry," I say. "I broke my ribs. I can't sit in a sidecar. Plus, motorcycles are dangerous."

"I know, but—"

"At least I'm letting you drive," I say. "I'll still be your sidekick. That sounds like fun."

"I know, man, but a Cadillac! It's so square."

"My father always said it's the greatest negotiating tool ever."

"I don't want to negotiate, dude. I want to get beer and girls."

— • —

We find a place in Stillwater County, on an outcropping that over-looks the Yellowstone River, and we eat chicken wings and drink root beer on the hood of my Cadillac DTS.

"So the guy just hauled off and punched you for nothin'?" Scott Shamwell asks.

"Yes. You can still see a little bit of the bruise under my eye."

Scott Shamwell peers in and crinkles his nose.

"I think it's gone."

I walk around to the side-view mirror and take a look. Scott Shamwell just didn't look closely enough. The bruise is still there. I guess it helps to know where it was in the first place.

"I wish I'd have been there," he says. "I would have stomped a mud hole in that dude's ass."

He flexes his freckly arms and gives each bicep a kiss. He's pretty funny sometimes.

— • —

When I tell Scott Shamwell about Sheila Renfro, he becomes excitable. He says, "Oh, yeah, Big Ed," and then he gallops around the car twice, pretending that he's slapping a horse on the hind-quarters.

Finally, he stops and says, "Did you screw her, dude?"

He moves his hips forward and backward.

"Did you get it on?"

"No."

I say this abruptly. I'm annoyed with Scott Shamwell.

"Dude," he says, and he slaps me on the shoulder. "You got to bone it like you own it."

I'm more than annoyed. I'm angry.

"You shut up," I say. "She's my friend. You don't say mean things about her."

Scott Shamwell looks shocked. Then Scott Shamwell looks ashamed. More than that, he looks hurt.

"She's important to you," he says.

"Yes."

"Well, Ed, that's—I'm sorry. Really. I'm sorry."

He gathers up our trash and bags it up.

"Do you want to go home?" he asks.

"No," I say. "Let's get stupid."

— • —

We're on a side road in Carbon County, a long way from the highway, and Scott Shamwell has decided that he wants to see how fast the Cadillac can go. He finds a straightaway and brings the car to a stop.

"Ready?" he asks.

"I wish you wouldn't."

"Well, dude, wish in one hand, shit in the other."

He stomps down hard on the accelerator, the back end of the Cadillac drops just a bit, and we're off.

"Nice takeoff," Scott Shamwell says, and then he lets out a whoop. "WEEEEEOOOOOOOOOOOO!"

He looks over at me. I wish he would look at the road.

"Yell, Ed!"

"Woo," I say.

"Really yell, dude! WEEEEEEOOOOOOOOOOOOOOOOO!"

"WEEEEEEOOOOOOOOOOOOOOOOO!" I say.

Scott Shamwell lets off the accelerator.

"Hundred and fifteen," he says. "Pretty bitchin'."

— • —

It's 6:17 p.m. and dark when we get back to my house. Scott Shamwell says he loves my Cadillac and wants to find one of his own and "soup it up."

He shuts off the ignition but still holds on to the steering wheel. He is staring at my garage.

"Edward," he says, "I need to tell you something, because I think you're fucking this whole thing up."

"OK."

"You don't want to go to work for that donkey-nuzzler Lamb guy, do you?"

"No, not really."

"Not really, hell. Not at all."

Scott Shamwell is correct.

"You ought to kick his ass," he says. "That's horseshit, man, making you come to work for him while he's boning your old lady. And it's horseshit the way they treat you, making you come back from Colorado like you're some kind of little kid or something."

Scott Shamwell's indignation amuses me, but the image of my getting into a fistfight with Jay L. Lamb, or anyone, is absurd to me.

"But what if he loves my mother?" I say. "And what if she loves him?"

Scott Shamwell doesn't say anything for several seconds.

"Scott Shamwell?" I say.

"Love is something else, man," he finally says. "If she loves him, you gotta let it go, because she'll never forgive you if you don't, and you'll never forgive yourself if it's real. Love is bullshit and weird and stupid, but shit, man, if you have love, everybody should leave you alone and let you keep it for as long as you can."

Scott Shamwell looks sad as he says this. He breathes in, and then he expels his breath in a sigh.

"If you ever want to sell this car, you let me know, dude."

"I will, Scott Shamwell."

He opens his door. I open mine. We both step out.

"Happy New Year, Ed," he says.

"In a week, yes. It's still 2011 now."

"Whenever, man. You take care of yourself."

I watch as he walks over to his motorcycle, and I wish my ribs didn't still hurt so I could ride in his sidecar. I think it would make him feel better. I also don't think I'm going to see him again for a while, and that's strange. It's conjecture, which I dislike, and imprecise, which I dislike even more.

By the time I've worked out the uncertainties, Scott Shamwell and his motorcycle are a noisy dot three blocks away on Clark Avenue.

TECHNICALLY TUESDAY, DECEMBER 27, 2011

A bizarre dream wakes me up at 2:21 a.m. In it, I see Scott Shamwell's face but hear Sheila Renfro's voice, and she says one word over and over and over: "Love. Love. Love. Love. Love."

When I finally pull out of the dream, I make an instant trip into the clarity of the waking world. For the first time, even as I remember the psychedelic aspects of my dream that would be absurd here in the conscious world, what I saw and heard makes complete sense to me. I can't believe I didn't realize this before.

I've worked hard to keep my life contained—in this house, in this town, in my job at the *Billings Herald-Gleaner*. But no matter how hard I've worked, the circumstances of my life have not been as airtight as I would prefer. My job went away. My friends went away. My mother is going away, and, from the looks of it, so is her new boyfriend.

And I'm lying here in my familiar bed, in the room I sleep in every night. Outside the door, my things are where I've put them and where I expect them to be. My notebooks record all the things I've tracked for all these years, and I'm no closer to controlling those figures than I was the day I started them.

I don't want to do this anymore. Everyone I know has found where they want to be. I'm still adrift. But there is something I can do about that.

— • —

I pull on my shirt and jeans and socks and slip into my shoes. In the garbage bin behind my house, I find my mother's Keurig. The box is dented and wet, but it's otherwise OK.

I put the box into the trunk of my new Cadillac DTS and drive to my mother's condo, with right turns on Seventh Street West and Lewis Avenue and Broadway. It's dark and the roads are wet, which makes the reflections from the streetlights look like smudges of yellow paint across the asphalt.

I ring the buzzer on my mother's condo once, and then once more.

Finally, her groggy voice answers: "Yes?"

"Let me in, Mother."

— • —

Telling my mother that she has violated my sovereignty is not the ordeal I thought it would be. She listens to me intently, her eyes following me as I pace the living room of her condo. I do not like looking people in the eye when I speak to them, especially when the topic is something like this, but I make myself finish.

"I'm not a child, Mother. I'm not incapable of making my own decisions. And you need to stop treating me as if I am."

Her eyes are clear and unblinking. "You're right."

"I am?"

"Yes, of course you are. I thought I needed to protect you—"

"I wasn't in danger. And I'm forty-two years old. I can protect myself. I'm developmentally disabled. I'm not stupid."

"I know. You're right. You're absolutely right."

I had prepared to say more on this topic, but now it seems like piling on, so I don't.

"I was wrong about something, though, Mother."

"What?"

"I was wrong about Jay L. Lamb."

"No, you weren't. You deserved to know before this. I just—"

"Do you love him?" I ask.

She looks at me as if she didn't expect the question, which is OK. I didn't expect to ask it, not like that.

"Yes. Very much," she says. "It surprised me. I didn't think I had it in me to love again. But...yes. I love him."

I surprise myself with what I say next.

"I'm glad."

I surprise myself further by realizing that I really am glad. I wouldn't have chosen Jay L. Lamb for my mother. I have to be honest about this. But I don't get to choose. If I did, I would want my father back. There are so many things I've learned. I would like to tell him about them. I would like to be his friend. I'm good at it now.

— • —

We talk about one more thing before I leave, and that is my father. I tell her how he's been in my dreams, and as she listens, she keeps curling the knuckle of her index finger into the corner of her eye.

"It upset me that you said you don't miss him," I tell her. "I miss him all the time. I wish he hadn't left us."

My mother invites me to sit down next to her on the couch. I do.

"I was tired," she says. "It was hard to be married to Ted Stanton. It wasn't just the drinking, which was bad and getting worse, or what he did to you, although it will take me a long time to forgive him for that."

"I forgive him."

"You're a good boy. But, listen, Edward, it was all-encompassing. Being married to your father was like being married to this city, and to every thought he had or word he said. Since he's been gone, I've done what I want to do. Do you understand? I make the rules now. I choose what gets my time and attention. I never did that before."

I understand. I should. It was my most common complaint about him when he was alive. How does the saying go? It was his world, and we were just living in it? Something like that.

"Did you love him?" I ask.

"Of course I did."

"I did, too."

"And he loved us," she said. "He'd be proud of you now, seeing you do the things you want to do."

There's nothing I can say about that except that hearing it makes me happy and sad all at the same time. That's peculiar.

OFFICIALLY TUESDAY, DECEMBER 27, 2011

At 6:18 a.m., I walk out to a spot where I can see the city lights below me. I've been driving for two hours, and my muscles are stiff. The first hint of sunlight peeks in from the east. The smell of pine and grass, even in late December, teases my nose. My left hand, cold and not yet limber, holds my bitchin' iPhone.

I dial the number. Traffic below me slowly rises from the trickle I watched from the parking lot as I ate my breakfast sandwich. Big rigs move east and west across the highway below me.

The call connects.

"The Derrick Motel. How can I help you?"

"Hello, Sheila."

There is a pause and then a tiny gasp.

"Edward?"

"Yes."

"You didn't call me Sheila Renfro."

"No."

"Where are you?"

I look at the city, gleaming in the first light.

"Sheridan, Wyoming."

"What are you doing there?"

"Wondering if you have a vacancy."

"You're coming here?"

"Yes."

"But your mother—"

"My mother says she is looking forward to seeing you in the spring when we go to Texas to see her and her new boyfriend."

"You want me to go to Texas with you in the spring?"

"Yes. We can close up the motel for a few days for that trip."

"That means—"

"Yes."

Sheila screams. She says "Oh my God, oh my God, oh my God!" And then she says, "Edward Stanton, you are the special man I've been waiting for. You are."

"I know I am. You were wrong when you said I wasn't."

"Edward, I am so happy to be wrong about that."

"I'll be there in nine hours," I say, and the words are hard to form because I'm grinning so widely. "Nine hours depending on the vagaries of traffic and gas stops." I think my face is going to break.

"I'm so happy," she says.

I begin walking back to the car, which sits alone in the rest area parking lot.

Sheila talks excitedly into my ear.

"Now, Edward," she says, "from now on, when I put my hand on your knee, I want you to put your arm around me. That's how you make a girl feel good."

"I will," I say. "And I want cable or satellite television at the motel."

"OK, but you have to kiss me sometimes, especially when I don't expect it."

"I will."

"And please don't always tell me about how mouths are gross, OK? Because I know that and will try to keep mine clean."

"Yes, dear."

She gasps again.

"You called me dear!"

"I thought I'd try it out. Do you like it?"

"I like it. I like it very much, Edward."

And that's how it goes for the next four minutes and thirty-seven seconds. Sheila instructs me on how to love her and make her happy, and I circle the parking lot and wait for her to finish so I can get there, only I don't want her to ever hang up, but I know that she must if I am to reach her in approximately nine hours.

She asks me why I changed my mind, and I say, "Because I asserted my sovereignty."

She laughs and says, "I don't know what that means, exactly, but promise me that you'll call every time you stop."

"I promise."

"I don't want to hang up."

"I know. But we have to."

"Hurry here to me."

"I will."

"I'll see you soon, Edward."

"Yes, you will, dear."

She giggles and then she hangs up, and I leave the parking lot and head for the interstate. I know exactly where I am going. As I guide the car onto the ramp and hit cruising speed, Michael Stipe is telling me that she is beautiful and she is the everything.

I know she is.

ACKNOWLEDGMENTS

So many to thank, so little space.

The "beta" readers: Jim Thomsen, Celeste Cornish, Jessica Park, Jill Rupert, Amy Pizarro, and R. J. Keller. Your earnest and eagerly offered feedback made this an immeasurably better book. I am indebted.

Elizabeth Holleran, you're funny as hell and you provided one key line of dialogue I could have never conjured on my own. You know the one. Thank you.

Alex Carr, Jessica Poore, and the team at Amazon Publishing: Thank you for believing in Edward and giving him a home. It's good to be with you again. And Charlotte Herscher, my developmental editor, you made this book so much better than it would have been otherwise. Thank you.

Chris Cauble, Linda Cauble, Janet Spencer, the team at Riverbend Publishing: It would have never happened in the first place if not for your hard work. I'm so thankful.

Mollie Glick and Foundry Literary + Media, the finest agent and agency in the land: It all comes back around. Thank you for your tireless work, your wisdom, and your cheer.

And, finally, to the readers and those who put the books in their hands: Thank you, thank you, thank you. I could never possibly say it enough.

ABOUT THE AUTHOR

Craig Lancaster is a journalist who has worked at newspapers all over the country, including the *San Jose Mercury News*, where he served as lead editor for the paper's coverage of the BALCO steroids scandal. He wrote *600 Hours of Edward*—winner of a Montana Book Award honorable mention and a High Plains Book Award—in less than 600 hours during National Novel Writing Month in 2008. His other books include the novel *The Summer Son* and the short story collection *Quantum Physics and the Art of Departure*. Lancaster lives in Billings, Montana, with his wife.